DON'T BLAME THE RECKLESS

Don't Blame the Reckless

MADDYSON WILSON

ZENITH PUBLISHING

Prologue
Ember

I hadn't seen the sun in 365 days.

It looked different, somehow, after I'd been kept in the dark for so long. Brighter, I think. Happier. I used to dream about the sun every night. However, in my dreams, I was free, and my sister was by my side. In my dreams, I was not minutes away from death.

Dreams never mirror reality.

I have the blood of fourteen Imperial Officials and twenty-two soldiers on my hands. All those wardens, those guards, those men ten times my size and twice my strength who screamed curses at me as their whips licked my bare back. They told me I should be dead. They told me it was only by some mercy of the gods that I was alive. They told me I should regret what I've done.

I don't.

I don't regret a single second.

I don't regret a single kill.

I'd do it all again.

The people know me as the Bloodhound of the East Sector. Champion of the folk without a damned cent to their name. Champion of all those without a voice. My name was once a whisper in the winds, something to mention only in secrecy. They said my name hushed like a curse. I wear my

title proudly, even now. I wear it like a necklace of gold, dripping around my bruised, scarred neck. Even now, as I look
back. I am the warrior that brought Kadjar to its knees.

And this, reader, this is how I did it.

Chapter One
Ember

The guard shoved me to my knees. He whispered in my ear, breath heavy, smelling of onions and cigarette smoke. "My brother is dead because of you. I am going to enjoy this."

I twisted around, the ends of my silver ponytail whipping in front of my eyes. The late afternoon sun burned against my eyelids. I squinted. What I could see of the guard's face wasn't familiar to me. He was just another carbon copy of the rest: dressed in the same chrome jumpsuit, short-cropped hair with a belt of weapons clipped to his waist.

There was no way I could have known the brother he was talking about, but messing with people like him was always fun, so I bared my teeth. "Your brother was filthy pig," I spat at his feet. "Bet you are, too."

He slammed his hands into my shoulders, sending me to the tile of the balcony we stood on. A gasp rose from the crowd below me. I couldn't bring myself to look at them yet. No, not yet. I couldn't see the disappointment on the faces of my people.

There were too many deaths running through my mind now to worry about the crowd. Names. Faces. Places. I remembered them all like every single one had just happened yesterday. I remembered their screams, their pleas. I remembered my own sick satisfaction at their last few gasps of breath.

The guard jerked me upright and latched a white muzzle around my mouth, tying it so tightly that I could feel the fabric digging into the back of my head, through my hair. I stared out into the dying light of the sky. Soon, it would be nightfall. Soon, I would be dead.

Wonder where they'll bury me. Hope it's somewhere with a view.

I sucked in a breath of air and let my gaze drift down, toward the crowd. Every inch of the street was covered with people, all looking up. I could see them, my people. Dressed in their rags. Dirt on their faces. Fathers, hoisting children on their shoulders. *Who brings a child to an execution?* Mothers—maybe some of them knew mine. Was Mama in the crowd? My father? My sister?

There was a clear divide between the East Sectors and the North Sectors. Those North Sectors, dressed in all their golds and silvers and purples and reds, stood at the front of the crowd. I could only see them if I bent my head down. I killed people like them. I slit the throats of their fathers and brothers and mothers and sisters.

And, somewhere in between, there were the South Sectors. Those with just enough to live, not to survive. Those who didn't have to wear rags. Those who couldn't afford the North Sector private schools but didn't have to send their children to the one-room schoolhouses that we had in the East Sector. Growing up, I always hated their kind the most.

The balcony door slammed. I didn't turn around to see who it was. I knew that it was the executioner, the only other

8

person granted access to this balcony.

His boots pounded against the tile, making his way to my side. He wasted no time.

"Today," his voice shot through my body like lightning. "Justice will be served for all thirty-six innocent Kadjarians, mercilessly murdered by Ember Faye Levin, also known as the Bloodhound of the East Sector."

Again, the divide made itself known. Waves of cheers and shouts pumped through the North Sectors. The East Sectors did nothing. I don't know what I was expecting, but it wasn't what I got. The North Sector cheers died down, and there was nothing but silence.

Choking, deadly silence.

It was kind of funny, actually. I never noticed how loud silence could be up until that moment.

The executioner pulled a silver knife from his belt. It sung as he sliced the air. He took his place behind me, grabbing a fistful of hair and pulling back. I tensed as pain trickled down my spine. He pressed the gleaming knife to my throat.

My heart began to pound.

I shut my eyes tightly, waiting for the knife to cut through my throat, waiting for the pain, just waiting for the next move. I only hoped that Death would welcome a monster like me.

"Stand down!" a familiar voice barked. That voice: I remember her screams in the dead of night. I remember her crying out for guards as I held a dagger to her throat. I remember that voice telling me she couldn't wait to watch the life

9

drain from my eyes.

The knife fell from my throat, and I turned my head to find the empress standing in the doors of the balcony. Murmurs rose from the audience below. Her dark skin glowed in the afternoon sun as she snapped her fingers, ordering the guard and executioner inside.

"But—?" The executioner looked from me to the crowd below. The empress rolled her amber eyes. She stalked to the stone railings of her balcony and spread her arms wide.

"People of Kadjar! I know what you came to see here today. You came to see the death of the menace that terrorized our great nation for two long years. I regret to inform you that there is business that I must conduct with the Bloodhound. The execution will be rescheduled. I will share what information I can when I have it. Thank you, and goodnight."

She turned around, looked pointedly from the guard to me. The executioner stepped out of the way as the guard pulled me to my feet with an iron grip on my shoulders.

When he shoved me inside the throne room, I fell flat on my face. I scrambled to my feet, pain beating through my nose, as the guard retreated to the side of the empress' throne. The executioner was gone, but I wasn't safe enough to let myself rejoice in that fact.

"What is this?" I rasped.

Empress Analita stood in the middle of the wide throne room, arms crossed over her chest. She looked like a goddess—there was no denying that. As spiteful, evil, and manipulative as she may be, she was beautiful. Dark skin covered in the maroon cloth of a form-fitting dress, golden tattoos snaking up her arms and neck.

"Hm. I would have imagined your first words to be *something* of a thanks," Empress Analita said. "But I must be forgetting just who I'm dealing with." She turned to the guard by her throne, dismissing him but ordering him to leave his knife laying on the arm of her throne. Panic rose in my throat. This was going to be a private execution.

Empress Analita's throne sat ten feet in front of me, perched on a maroon platform the same color as her dress, clad in rubies and emeralds and diamonds. Two velvet curtains sat behind the throne, stretching all the way up to the tall domed ceiling.

"Tell me, Ember, do you feel any guilt for what you've done?" she asked, striding toward her throne.

"No." I answered, inching toward the throne.

"Why?"

"They deserved it."

"And who are you to play gods?"

"Who are you to ignore the embezzling? The lies? The violence? Who are you to ignore every awful, evil crime that was committed by your friends and colleagues?"

The empress took a minute. I stopped walking just short of the steps that led to her throne and stared down at the golden platform. I bet just a chunk of this could feed the entire East Sector for a year.

"So, that's what all of that was about?" I didn't respond

11

to her. She continued. "You think that just because some man took a few gold bars from the Treasury, he just deserved to die?"

"I didn't decide. The people did. They felt cheated. Look at what the North Sector is allowed to get away with while we starve. It's a slap in the face."

"How did the people decide?"

Might as well squeal. I'm not getting out of this alive. "I found a note in a bottle, washed up in the river behind the East Sector. It was a letter to the gods, written by Kater Hanover's wife. It listed every dark and awful thing that he ever did to her. She begged for the gods to kill him. I figured if I didn't do something, that woman was going to end up dead by her husband's hands. I just wanted to scare him. But I was a fifteen-year-old girl holding her father's handgun—not very frightening. I ended up shooting him because he mocked me. A few weeks later, I started finding more bottles in the river when I went to fetch water for the day. That's how the people decided—they directed me where to go."

Again, she thought. "You think of yourself as some kind of god, don't you? Some kind of savior?"

"No."

"Why'd you do it, then, if not for glory?"

"Because if I didn't, no one would. It started off with people like Kater, then it progressed. I received bottles about soldiers. Generals. Officials. I kept those bottles under my bed, at first, because I was too scared to do anything with them. Right after my sixteenth birthday, I killed my first Official. And then I realized that's how I could get your attention."

"By killing my friends and colleagues?"

"Every other way has failed."

"You want my attention? For what?"

"I need you to see that the East Sector is *dying*. Your people—the very people you're supposed to protect—are dying. We don't have clean water. We don't have enough food. We don't have access to proper housing or education, and you just don't care."

The ghost of a smile danced across the empress' lips. A smile. An actual smile. I wanted to punch her so badly that my fists ached. "Tell me, Ember, what exactly would you do to be free?"

"Don't change the subject."

"Ah, I'm the one with the knife." She let the blade swing between two fingers. "I get to control this conversation. Answer my question."

"No."

Empress Analita raised a thinly plucked eyebrow. "Are you defying me?"

"Defying the same empress who let half of my people die in a useless war? Yes." I pulled every inch of emotion from my face.

"You were barely three when the Angelesan war happened. What do you know of it?"

"I know that you deployed almost every able-bodied

adult in the East Sector to fight, and you barely touched the North Sector. I know that when less than a third of them came back, you didn't even acknowledge that the East Sector was in ruins."

"It was a *war*, Ember. Of course people died. Of course people suffered. That's what happens in war."

"What shouldn't happen is neglect of the government. You should have helped the East Sector get back to what it once was."

"Why do you even care?"

"Why do I *care*?" I roared. "I care because I am so goddamn *sick* of people like you creating useless wars for people like me to die in!"

The silence between us was enough to kill. Empress Analita spoke, slowly, meticulously. "You want to paint me as the villain so badly, don't you? You want me to say that the East Sector is some kind of shit-hole. You want me to pretend that I don't care about the people dying. I do. I want to change things. I just—I can't."

"Why?"

"Because! The East Sectors work. They're the ones who sacrifice their sons and daughters to my military academy. They're the ones who work in the mines and the fields. The South Sectors supervise. They're the managers and the bosses. They're the ones who make sure you all don't step out of line while the North Sectors lead. They run the businesses, the fields, the mines your people work in. I can't afford to mess with the delicate nation that I have crafted."

I seethed. "People are *dying*. Babies are dying because their parents can't afford vaccinations. Parents work themselves to death just to put enough food on the table. Is that what you want? Is that the delicate nation that you have crafted?"

"I'm choosing my battles wisely. And I'm choosing not to upset the balance."

I couldn't fathom a response. How do you respond to a woman who cares more for keeping her friends and colleagues in power than saving the lives of her people? So, instead, I changed the subject. "Why did you keep me alive? To taunt me? To mock my cause?" I clenched my fists at my sides.

"You have a certain...talent," the empress drawled, "that I'd like to use."

"Talent?"

"You seduced—"

"I *never* seduced any man or woman. I caught them off-guard and I tricked them. I didn't seduce anyone."

The empress waved my words away dismissively. "I need something from you. I need you to complete a task for me."

"No." I said, without thinking. "I'm not working for you. You and I will remain enemies until the East Sector is restored to what it was before the Angelesan trade war. Kill me for it if you want."

"What if I could offer you that change and pardon your charges along with it?"

I couldn't stop the odd sense of joy rising in my throat. "What do you define as change?"

The empress went silent. She shifted her weight in her throne, then spoke. "Better housing. Better healthcare."

"Better education," I continued. "More job opportunities for my people. I want all public aqueducts to be fixed and the roads repaved. I want free vaccinations and affordable healthcare. I want more homeless shelters and better rations."

The empress shut her eyes. She lowered her head in her hands and rubbed her temple with two bony fingers. "Would you work with me here? I'm trying to compromise." She finally asked, raising her head.

It was my turn to fall silent. "We are far past a compromise. I get what I said or there is no deal." I finally answered.

"The King of Angeles has a prisoner—a Kadjarian prisoner. I thought they were killed right after they crossed the Angelesan border—that's what he does to all of his prisoners of war anyways. But I received a letter and a proof of the prisoners' existence. I leave no man behind. I want that prisoner back."

"And you expect me to go get them?"

The empress nodded.

"No. I'm not doing it."

"Why not?"

"How do I know that this isn't a suicide mission?"

The empress rolled her eyes as if she couldn't believe my distrust. "This is our last resort. I can't afford to waste more valuable lives of my soldiers by having them sneak into

Angeles. I need someone smart, experienced, yet expendable. I need you."

"And why do you trust me?"

"I trust you because I don't have a choice. I'm not risking the lives of my soldiers any more than I already have. If you die, there's no skin off my back. If you live, I'll give you what you want. Do we have a deal?"

I fell silent.

Empress Analita continued, "Are you *really* going to give up the chance to get the change that you seem to want so badly? Think of your people." Her words were slow like molasses, taunting me with every aching syllable.

My silence seemed to be enough of an answer for her. She called for the executioner. I watched as he entered the room, looking from me to the empress. "Continue," she said.

The thud of his boots echoed throughout the wide throne room as he walked toward me. He took his place: one hand digging into my shoulder so hard I was sure he'd break skin, and the other gripping another knife against my throat. Cold silver danced against my skin.

I sucked in a breath, waiting for the pain of the final slice. Each passing second felt like a lifetime—what was he waiting for?

My mother's sun-weathered face flew through my mind.

My father's ash-stained hands.

My sister's crooked smile.

I could have been their final chance at a good life. I

could be throwing everything away, and for what? For my own fear?

Was I wasting their one shot?

"Stop!" I choked out. "I'll take it. I'll go to Angeles."

The Empress of Kadjar smiled.

Chapter Two
Roman

I live by two rules. Two rules to keep me safe. Two rules to keep me sane.

One: Never trust a king. Especially when that king is your father.

Two: A prince should be two things—obedient and silent.

My entire life, I've worked my ass off to make sure I'm always both. Most of the time, though, it doesn't work out.

My father, King Nero Stone, sent me to the Healing Room twice a week: Mondays and Fridays. I never even understood why I needed to go. It's not like I could ever heal. You have to face your secrets to do that.

I'll go to my grave with mine.

The Healing Room sessions were like clockwork: I went to the Healing Room at 4 PM; I listened to my therapist spew some bullshit about "recovery" and "my body aligning with the stars" for an hour; and then I went home.

Today was no different. I sat with my chin in my hand while my therapist, Natasha sat across from me. She was a slight woman practically drowning in an oversized sweater, scribbling something down on the legal pad in her lap. Though she was speaking to me, her voice sounded a million miles away.

"Prince Roman?" She snapped her fingers. I jerked to

attention.

"Huh?"

"What do you think?"

"Yes." I blinked.

"I—what?"

"Sorry, what was the question?"

Natasha furrowed her eyebrows. "I asked what's on your mind. Not a yes or no question, Prince Roman." She forced a small laugh, trying (unsuccessfully) to diffuse the awkward situation.

I opened my mouth.

"And I want the truth this time. Not some sarcastic answer." Natasha interrupted.

I closed my mouth. She deflated, setting the legal pad aside. "I'm being serious, Prince Roman. Nothing is ever going to get done if you're not honest with me."

"Nothing has ever gotten done." The second those words left my mouth, I wanted to rip them back in.

"On the contrary, you've grown a lot in the past year, but I'm afraid you're going to lose that progress. You don't seem any…" she drifted off, trying to grasp for words. "You seem like you're losing yourself lately."

"What's that supposed to mean?"

"You're preoccupied. You're seventeen, and you have your whole life ahead of you but you just—you close yourself off. You hide so much, Prince Roman, and it weighs you down. I can see it in your eyes. That's why your father started to send you here, isn't it? Because he saw what your secrets were doing to you?"

My father sends me here because he's afraid I'm going to snap and tell the world what he's done if I don't have somewhere to vent. Though, he'd never admit that.

"I have no secrets, Natasha. I'm an open book. I'm just tired lately. You know how a prince's life works: the older I get, the more responsibilities I have. My father turns fifty in five years, and then I'll take the throne. I have a lot to prepare for."

Natasha nodded, picking up the legal pad again. "You know I don't believe you."

"I'm telling the truth."

"I don't think you are. I think you're a master liar. I think most politicians like yourself are. I think you're hiding yourself from the world, and I think it's slowly killing you." She glanced up at me. "Ivelisse came to see me."

My heart sunk. "Why?"

"She's worried about you. I told you—you're not yourself lately," Natasha leaned in, her voice dropping. "People are noticing."

"What did she say?"

"She wanted to know what she could do to help. She said that she and Ky would do anything for you. They're your friends. They know you better than anyone in this world, and even they see that you're slipping again."

"I'm *fine*." I insisted.

"Then why are you here?"

"Hell if I know." I snapped. I averted my eyes, not

wanting to see the disappointment on Natasha's face. "I'm sorry. I shouldn't have said that."

Natasha took a deep breath. "We're out of time," she exhaled and stood, going for the door. I followed her. "Are you going to show up to our next meeting? Or are you going to skip again?"

A pang of guilt pounded against my chest. "I'll be here. Friday at 4, right?" That was a stupid question. It was always Friday at four.

Natasha nodded.

I hadn't noticed my fists were balled so tightly until my index finger slipped and flicked against the metal flask in my jacket pocket. My breath hitched in my throat as a sharp pinging noise resonated throughout the Healing Room. I froze.

Natasha jerked her chin toward my pocket. "Whatcha got?"

"Um...a drink."

She looked me up and down, eyebrow raised in the air. "Water, right?"

"Water. It's water, yeah. Dehydration's a bitch, you know?" I patted the flask.

"And you just smell like booze because...?"

"I do not—" I brought the collar of my shirt to my nose. The stark stench of beer flooded my nose. "It's...this isn't my shirt." I scrambled for an excuse. "I swear it's water."

She opened her hand. "Can I see the flask?"

I slipped out into the hallway. "No."

"Hey—Prince Roman!" I was halfway down the hall

when Natasha's words stopped me dead in my tracks. "Roman Stone!"

I froze once more. A civilian leaving a royal's title off of their name was a crime. She could have been jailed had there been anyone else in that hallway but me. I turned around slowly, fear thumping through my body.

"What's wrong with you?" She said through gritted teeth, walking toward me with a hand out. "Do you know what the media would do to you if they found out what you've been doing?"

"What? Drinking beer? Going to raves? I'm seventeen. Most kids my age are out partying until the break of dawn. Don't I get to live my life too?"

"Most seventeen-year-olds aren't the heir to the throne of Angeles. I'm serious, Roman, you've got to get yourself in check. You can't keep living your life like this." She held out a hand. "Give me the alcohol."

"I told you, it's water."

"I don't believe you."

I held the flask as tightly as I could. I had two choices, each one digging me an early grave. Either I showed her and she told my father, or I didn't, and she'd tell my father. I took the metal flask out of my pocket.

"Here." I said through clenched teeth. Natasha flipped the top open. She stared down into the flask, then emptied it out in her hand. A single black cigarette fell in her palm. Her eyes widened.

"Prince Roman," she breathed. "What is this?"

The old tale goes something like this: these black cigarettes hold the power to give life and take it away. Created by a man who mixed some of the most powerful drugs in all of Angeles together, you can only smoke two of these cigarettes. Both times you smoke, you'll gain the highest buzz of your life.

You can never smoke more than two. If you do smoke a third cigarette, you'll die. Some people die trying to chase what they once felt.

I don't want to die. I can't. I have a little brother who needs me. I have a nation that needs me, though I seldom want to accept that fact. This little cigarette holds the power to kill me, and I guess I keep it around as a final escape. I don't control most of my life. I am simply a microphone for my father and for the Senate. I don't control what I wear in public. I don't control what I say or do in public. The only time *I* get to control everything is when I'm tucked behind the four walls of my bedroom. I think it's nice to know that, at least, I get to control my own death.

I've smoked two black cigarettes before. Once, with my best friend Ky and another on my sixteenth birthday.

"I've never smoked one before," I lied. "I was just curious."

Natasha closed her hand around the cigarette. I grabbed her wrist, trying to pry it from her hand. I don't know how I'd get another if she took this one. "Please," My voice was gravelly, desperate. "Don't tell my father. Give me the cigarette back."

"Look at you," Natasha said. "You're turning to drugs." Her fist tightened as she jerked out of my grip. "You need to let me help you. You need—"

"Don't say it."

"It would just be for a weekend. The staff would keep it hushed so the media doesn't find out. Nothing major. You just need a break."

"I don't want your stupid retreats or your mental hospitals. I just—I just need time. I can figure things out on my own."

"You don't *get* time, Prince Roman, don't you see that? You only have a few months until you turn eighteen and then for the next five years, you'll be training day in and day out and then you take the throne. There are no breaks for you from here on out."

I shut my eyes, trying to tell myself that she was wrong, even though I knew that she wasn't. "Promise me, Natasha, that my father won't find out what you know."

She took a deep breath. "He won't." She exhaled. "But this is the last time I'm covering for you. I can't do this anymore. I can't let you ruin yourself."

"One cigarette is not going to kill me. I was just curious."

"You were—"

"Stop! Natasha, please stop. Stop telling me what you *think* you know about me. You don't know what I've been through. What I see. What I have to deal with. And I can't tell you, so I don't even know why the hell I come here. I'm fine

25

on my own. I'm done with this. I'm leaving."

I turned, not able to look at her face any longer, not able to stomach the disappointment. I hated it—I hated disappointing her just like I did everyone else.

Natasha called out my name, but I was almost at the elevator. Too far gone to care.

Chapter Three
Ember

The sky is different when you're free.

For the past three hundred and sixty-five days, my sky had been a damp, brown ceiling dripping with water, laughing at me, laughing at the trapped bird I had become. You are mine, it growled. You are going to die in my embrace. I'd close my eyes tightly and pray for the voices to pass. They would always come back.

The sky is different in prison. It's a damning thing, a painful reminder that you are a finite being with a beginning and an end. But when you're free? There is no end to the sky just like there is no end to the possibilities. I have no end. I can live forever and ever and breathe in the air of my city and take in the faces of my people.

I want to spread my arms wide and run for miles until the air sears my lungs and burns my throat with every inhale. I want to run to the ends of Kadjar and scream until my voice gives out. I want to tell anyone who will listen that the walls and the ceiling and my prison sky didn't win. I won.

I'd dreamed about this scenario enough: riding home in a limousine. I just never pictured the empress to be sitting beside me. Traveling through the smooth roads of the marketplace and the streets where the rich owned all their businesses, transitioning to the potholes and gravel roads of the East Sector, didn't feel as freeing as I dreamed it would.

The East Sector was protected by a chain-link fence. I remember my sister, Mara, always used to ask if it was to keep us locked in rather than to protect us from whatever was outside. People gathered on the sides of the road in their ratty clothes and bare feet, shielding their eyes from the sun. For some of them, they'd only ever seen an automobile once or twice in their life. I sure as hell had never ridden in one.

I leaned forward to watch through the windshield as the driver swerved onto my narrow road. It was identical to the rest of the backroads in the East Sector. It was made of orange dirt that kicked up a windstorm of dust and cluttered with debris. The houses were crushed together, made of mismatched boards of wood and cracked concrete.

"Go before I change my mind," Empress Analita nodded toward my house that the driver had halted in front of.

Melancholy hit me like a ton of bricks as I stepped out of the car and into the hot, soupy air. My hands shook. This house, these walls. These forgiving walls so different than the prison ones I had known had raised me and tried to save me. This house showed me nothing but love in the midst of destitution, and I rejected it. I let the wild evil race through my blood and force my hand to kill. I never wanted to kill. But I needed to. For my people.

The porch boards creaked under my feet. Once upon a time they were a dark brown, but now they were a sun-weathered tan.

I stood at my front door, unable to bring myself to knock. I was not the same girl I was a year ago. I don't look like the girl I remembered. This girl, standing in front of her old home, is covered in bruises and scars. This girl shakes with the pain of memories flooding through her like wildfire. This girl is broken. Just like the sector that raised her.

Tendrils of a conversation floated through the doorway.

"…must know something." Mama.

Angry—her voice was angry. The same voice that used to sing me to sleep now sounded like it had spent an entire year screaming.

"I told you, Rosalie. I went to the prison myself. They won't tell us anything." Father. His voice was like ice against the fire of my mother's. My father was not a cold man. This was the man who learned how to sew so he could make dresses for Mara and me when Mama's hands were worn raw from working in the fields all day. The ice in his voice frightened me.

"We are her parents. How can they deny us the right to know the fate of our child's life?"

"I know just as much as you do."

"It's not fair! They can't keep giving us hope and taking it away. I just—I want my daughter back." Her voice cracked.

"I know. I know, my love, I know."

Muffled sobs tore at my heartstrings. Before I could even think about what I was doing, I knocked.

Someone sniffed. "Coming!" Mama's voice had changed in a split second. It was happy, now. That was Mama. She didn't cry in front of people. She didn't allow the world to see her hurt.

The door opened.

Mama blinked. Her face was unreadable. My father stood behind her, eyes bloodshot as well. My chest grew heavy at their sight: they looked old. Gray hairs peppered through Mama's brown tresses. I didn't remember the crows' feet next to her eyes or the laugh lines around her mouth.

"Mama," I whispered. I couldn't raise my voice to a normal volume or else I might've cried. "You look so sad."

She still didn't move. I wanted to see myself in her, like Mara could. They were spitting images of each other. I wanted to see her tan skin and auburn hair, her wide smile and upturned nose, and I wanted to find myself. I couldn't. Father used to say that my mother's beauty was the sun that made the world go 'round.

I was not beautiful in the way she was.

I was like my father—sharp edges and intimidating gazes. I was all pale skin and white hair, glassy blue eyes and unsettling words. I made people uncomfortable, and I used to relish in that fact. It made me different. I never minded it. But Mama used to say that I was her ice queen. I was her little spot of cool in a world on fire. And she loved me for it.

Would she, still, now that she knew that my cool is capable of murder?

"Ember," she rasped. "My baby." A single hand reached out to graze my cheek. She pulled away the second she touched my skin. To her I was part girl, part ghost. I took her hand and brought it to my face again.

"I'm home, Mama."

She pulled me into her arms. My mother was a slight woman, barely five feet tall. I was exactly six inches taller than her but standing there, I was a child again. I was a child with a scraped knee, a child who had a bad dream, a child who needed nothing more than a mother's hug. I couldn't let myself cry. I couldn't let them see my weakness.

So, I shut my eyes tight to keep the tears from pouring I felt my father wrap his arms around the both of us.

"Every night," my mother whispered. I opened my eyes, still struggling to keep tears at bay. "I prayed for you. I prayed to the gods, that they'd bring you home to me again, and they did. Look at you, my girl."

I had gone over this scene a million times—how I'd find the words that would heal all the hurt I had put them through, but no soul-healing words came to mind. No words came at all.

Father pulled Mama close when she folded in on herself, sobbing. He stared at me, smiling. That was enough. I didn't need words. I just needed to know that he didn't hate me.

I can't stay. I mouthed.

He furrowed his eyebrows.

The empress. We have a deal.

My father stopped smiling. I was afraid to say anything else, should Mama hear. She pulled herself out of my father's arms to take another look at me, as if she were afraid I was going to disappear.

"The empress has offered me a deal in exchange for my

freedom, and for real change in the East Sector. Everything I was hoping for."

"A deal?" Father echoed.

"I have to bring back this prisoner of war."

Mama wiped her tears away with the heel of her hand. "From?"

"Angeles."

"No." Father said immediately.

"The empress wants me to infiltrate Angeles to retrieve the prisoner, and she'll give me everything I wanted in return. I can live. I can help the East Sector. Things will finally look up for all of us. This is a chance that I have to take."

Father shook his head. "No. You're still a child. She can't expect you to risk your life in a world we know nothing of. You'll stay here with us—safe."

"She does, and I will. I don't want to die, and I don't want the East Sector to suffer. Don't you want what the North Sectors have?"

"I want my child alive. End of story."

"I don't care what you want."

My father blinked. "Excuse me?"

"I have to go because no one else will."

"Why does it have to be you?" Mama choked out. "Why you? Why—after everything we've lost. Why you?"

"Everything you've lost?" Silence filled the small house. My parents looked at each other, an unspoken conversation drifting through them. I repeated my question.

"Mara…" My father started, then stopped. Mama covered her mouth with her hand, slamming her eyes shut.

"—Is dead." she finished for him, her words tight.

My world was knocked off its axis.

"She was killed the week after you went to prison. Her body was found in the same river you got your notes from." Father's eyes were trained on the ground. I wanted to force him to look at me, to tell me that he was just playing some sick joke on me.

"How—what?"

"We don't know anything. Her death was ruled as a homicide, but the guard hasn't looked into it further. Said there's more important cases to be looked at." Father's eyes met mine. "We can't lose you too. We can't lose two children. Let someone else save the world." While Mama sobbed into her hands, he kept himself calm, back straight as an arrow.

Half of me was screaming I have to save everyone while the other half was screaming I want my sister, and I had no idea which to listen to.

"No one told me," I said to myself more than to them.

Without thinking, I turned and barreled out of the house. The afternoon sun was scorching hot. I flung the auto-car's door open. "No one told me!" I cried. Wind mixed with sand and orange clay whipped my hair around my head. I had to fight to keep it out of my mouth.

"What?" The empress stepped out of the car.

"My sister. My sister is dead, and no one told me." I don't know why I was telling her this. She was the empress of a cold, unforgiving nation. Why should she care about my dead sister? When has she ever cared about her people?

"Mara?" She asked, like it was the simplest thing in the world. "I couldn't tell you. It would have made you weak."

"Made me—what?"

"News like that would have driven you to the brink. You think I don't know the torture my guards put prisoners through?"

"Why tell me now?"

"Prison has made you strong. It's broken you and re-built you. Now I trust you to handle the news; whereas before, you would have fallen apart. I only thought it fair to let you know before the mission. I am nothing if not fair."

Rage burst through my veins, igniting my every sense. "You killed her!" I roared. "You're a murderer!"

If it hadn't been for the hands I felt wrapping around my shoulders, hands that I knew belonged to my father, I would have ripped the empress limb from limb, right then and there. Mara was dead.

My sister.

Dead. Gone.

And there was no killer to blame. There was no man behind bars whom I could throw all my rage at. All I had was blind anger loosely directed toward the woman who built this broken system in which we live.

"You want your sister's killer found?" The empress asked. I nodded. My father's hands fell from my shoulders. "Complete the mission. I'll take the civilian guard force off the case and put the military guard on. They'll find the killer, but you must complete the mission first."

I shut my eyes.

Chapter Four
Roman

Ivelisse was waiting for me in the rose garden, the one place in the world where a prince and his betrothed could be alone.

The gardens had been Mom's project. She always smelled like flowers and fresh soil because for as long as I could remember, she was always gardening.

The gardens were a maze of rose bushes stretching high into the sky, leading into a single clearing with a stone fountain in the middle that had benches along the sides.

Ivelisse and I usually made plans to meet here whenever something happened with my father, so we knew the other was safe.

I had first met her here. Back then, though, the gardens weren't as lavish as they were now. They didn't block out the outside world but were a skeleton of the giant they stood as now.

I remember the scene so clearly: Mom introduces Ivelisse, a wide-eyed six-year-old in a dirty dress. I back away from her as she holds out her hand to me. Mom bends down and says "no, love, you curtsy to royalty." Ivelisse furrows her eyebrows like she can't fathom the idea of curtsying to me.

Mom tells us what it means to be promised to each other. Ivelisse cries, and I try to slip away to the palace. Mom holds us both on the satin fabric of her lap and tells us a story—one of a dashing prince and his beautiful wife saving the day in a land of peril.

How different things would turn out to be.

I inhaled sharply, waiting for the pang of grief to pass. I took a seat beside Ivelisse on one of the benches. She glanced up from the book she had been reading to finally notice me. A sharp gasp escaped her throat, and she reached a hand up to touch my neck.

"What is it?" I asked, as if the past thirty minutes hadn't happened.

"Did he strangle you?" Her words were almost inaudible.

I shook my head. "No."

"There's a mark on the side of your neck—god, it looks like claw marks. They're bleeding." Her fingers grazed across the marks that my father's nails had left on my skin. I jerked away from her.

"I'm fine."

"No, Roman, you're not. You're bleeding." She pulled a tissue from the purse at her side and began wiping away at the sparse blood on my neck.

"I just fell."

"On your neck?"

I shut my mouth.

Ivelisse crumpled the tissue up and stuck it back in her bag. "How are we going to cover this up?"

"How am I going to cover this up," I corrected.

"We." She insisted with an exasperated huff. "You

can't shoulder the entire weight of governing by yourself. That's why you have me. And Ky. And the Senate. You're not supposed to be alone."

"I'm fine. I don't need—"

"You're going to make all the laws? You're going to listen to every concern your people have? You're going to pass every bill and attend to every broken district? All by yourself?"

"Can we not talk about this now?" I snapped. My words came out harsher than I expected them to. Ivelisse blinked. Once. Twice. Her face went blank. I never learned how to mask emotions like she did.

"Alright," she pushed her book down in her purse and pulled out a pastel pink binder. She flipped through the pages, each sheet kept neat and clean with sheet protectors. She stopped at a sheet titled 18th—September 25th.

"You have my birthday marked?" I asked.

Ivelisse nodded. "It's an important birthday. I have yours and Ky's marked down. It's when you become a full-fledged member of the Court, and on yours, you'll be officially recognized as heir to the throne."

My eighteenth birthday was nothing other than a ceremony for the people. Religious leaders would gather at my party so they could bless me as I began training for the throne. It was just another spectacle for the paparazzi.

"We have a month and nine days until the ball. Is everything in order? You've written your speech?"
"Not yet."

Ivelisse rolled her eyes. "I could kick Ky off the reception team, and he could help…oh, that'd never work. You two wouldn't get anything done." The ghost of a smile danced across her maroon-stained lips. Long, black eyelashes coated in mascara brushed against her cheeks when she blinked.

Look at her. She did everything she was supposed to. She smiled for the paparazzi, she held my hand in public, she knew all the right things to say. I should be in love with her. After all, she's in love with me.

She was going to be the perfect queen. She loved Angeles, and she loved her people. She could do press conferences and photoshoots all day. She thrived under the lights, where I lacked.

"Ky and I do get stuff done. We won that one speech and debate competition in school."

Ivelisse scoffed, a little laugh escaping her throat. "Only because Ky tricked all the other participants into forfeiting. That doesn't count."

"The trophy on my bedroom wall would say otherwise."

"You still have that thing? The tournament was almost two years ago. I never knew you were a pack rat." She teased.

"What else am I supposed to do with it?"

"Throw it away?"

I feigned shock. "And lose my only evidence of the legendary speech and debate tournament? The very one where Ky Amadeus McKenna lost half of his savings account bribing the other contestants into quitting? God above, Ivelisse, you've gone mad!"

Her mouth broke out into a stunning smile. "I supposed you're right. I wonder if he ever got that money back. You know, after the headmaster found out."

I shrugged. "Charlie Nakamora did have a new diamond wristwatch after the tournament."

"Oh, you're right. He did! I remember him shoving it in my face at lunch. What a show-off. Ky can't bribe anyone at your ball, especially not Charlie. If he did, I might have to kill him."

"You and my father both," I grumbled. Ivelisse crossed one leg over the other and began flipping through the pages of her planner. The pages were covered in her neat, curling handwriting, detailing every milestone until the day that we took our thrones. She stopped abruptly and shut the book.

"Can you believe it?"

"Believe what?"

"We've waited for this ceremony—for your eighteenth birthday—our entire lives. It's only a month away. After that, we'll be indicted as full-fledged members of the Court. We can sit in on Senate meetings, we can vote on legislation. It's what we've dreamed of for so long."

It's what *you've* dreamed of. I wanted to say, but, like always, I kept my mouth shut.

"Right," was all I said back.

It's not that I don't want to lead. I do. I want to lead, but only in a world where my father is dead. I only want to lead in a world where I can focus on my people. I don't want to constantly look over my shoulder. I don't want to have to worry about my father snapping again and killing me or my brother in the same vein he took my mother. But, I guess I have no option. So, I suck it up. I wake up every day, and I fight. That's all I can do.

"Can I ask you a question?" I said, eager for a change in subject. I didn't want to have to think about my stupid birthday if I didn't have to.

"Sure." Ivelisse stuck her planner back in her bag.

"Why did you go see Natasha?"

Ivelisse paled. Her gaze fell to her shiny lavender heels, the same color as her sweater that was neatly tucked into her cream skirt. She dissolved into a sigh. "I hoped you wouldn't find out. I asked her to keep it a secret."

"Why? What did you need to know so badly that you couldn't have asked me?"

"You'd hate me if I told you."

"Tell me." I insisted.

"It was part worry, yes, but I'd be lying if I said I didn't go for selfish reasons. I'm sorry." Her apology made my heart race.

"Which are...?"

Ivelisse opened her mouth to speak, then closed it like she was having some kind of internal battle. Finally, she spoke. "I wanted to see if you had confessed what I already know. Natasha said she couldn't tell me, though. Patient-doctor confidentiality or something like that."

"What do you know?"

My eyes trailed down to her hands that were gripping her knees, knuckles white. I remember how much she hated me when we were little. She used to push me into puddles if I tried to walk beside her, or she'd scratch me when I got too close. I tried complaining to Mom, but she told me that Ivelisse was only scared. Back then, Ivelisse's hands had been dirty—nails bitten down to the quick, laden with dirt and painted with cracked pink nail polish. Now, her hands were clean. Her fingers long and slender, manicured with white tips.

"I think—I know that you don't love me." I froze. "I've known for a while." She continued.

"You went to Natasha to ask her if I loved you?"

"When you say it like that it makes me sound like a stalker. No, I didn't ask her that. I just asked her what you'd said about me in your little sessions."

"It does kind of make you sound like a stalker."

"You're missing the point, Roman."

"You went to my therapist—"

"Roman!" Ivelisse slammed her hands down on her lap. "I love you, Roman Stone. I love you in the very worst way." My heart beat so loudly against my chest that I was sure all of Angeles could hear it. "And I know…I know that my confession is just a shout into a very dark void, but I thought you should at least hear it. I only thought it to be fair."

I was raised to always have soul-healing monologues on hand. From the second I could speak, my father was coaching me. I always had the right words to say to someone, from a hurting citizen who'd just suffered a tragedy, to a friend who simply needed a kind word. I was always supposed to have the right things to say.

But now, I didn't.

"I'm sorry," was all I finally said.

She waved a dismissive hand, clearing her throat. "It's fine. I just—I just wanted to tell you."

"I wish I could say it. And mean it." I said, trying to fill the silence. God, I hated this aching silence. I hated it with every fiber of my being. She wasn't crying. She was trying not to, I think, and I was left in an awkward limbo between wanting to run and wanting to comfort her.

"I do too. I've spent the last few years wishing that very same thing."

"Have you?"

"Yes, Roman, of course I have. It's not like I could have just ignored it. I could light the world on fire with what I feel, and you could barely light a match for me. Imagine how that feels."

She wasn't angry. Just defeated. Still, her words stole the breath from my lungs. How lucky I am to have another person that feels such a fire for me—and look at me, the broken shell of a prince that can't even manage to say three simple words and mean them.

"If I said it once, would that…" I trailed off.

"No. That would be like opening up the wound I've tried so hard to patch up. I just wanted to tell you and get it out of my system before everything happens. You know the

Court is going to push for us to get married as soon as I turn eighteen. My birthday is only three months after yours. I just needed to know that you didn't feel what I feel. I had to be sure. I don't want to go into this putting more effort in than I'm getting back."

"And you won't be. It'll be like my parent's marriage. Business only."

"Right. Love is for the common people."

"Exactly."

She stood, hiking her bag up on her shoulder. I followed her. "And by this time next year, we'll be planning our wedding. Strictly business. In five years, we'll be sitting on the thrones of Angeles. Then the Court will push for us to have children."

"And we'll have children." I filled in the silence as we began our way through the maze of the rose gardens. I could faintly hear the buzz of the city growing as we neared the exit.

"And we'll grow old together. Strictly business." Ivelisse stopped. A long stretch of tall rose bushes stood between us and the palace. "I don't want this, Roman." I hadn't realized she was crying until I turned to see tears streaking down her face.

"Wh—what?"

"You. I don't want you. I mean—I do want you. I want you more than I've ever wanted anything in my entire life, but not like this. Look at you." She threw a hand in my direction and hastily wiped at her face with the other.

"I'm not following you."

"You're cold and callous. You're distant. You don't talk to me or Ky like you used to. You're going to rule an entire nation, and you're becoming just like him. I'm so afraid for what's going to happen the second you get on that throne," she paused. "I'm afraid...I'm afraid the throne is going to drive you mad like it did him. I'm afraid for myself and for our future children. I don't want to marry you until I get the Roman I know back."

"Nothing is wrong."

"Really? You show up today with bruises and scars on your neck. You give one-worded replies and smile just like you're standing in front of cameras. You're not. You're with me. I've been by your side since we were six and now—only a year away from our marriage—you're treating me like a stranger?"

"I just...I have to figure things out."

"How long is that going to take? How long am I going to have to wait? I am sick of being cheated by you."

"Cheated?"

"Before you're my husband, you're supposed to be my friend, and you can't even do that. You can't even get over yourself long enough to realize that you don't get to have emotions like the rest of them. You don't get to mope around all day. You don't get to hide yourself away because you're afraid of him."

"I'm afraid? I have never been afraid!"

"Really? Because I have a whole list of reasons why that's a lie."

Anger shook through my body. I turned away from Ivelisse, trying to stop myself from seeing red. I pressed my pointer finger and my thumb to the bridge of my nose and waited for the wave of anger to pass. "I am so sick of you."

"What?"

"You act like you're God's gift to the palace. Let me let you in on a little secret, princess. You're no better than the rest of us. You aren't special. You don't get to point fingers at me while acting like you don't have your secrets, too."

"I have no secrets."

"Really? Should I order Killian to take a paternity test, then? Don't you think we'd find a few skeletons in the closet?"

She didn't realize that I knew. I had overheard Li Grace discussing it when her mother came to visit the palace once. Killian wasn't Ivelisse's father. Ivelisse's father was a farmer in the Agricultural District. He didn't have the money that Killian had, so Li sacrificed love for opportunity.

Killian didn't know, and Li swore up and down that he could never know. Ivelisse only found out when she was going through her mother's things and found a letter from Li to Ivelisse's biological father.

Ivelisse's face grew red. "You asshole!" She shoved two hands directly into my chest. I stumbled back a bit. "You're just like him, you know. You can act like you're some kind of troubled soul but you're not. You're just as evil and vindictive as the king."

"I—"

46

"Rot in hell." With that, Ivelisse turned on her heels and left.

Chapter Five
Ember

"This mission is simple, but it can only remain simple if you begin with the goal in mi—are you even listening?" The empress crossed her arms over her chest. I jerked my head away from the window of the jet.

Empress Analita looked utterly human while trapped within the small confines of the helicopter. I grew up hating this woman with everything that I had in me. She let my family run out of rations in the middle of famine. She let my cousins and uncles and aunts starve to death. I wanted her to be some vile monster with scales for skin and fire for breath. She doesn't look like that, though, and I'm slightly disappointed as I stare at the shockingly beautiful face of the vile woman standing across from me.

She looked just like any other North Sector woman, wearing a white shirt tucked into a pair of cigarette pants, paired with black flats. Seeing her without her ceremonial red robes and their embroidered golden swirls was odd and a bit unsettling.

"I'm listening." I lied.

"What did I just say?"

"Something about the mission being simple?"

Empress Analita set her hands on her hips and craned her head toward the metal ceiling. She shut her eyes and muttered, "Gods, you're going to be a piece of work." I wanted to fire something back, but an entire night without rest had cost me some of my wits.

She began to speak once more, and I zoned out. None of it was important, anyways. Just some backstory about the palace I'd be staying at, Angelesan history, and stupid rules about interacting with the Angelesan royals.

The helicopter I sat in was an old one—last used almost thirteen years ago in the war against Angeles. Everyone knows someone who died in that war. A war started over something as stupid as trade rules, ending in an Angelesan victory and over half of Kadjar dead. I wondered how many Kadjarian men and women bled out in this exact same plane, all for a war that they didn't start.

I wonder how many will continue to do so. I wonder how many people I've grown up with who will sacrifice their lives to a nation that never loved them. I wonder how many will do so because they know that false patriotism is better than starving to death on the streets because their families can't survive without the money.

"Repeat that back to me."

I snapped my head towards the empress. "What now?"

"What I just said. Repeat it back to me."

After a straight twenty seconds of silence, the empress let her head fall into her open palms. She huffed and repeated herself. "You have to know the hierarchy of Angelesan politics or else you won't stand a chance. Are we clear?"

"I'm only going to be there for three days. Why does any of this matter?"

"It matters because you have to get someone of importance to tell you where the prisoners who aren't dead yet are being held. This mission depends on you blending in. Can I trust you to act like a normal person for three days?"

"Obviously."

A flash of a scowl crossed her face before she continued. "Prince Roman is the heir to the throne. His younger brother, Prince Ian, has been sheltered for most of his life; whereas, his brother has been thrust into the limelight essentially from birth." She went on. "You will attend this party, find out where the prison is, infiltrate it, and get out. Am I clear?"

"Wait—what party?"

She ran a hand down her face. "The exact party I've been talking about for the past half hour. Gods above, are you deaf?"

"No. Just not interested in learning about this capitalistic machine you call a nation. Forgive me." My voice oozed sarcasm. Anger flickered behind the empress's eyes.

"Prince Ian is turning twelve. The palace is hosting a gala in his honor. You will attend the gala, rub shoulders with the nobility, and find out where the prison is. Once you've located the prison, you'll infiltrate it and get out. I'm giving you a three-day time limit because I've never had a soldier last beyond the first three days. If you can't do it in three days, then it's never getting done."

"Is the prison location not public knowledge?"

"No. King Nero does wicked and twisted things to his

prisoners. Once someone is convicted of a crime, they're never heard from again. No one knows where the prison is, and everyone in Angeles is terrified of the prospect. I have a hunch as to where it's at."

"Which is?"

"Under the palace. It's the easiest place for the king to sneak in and out of. If I were you, I wouldn't wait to infiltrate. I'd do it tonight at the gala, while everyone is occupied."

"How am I supposed to find out where it is?"

"That's not my problem. That's yours." The empress picked up her water bottle and took a sip before setting it down on the wooden crate next to her. "Let's go over your backstory once more. You are?"

"Helené Grace, cousin to Ivelisse Grace, who is the daughter of Killian and Li Grace. Killian serves in the Senate, and Li serves on the king's advisory council. I am the daughter of a wealthy banker from the Business District and was invited to the palace for Prince Ian's 12th birthday celebration. See? I did listen."

Empress Analita nodded curtly. "What do you know of the royal family and their inner circle?"

I shrugged. "Nothing."

"What do you mean nothing?"

"I mean that no one ever talks about Angeles back home. It's a dirty word. Kind of like cursing around children."

The empress huffed. "The royal family consists of the two princes and their father, the king. The queen resides in the Common District where she works with nearby charities, so she's never at the palace."

"Oh, that's nice. Seems like she actually cares."

If the empress noticed my jab, she didn't say anything. "The queen is dead."

"I—what? You just said that she—"

"The queen is dead, and my spies believe that the king killed her. The Common District is simply a facade so all of Angeles doesn't know what goes on behind palace walls. The people can't mourn what they don't know is gone, can they?"

"Guess not," I said.

"Nevermind that. Let's continue. The inner circle consists of the king's advisory council, Prince Roman's betrothed, Ivelisse Grace, and his best friend, Ky McKenna."

"Doesn't the king have friends?"

"No. Most royalty don't fraternize like common citizens do. If anyone is going to stand in the way of your mission, it's going to be Ky and Ivelisse. Ky is undoubtedly loyal to the royal family. Ivelisse is intelligent and quick-witted."

"I thought Ivelisse was on our side?"

"Her parents are. They were easy to pay off. Ivelisse, however, might be a bit skeptical. Keep your eye on her."

"What do I do if I think she's going to blow my cover?"

"Run."

"Is there someone I can call to come get me out?"

"No. You either come back with the prisoner of war or you don't come back at all."

A chill raced up my spine. I had to come back. I had to see my parents again and find my sister's killer.

"How am I supposed to find them?"

"My last informant managed to tell me that the prisoner is in a secluded part of the prison, and it's marked. You'll know when you get there."

I shook my head. "This is a suicide mission."

A jolt of turbulence almost pushed me off my crate, but I held on tightly. Empress Analita craned her neck to look out the nearby window. I hadn't dared to even peek at the window behind me.

"It's time to go. Get out."

"I—what?"

The empress stalked toward the door beside me and flung it out. A gust of wind pushed in, rocking the empty crates and rustling papers. I struggled to stand. The empress caught my arm just before I could step out.

"Come back with that prisoner." She said.

I jerked out of her grasp and stepped out, into the sun.

The helicopter hovered a few inches above some sort of concrete barrier that stood between Angeles and the outside world—a barrier that had been constructed just after Angeles' victory in the war, almost like they were afraid of Kadjarian retaliation. Who would've thought that the retaliation would come fourteen years later in the form of a disgraced assassin.

Wind from the helicopter blew my ponytail into my eyes as I stepped down to the barrier. For a second, all I could see was a silver whirl of hair. I pushed it out of my face and tried not to think about the eighty-some feet that stood between me and the ground.

53

Every inch of me wanted to look on this world with disgust. Every inch of me wanted to see the flickering, glowing advertisements cast upon skyscrapers so tall that they disappeared into the clouds and feel nothing but disgust. Yet, somehow, I felt nothing at all. No disgust, no sadness. Nothing.

In my mind's eye, though, I could only see the anti-Angelesan graffiti spray-painted over the sides of abandoned buildings in the main strip. I could hear the faint riots in front of the citadel as people demanded to know when the troops were coming home. I could hear my Aunt Hana's raucous sobs as a tiny white box of her husband's ashes was delivered to her door. I could smell the burning fire as all those with Angelesan blood were burned alive in the marketplace.

All over something as simple as a trade war.

A trade war escalated into years of ill will just because our empress couldn't stand to lose. She'd rather trade in tens of thousands of Kadjarian lives just so she didn't have to accept defeat at the hands of King Nero.

I couldn't find it in myself to hate this place. I couldn't make room in my soul for any more hatred.

The wild wind behind me lifted and vanished. I was alone. I dropped to my knees to figure out my next move—how the hell was I going to get off of here?

"I guess now would be a good time to mention that I am not the biggest fan of heights."

Two white heels appeared in my peripheral vision. I craned my head up to see a girl standing beside me. I clambered to my feet, brushing debris off of my jeans. The girl in front of me was dressed immaculately, in a pastel pink skirt and white shirt, her hair tied up in a ribboned ponytail atop her head. Careful tendrils of jet-black hair curled around her jaw.

She peered over the barrier and shuddered. "Lady Ivelisse Grace of the Court," she stretched a hand out in introduction, closing the space between us. "Future queen at your service. King Nero called an emergency advisory council meeting, and my father had a Senate meeting to attend, so they sent me. They send their utmost apologies."

I took her hand and shook it.

"And your name?" She asked.

"The Bloodhound."

Ivelisse blinked, then furrowed her eyebrows. "You're Ember Levin, are you not? The prisoner we're housing?"

Her words caught me off guard. "I—yes."

Ivelisse nodded. "Good. We have less than a day until the gala and—no offense or anything—but you look like you've gone dumpster diving."

"What?"

Ivelisse sighed.

~

I wanted to hate Angeles. I really, really did.

The city was breathtaking. Never in my life had I ever seen so many people gathered in one place. They shoved into each other, dressed in business suits and carrying briefcases and shouting and pointing at the yellow cars that drove past.

And the palace—there aren't words to describe it. It

55

was like every castle in every storybook I've ever read all twined into one. Two main buildings connected through a golden archway. The back building, Ivelisse explained, was off-limits to the tourists. That's where the nobility lived. The front building held the Senate hall, every Senator's office, and a little shopping mall for the tourists complete with restaurants and the works.

The people in the foyer of the front building were dressed the same as those outside in the city: professional clothes and carrying laptops and briefcases. They all would've fit right into the North Sector. Dressed in ill-fitting jeans and a baggy t-shirt brought to me by one of the empress' handmaids, I felt all too out of place.

No one paid much attention to the two of us as we stood against the marble wall. Ivelisse had told me not to move while she pulled out her phone. She made a call, speaking in short, clipped vowels that I didn't understand. I looked over at her, trying to make sense of what was coming from her mouth. She didn't seem to notice me.

"What was that?" I asked as soon as she set her phone down.

"What?"

"What you just said—all of that."

"Mandarin?" She asked. "Never heard of it?"

"No."

"What do you speak in Kadjar?"

"English. I've heard the North Sectors speaking French in the marketplace, but we don't learn other languages in our schools."

"Angelesan children are required to learn a second language. I chose Mandarin because that's the language I would have spoken if my mother's family hadn't moved to Angeles."

"What do you mean?"

"You really don't know anything about the outside world?"

I shook my head. "I've always assumed that Kadjar was the beginning and ending of the world."

"People started to form small tent cities after North America was pretty much decimated due to the plague that swept through. Kadjar and Angeles both come from those tent cities. Once, before the plague, though, people migrated to and from North America in extreme capacities for pleasure."

"Is that how your family ended up here?"

"No. My family was one of the few that moved here after the plague when they got word of how Angeles was going to take over North America once again. They, like many, had hope that North America would become what it once was, and so they left China in search of a better life here."

"What about your father's family?"

Ivelisse thought for a moment. "They came from Cuba. I don't know much about his family, actually. My father says we don't know much about how they got here, but I'm glad they did move. If they hadn't, I wouldn't be the future queen."

Ivelisse's phone buzzed. She started talking into it again, still in Mandarin, and I zoned out. I could spend hours in this place. It was all too easy to forget who I was amongst the mass of people. None of them cared who I was or wasn't. I wasn't a killer. I was just a girl, standing in clean, borrowed clothes with, albeit still dirty, but perfumed skin. I wasn't a girl who'd spent the last year of her life in prison.

Businessmen and women flooded in and out of elevators on either side of me. I could stay and watch them with their extravagant clothes and sleek hair and beautiful lives forever. If I concentrated hard enough, I could even pretend like I was one of them. I could really be Helené Grace, kin to nobility and owner of fancy evening gowns and said things like—

I snapped out of my daze to find Ivelisse gone. I tensed, my head swiveling from side to side as I pushed my way through the crowd of people, only to make it to the other side without a single sign of Ivelisse.

A force knocked me to the ground. "Wha—oh, I'm sorry." I rubbed my aching forehead to see a boy on his bottom a few inches from me. He clambered to his feet and held a hand to help me. I stood on my own.

"Forgive me," he said. "I was in my own little world."

"It's fine. I was too. Just looking for someone."

The boy staring at me took me aback—stunned me for a second. Sculpted perfectly as if out of stone: a sharp, sloped nose on a face of tanned, olive skin with full lips. He wore a neat blue polo shirt and a pair of khaki pants. There was a golden watch on his wrist that practically screamed money. The only messy thing about him, though, was the mop of curly brown hair atop his head.

"Who?" He asked.

"My cousin. She was here one second and gone the next. This place is a little…busier than I'm used to."

He laughed. "I hear that a lot from visitors. When you grow up here you definitely do have to work to find peace in all the commotion—something I'm still working at. Is your cousin a part of the Court or is she a visitor as well?"

"The what row?"

"The Court."

"I'm still not following."

"The Court. The Senate and their families." The boy looked at me like I was an idiot. Part of me wanted to slap him. I nodded. "Alright, what's your cousin's name?"

"Ivelisse Grace."

"Ivelisse! Oh, follow me. I can take you to her apartment." The boy jerked his head towards the back building. He bounded down the steps, through the golden archway, and into the second building. Immediately, the number of people died down. Two children chased each other across the foyer, and a woman followed them, calling out as they ran.

At the back wall, there sat a secretary at her desk, answering calls. Behind her was a pegboard of cards with barcodes on them. Across from the secretary's desk, in the direction of the running children, was a long row of elevators.

"You live here?" I asked as the boy walked up to the secretary. She smiled and raised an eyebrow toward him, then spoke into the phone. "I need the Grace's card, please." He whispered. The woman plucked a card from one of the pegs and handed it to him. He thanked her and led me to an elevator.

"To answer your question," he said as the elevator closed in front of us. "Yes. The Court lives here as well. Everyone else, who doesn't serve in the Senate, works out in the Royal District."

The elevator jolted and shot upwards. I gripped onto the railing. "Have you ever been to the palace before?" He asked, staring at my hands.

"Yes, once, when I was younger. I was invited back for Prince Ian's party. My parents couldn't come, so they sent me."

He nodded slowly, shoving his hands in his pockets. "Yeah, the Graces invited almost a hundred people. Each Court member invited every distant relative they have. I don't know how we're going to fit all these people in the palace."

The elevator opened to reveal a narrow hallway with golden wallpaper and maroon carpeting. We must've passed at least twenty doors before the boy stopped in front of one. "Since you're traveling alone, I'm assuming you're staying with the Graces?"

"Yes."

He handed me the card with the barcode. "You'll need this, then. Just return it to the main desk when you leave. Li and Killian should have spares if you lose this one."

I took the card from his hands and stared down at the

door. There wasn't a knob anywhere, just some kind of scanner. I looked from the card to the door, trying to figure out what the hell I was supposed to do to get the door open.

"You scan the card." He said, flatly.

"I—what?"

He took the card from my hand and pressed the barcode against the metal scanner. It clicked, and he pushed the door open.

"How did that happen?" I asked.

"Every apartment door is like that for security reasons. If you need to get into someone else's apartment, you'll have to have their card. The secretary can check identities through her computer system, and if you're not on the apartment owner's record, you can't have their card. It's fairly simple once you think about it."

I turned to walk into the Grace's apartment, but his voice stopped me. "I never caught your name."

"Excuse me?"

"Your name."

"Oh, it's Helené. Helené Grace. And you?"

The boy nodded. "It's nice to meet you, Helené. I'm Roman."

I gaped. "As in…Prince Roman?"

"Yes. I apologize—I should have introduced myself as such. It's not every day that you meet someone who doesn't recognize their prince."

I fumble for words, afraid that he's caught me in my lie. "I'm just a bit out of it today. Forgive me, Prince."

I couldn't hide my confusion. Him—a prince? The very thought hadn't even dawned on me. He didn't move or speak like I had expected a prince to. He spoke very matter-of-factly. There were no grandiose gestures or beautiful analogies twined into his words. Maybe I caught him on a bad day. He walked like there were shackles around his ankles, like a bird that had been caught and caged.

"Don't mention it. I'll see you again, Helené, alright?"

"Yes. I'll see you again."

Chapter Six
Roman

The only thing that separated me and my brother from a crowd of four hundred and eight-five Court members and their guests was a glass door and a velvet curtain.

Ian and I met in the hallway just outside the ballroom, where we each had our own dressing rooms. He didn't speak to me at first, just presented me with the cuffs of his shirt that weren't buttoned.

"Where are your cufflinks?" I asked, buttoning his sleeves.

Ian shrugged.

"Here, hold on a second." I reached into the pocket of my blazer and pulled out two golden cufflinks with the seal of Angeles stamped into them: a tiger rearing on its hind legs, circled by a barrier. "These used to be Dad's."

Ian's eyes widened, and he jerked his wrists away from me. "You took Dad's cufflinks? No, Roman give them back. He's going to be so mad. I don't want him to be mad at me."

"Calm down," I said, pulling on Ian's wrists. "He doesn't care about these cufflinks, I promise."

"Why?"

"Mom gave them to him."

Ian's face softened as I took his wrists and put the cufflinks through his sleeves. He watched my face carefully. "I thought Dad threw all of Mom's stuff away?" I shook my head, not trusting myself to say anything.

Dad never actually got these cufflinks. They were a birthday present that he never received. On the only night that I ever saw my mother angry, she gave them to me instead. She told me to take care of them, and she'd rather give them to someone who deserves to wear such precious metals.

I finished putting Ian's cufflinks on and opened the glass doors as trumpets began to blare. My father's voice filled the hallway, booming out of a microphone. "Citizens of Angeles, please join me in welcoming my sons, Prince Roman Oliver Veres Stone and Prince Ian Alexander Harlock Stone."

The curtain flew up and away. The crowd erupted in cheers. I knew better than to squint under the stage lights as I walked to my father's side. Ian and I parted ways to stand on either side of our father. We both stood as we were taught with hands clasped behind our back and smiles bright as we stared down at our subjects.

Look at them. They have no idea what a monster their king is. Oblivion truly is a gift.

My father spread his arms wide and the cheers subsided. "My friends, thank you for attending the celebration of my youngest son's birth. Ian truly is a gift to the royal family. We thank you for being here with us." I faded out of focus as he went on to talk more about Ian and his favorite memories of him that hadn't even happened. I don't remember the last time my father spoke to Ian in a way that wasn't scolding or passive-aggressive.

He thanked the crowd a final time, and they burst into

another round of jarring applause. My father spoke again, talking about an amazing era that our family was going to bring Angeles into I wondered when the people would grow tired of hearing the exact same promises at every celebration.

That's the harsh truth that everyone seems to ignore My father was a terrible king. He rarely ever attended the Senate meetings that he was supposed to. All government affairs were left to his advisory council to handle. He only cared about making himself look good. He spent his days shooting magazine covers and appearing on stupid daytime talk shows. He didn't care about his people. My father was the greatest showman.

"Now, please, enjoy yourselves in the name of my young son." My father knelt down to Ian's level as the crowd dispersed. I immediately moved to Ian's side. King Nero looked up at me with the same face that haunted my nightmares.

"There is a throne by the gift table that you are to sit at and accept gifts. You will smile at all the people, give a kind word, and shake hands. You will not get up or leave. Are we clear?"

"It's his party, that's not—"

Ian put a hand on my arm, stopping me dead in my tracks. "Stop it, Roman. It's fine." He snapped.

I stepped back. My father stood. For years, he had towered over me. Now, we were at eye level. How I wish that would be enough to deter him from hurting Ian, but I doubted so. His eyes studied every feature on my face, scrutinizing every imperfection until he fixated on the fading scratch marks.

"If anyone hears about what happened yesterday," he growled, voice low and dangerous. "I will find out, and I will make you regret it."

In a split second, his face changed. He plastered on a fake smile and turned sharply for the crowd. He called out toward a nearby Senator who patted my father on the back as he came close.

"Roman!" I turned to find Ivelisse at the edge of the stage, waving to me. I started for her, not taking my eyes off of Ian who was making his way toward the throne next to an already half-full present table with golden cloth over it. Two guards stood next to the throne.

Ivelisse kissed my cheek as I came close. "Cameras. I still hate you," she whispered in my ear. I plastered on my best smile and took her hand as we entered the crowd.

Sure enough, I caught glimpses of the back wall laden with paparazzi, cameras hanging off their neck. Some of them aimed their cameras at the crowd, desperate to get a shot of Ivelisse and me. Most of them didn't bother, pointing their cameras up at the diamond-encrusted chandeliers above us. Reporters with records and pads of paper pushed their way through the crowd, talking to whatever important-looking figure they could find.

I pulled Ivelisse away from the thick of the crowd toward the wall. "I'm sorry about yesterday. That was a low blow."

"I know. You should be sorry."

"We could have talked about it at Auria. You kind of stood Ky and I up. We tried to call you, but you didn't answer."

"Yeah. I had work to do. Sorry." She said without an ounce of remorse in her voice. She crossed her arms over her chest, eyes trained on the floor.

"Don't be. Do you think I could win you back if I said I bought you a latte and a pretzel? They're sitting in my fridge. Just say the word and I'll be there with them."

She glanced up at me. "Maybe. Only if it's—"

"Vanilla latte with an extra shot and coconut milk and a pretzel with honey mustard?"

A smile broke out on her face. "For some stupid reason I can never be mad at you for too long. It's almost as infuriating as you are."

Ivelisse grabbed my hand, and we made our way back into the crowd. Her hand was warm around mine. It sent a round of guilt through my body.

She knows now. I told myself. She knows your secret, she knows you don't love her. She's just joking. She's just being friendly.

"Uh, hello, the coffee and pretzel were my idea, you're welcome. Stop taking my brownie points, dude." None other than Ky McKenna broke through Ivelisse and I. He looped his arms through Ivelisse's and mine, steering us toward a group of our friends at the back of the room.

"But I bought them." I remarked.

"Still, my idea. My copyright."

Ivelisse hummed. "I don't think that's the right use of the word copyright." Cameras flashed as we passed the wall of paparazzi.

"Who manufactures dictionaries? I'll buy them out, so I can change the definition. That, my friends, is why I am a level ten genius."

"Since when are we classifying intelligence through levels?" Ivelisse asked.

Ky thought for a minute. He stopped walking, stopping Ivelisse and I as well. "Since I made up a foolproof system, obviously."

"If we're going by levels, I think I'd classify you as a level ten dumbass." I said. Ivelisse snickered, and we joined the group of people waiting for us.

"I can't seem to find a waiter. I need a glass of champagne." There was a boy with glitter smeared across his cheeks. He ran a hand through his fire-red hair and stood on his tiptoes to look through the crowd for someone carrying a silver platter of champagne.

"The very last thing you need is champagne. You can't even drink yet. You have to be eighteen, stupid." The girl next to him huffed. She untangled a red curl from her headband as she spoke.

"Oh, please. No one cares if we drink. If they do care, just toss them a few hundred Notes or so."

"Markus, why do I get the odd feeling that you've done that before?" Ky asked, narrowing his eyes.

"Oh, don't be jealous, Ky. We all know that dear old mommy found out about your little escapade on your seventeenth, and now you're too scared of being caught again." Markus retorted, voice dripping with sarcasm. His sister, who I recognized from our younger years, elbowed him in the ribcage, but he didn't bend. I think her name was Allie or something. She used to be friends with Ivelisse.

"Yeah, because someone snitched." Ky turned his attention towards the other boy in the circle, whom I only barely recognized as Kenneth Nakamora, brother to Charlie Nakamora, whom Ky had bribed in school.

"I didn't snitch!" Kenneth threw his hands in the air. "Your mom asked me if I had a good time at your party, and I told her I didn't remember anything."

"That's snitching!"

Just as Kenneth was about to defend himself, his brother waltzed up. I could practically smell the whiskey on his breath as he tossed an arm around my shoulder. Some of the guys my age snuck away hours before celebrations so they could pre-game at places where they wouldn't get caught, and then they'd show up to galas and balls drunker than all get out. Most guards were easily swayed about smaller things if you handed them fifty Notes. Not that I have experience with that, or anything.

"You seen the new girl?" Charlie slurred. "She's hot but she's weird and a little mean. Almost bit my fuckin' head off when I tried to get her to dance with me."

"Well, were you a jerk about it?" Ivelisse said at the

same time I asked, "the what?" I ducked out of Charlie's grip. He leaned on Ky, who tried to no avail to get out from under his arm.

"The new girl. And no, I wasn't. At least I don't think so. She's one of Ivelisse's guests, I think. They have the same last name." He pointed a shaking finger toward Ivelisse.

"Which one? My parents invited all of my cousins, even the ones from the Common District. If she's weird, she's probably from there. Just…ignore them." She looked down at her phone.

"That's a little rude, don't you think?" Allie asked.

"Not when they're from the Common District. God, they all probably have lice or something." Ivelisse answered back flippantly without glancing up from the screen in her hand.

"If all your cousins are as hot as this one, I think I'm moving to the Common District." Charlie said, plucking a glass of champagne from a passing waiter's tray. Markus tried to grab at the tray but was too late. He took Charlie's glass from his hand, eliciting a grunt of disapproval from Charlie.

"Which one are you talking about?" Ivelisse stuck her phone back in her pocket.

Charlie whirled around, almost tripping over his feet, and pointed. I followed his finger to find a girl whom I just barely recognized as the girl I'd led to Ivelisse's apartment the day before. She stood next to Li and Killian. I watched her for a second as she shook hands with my father and another one of his advisors. She smiled, let out a laugh and a wave,

70

and disappeared back into the crowd.

"Oh, I know her. I met her in the hallway earlier. Her name is Selene or Celaine or—"

"It's Helené." Ivelisse said. "My dad's sister's kid."

"Since when do you have a hot cousin?" Markus asked.

Ivelisse turned around to smack his shoulder. "Is that all you think about?"

"No. I think about other things. I think about dinosaurs a lot. Why don't we have dinosaurs? We have flying trains and robots that do our laundry, but we don't have dinosaurs? I think it's a travesty, really—"

"Markus, with all due respect, stop talking."

Allie started to speak, something about her brother being embarrassing. I watched as Ky ducked away from the group and disappeared into the thick of the crowd. I turned back to Ivelisse, assuming Ky to be lost to the crowd. On her phone again, I could see her texting someone—a number she didn't have saved.

I'm not getting my hands dirty. Not in this. It's not my problem.

She shut her phone off before I could read the rest of the message. I wasn't risking asking her what she meant and get accused of being a stalker. Still, something about the message didn't sit right with me.

A voice from behind dragged me out of my thoughts.

"Everyone." Ky introduced. "This is Helené Grace, Ivelisse's cousin. She's staying at the palace for the gala, and we're all going to be nice to her. Markus, Charlie, if you hit

71

on her I'll throw you over the barrier."

"Do not hit me," Helené warned in a sharp tone.

"No, he said hit on you." Ivelisse pulled her cousin over to where she stood. Helené's face was stoic. Ivelisse let out a forced laugh in an attempt to disperse the tension in the group. Ky glanced at me sideways, almost as if asking if bringing her over here was a good idea. I gave a small shake of my head to let him know to drop the question.

"What's the difference?" Helené asked.

"It means—you know what? It's not important."

Another waiter passed, this time carrying a tray of sushi rolls. Ky reached over and plucked one off the platter, popping it into his mouth. "So, Helené, where are you from?" he asked.

"She's from the Business District." Ivelisse answered before Helené could even open her mouth.

Ky motioned towards Helené. "I was trying to drag some conversation of out her. What does your family do?"

"My father runs a business."

Ky gave a friendly laugh. "That's what people do in the Business District, don't they? What does he sell?"

I elbowed Ky in the ribs lightly. "Dude, let up."

"What? I'm just trying to be nice."

"You're not supposed to interrogate the guests. Unless they're criminals. In that case, we leave that to the prison warden."

Helené tensed. "Jewelry. He outsources jewelry to shops in the Common and Royal districts."

"So, he makes cheap, tourist jewelry? Plastic, I'm assuming?" Allie asked, her lip curling.

"Um, no?" Helené's words came out as more of a question than an answer.

There was something about the way her eyes shifted to meet Allie that I didn't trust, almost like something was wrong. Ivelisse's family was huge, but I still knew almost all of her cousins. I could name the majority of them. Surely, I would have remembered a cousin like Helené.

Ky nudged me. He nodded towards my father who was making a beeline for Ian. Without speaking, I took off to meet my father at Ian's throne. I saw the malice in his eyes. It wasn't like it ever fully went away, though. My father bent down and whispered something in Ian's ear as I walked up.

Reporters were gathered around Ian's throne, holding recorders in his face as the guards pushed them back. I squeezed my way through the crowd. Ian looked over at me, worry across his face. Gods, he was only twelve. He shouldn't have to be worried.

Cameras clicked like crazy and shouted questions flooded through my ears. Stars danced in my eyes with the flash of cameras.

What did you say to him? I mouthed to my father. My smile never wavered. My father ruffled Ian's hair, and an ocean of clicks and flashes flooded my senses. Poor Ian was fighting to keep the grin on his face as he accepted gifts only to hand them to the guards. They set them on the table and pushed another wave of reporters back.

He is faltering. My father mouthed bad.

He is a child. Don't hurt him.

My father turned to the guards. "Take the paparazzi away. I want them out of the gala. All of them."

The guard repeated his order to the crowd. Both guards dispersed with the reporters, herding them like cattle as their cameras clicked one last time.

My father set his gaze on me. "I will do whatever I want with my son."

"If you do so much as touch a hair on my brother's head, I will rip you apart limb from limb and feed you to the dogs."

The King of Angeles reeled away from me. The smile fell from his face as the last camera clicked. Ian grabbed my wrist that was holding the arm of his throne so tightly my knuckles were turning white.

"I'm okay, Roman." He said. "Everything is okay."

My father clamped a hand down on Ian's shoulder. I set a hand on my father's. "Leave," I spat. "Leave him alone."

"Prince Roman. King Nero." A sharp voice in front of us broke our stare-down. Ivelisse stood in front of us with her arms clasped behind her back. "There are still reporters in the ballroom. Reporters taking pictures. May I speak to Prince Roman privately, please?"

I took Ivelisse's hand and followed her to the corner of the ballroom. "You need to take a breather."

"A breather?"

"You look like you're about to pass out. Someone is

going to notice. Someone with a camera."

"King Nero told them all to leave."

"You know some of them are going to find a way to sneak in. You can't be walking around like you've just seen a ghost—you're sweating, and your hands are shaking. Go. Collect yourself. I'll stand with Ian."

"I don't need a breather."

She raised an eyebrow. "What we don't need is someone to take a picture of you and try to pass off a headline about you being sick. You know how the paparazzi are. Just for five minutes. Go take a walk or something."

I started to protest but decided against it. I thanked her and pushed through the crowd, out the door.

Getting out was a sigh of relief.

I shouldn't want to get away from it all. The hustle and bustle of galas like these should excite me like they do everyone else. I should love people, but I don't. I'm not Ivelisse. I'm not hospitable. I can pretend to be all I want, but at the end of the day, it's not who I am.

I shouldn't want to get away from Ian especially. He needed me. He always needed me. There were times when I felt like I was failing him, like he wasn't growing up how he was supposed to. He was already cheated out of a mother by a father who never loved him. I should be able to fill in the pieces, the cracks in his soul that our father made, but I can't. I don't know why I can't.

Ian doesn't remember our mother, but I do. I remember

how she and I used to go to her great aunt's house in the Common District when my father would get angry. We'd spend nights sitting by the fire and telling stories of what the world was like before Angeles. Ian was seven when she was killed. I was twelve.

I tried to tell him stories of the woman who loved like no other, who loved with a fire and did everything she could to protect those that she loved. Sometimes, I don't think that's enough. Sometimes, I wonder if she'd be disappointed in me for the way I'm raising him.

I used to try and tell myself that I didn't belong to the tragedy or the bloodshed. I tried to lean into the pain and wait for it to pass, but there were days that I truly believed that my past was going to swallow me whole.

The cold marble floors of the hallway were a blessing. All the bodies in the ballroom made it suffocatingly hot. Shocks of cool air washed over me. I made sure I walked far enough down the hall before I took a seat on the ground and rested my head against the wall. The ceiling was covered in a painting—cherub babies flew over half-naked woman, draping scarlet petals in their path.

I knew this painting well, since it was one of the only paintings that survived the plague and made it into Angeles. Angeles had once accepted trade before the barrier had been constructed after the Kadjarian war. That's how we got ahold of this painting, and the few like it.

I reached into the pocket of my suit. I promised myself I wasn't going to bring it with me tonight. I wasn't going to need it, but on my way out the door, I grabbed the flask on impulse. It was stupid. I was stupid for bringing it. Now, though, as the moonlight from the long window across from me fell on my hand holding the bottle. The little black cigarette tucked so neatly in its flask looked mesmerizing. I shook it out onto my palm.

What's it going to take to light up?

When it does happen, when that Great and Final Tragedy does happen, is anyone going to care if I do?

"Prince Roman?"

I stifled a groan and clambered to my feet. Helené stood a good three feet away from me, just shutting the doors of the ballroom behind her. She shut the door behind her before making her way to me. She was a bit startling, not just in the way she walked, but in the way she looked. She wore a form-fitting black dress with a sheer collar and waist—golden jewels peppered along the sleeves. A tumble of pale, almost white hair escaped her intricate updo that I'd only ever seen Ivelisse wear. I think it was her eyes, though, that caught me. They were a gunmetal blue, almost blending in with her pale skin, coated in thick black mascara and kohl eyeliner. I don't think I'd ever seen another person like her.

Had I been anyone else, my eyes might have skated over the poorly covered bruise on her neck or the cut on her chin covered with thin concealer. I wouldn't have bothered to notice the way she couldn't meet my eyes or the way her dark lipstick covered her chapped lips. Scars told stories—I wondered what stories this rich girl had been through.

"Is Ian alright?" I asked.

"Ivelisse is still looking after him I just came out here to see if you were alright."

"Oh, I'm fine. Thank you for checking on me."

Silence filled the space between us. "When you left, you looked—sick." She finally said.

"I'm afraid you've been mistaken, then. I'm quite alright." I straightened the cuffs of my suit. If my publicist were here, she'd be fixing my hair or pinching color into my cheeks or messing with my collar.

Helené turned around, and I waited to hear the close of the ballroom door before I returned to where I had been sitting. I waited. And waited, finding things to fix on my suit. When I looked up, she was staring up at the sky.

"They're so bright," she breathed.

"What?"

I stepped up to her. She crossed her arms over her chest, gaze intent on the sky like I didn't even exist to her at that moment. I looked up to see the night sky. Stars ripped through the very fabric of the universe, shimmering, shining, glittering millions of miles away.

"I said they're so bright."

"Because they're engineered to look that way."

She tore her eyes from the window, eyebrows furrowed. "They're what?"

Have you never sat through a science class? I wanted to ask. Maybe she was younger than I was—her face didn't exactly tell her age. She looked ethereal, almost. But it was the middle of the summer. She might've forgotten what she had learned in school that year.

"Scientists in the Business District cast holograms over the sky, over the actual stars, so they look brighter."

"Why?"

I shrugged. "It's nicer to look at, I guess. Hides the fact that our environment is dying."

"It—what?"

"Smoke from Angeles and surrounding colonies is killing the ozone layer. Air quality is down, stars are becoming less visible, temperatures are fluctuating. That's the first thing I'm going to fix when I'm on the throne. That, and taking down the barrier."

Helené blinked. She didn't say anything. She just turned her attention toward the sky once more. Something had to be up with this girl. And I had to find out.

"You said you haven't been here much, right?"

She nodded.

"Would you like a tour of the palace? I'm told I give the best ones."

~

Since she liked the stars so much, I took her to the roof. Ky would've killed me if he knew I brought Helené here because it was supposed to be "sacred ground." At least, that's what Ky always called it. The three of us came here when we were younger. We talked for hours about anything and everything. We played up here. But this was the only place I could think of where no one would bother us.

79

There was a small attic in my mother's bedroom that led straight to the roof. It was as close as I could bring Helené to the stars. I had to find some common ground to get her to trust me so I could find the crack in her lie.

She sat next to me, toying with the tulle fabric of her skirts. Her answers were vague, almost like she wasn't sure of herself. When she asked me questions, they were strange and made the hairs on the back of my neck stand.

What's it like being a prince? Are you ever afraid?

Is there anywhere in the palace you can't go?

"I take it Ivelisse never told you about our stars?" I asked, sitting down next to Helené and handing her a cup of coffee I took before we came up the stairs. I always had a pot brewed—never knew what politician or journalist my father had approved to stop by, and the prince always had to look hospitable.

Helené shook her head. "Is that what you call this place? Your stars?"

"Yeah. Ky, Ivelisse, and I used to come up here when we were little and play. We don't anymore, but Ky still thinks it's sacred ground or something. Though, I will say I don't think they appreciate the stars as much as you do."

The hint of a smile danced across her lips. "I don't think anyone does."

"It's not a bad thing. Not many people take the time to stop and look up, you know? Everyone's always on the go. No one ever thinks about the world around them. No one ever bothers to see the world as it is without cell phones or government or politics."

"I've had a lot of time to look up. I guess I've just never seen stars like these."

"How? It's not like you see a different sky than I do."

Helené went silent. I kicked myself for prying too soon. She brought her coffee mug to her lips. An idea began to form in the back of my brain. An idea that could get me killed—but still, I needed to know. I needed this to work.

"I didn't always see this sky, though. The stars in the Common District aren't as bright because it's hard to stretch a hologram that far. I used to spend most of my nights looking up at those stars."

"Why?"

"My mother and I used to hide out there when my father's outbursts became too much. She'd bring Ian and I to her great-aunt's house, but Ian was so little that he'd be sound asleep by the time we got there. She and I would sit out on the porch and watch the stars. I've always liked the Common District stars better than the ones here. They just seem more real, you know?"

"Your father's outbursts?" She asked.

I nodded. I didn't dare say anything else. If she left tonight and went straight to the papers with what I told her, I was going to be dead.

She blinked and picked her coffee cup again. She took a sip. "Why'd you tell me that?" She asked.

"What?"

"Why did you tell me that? You know what I could do with information like that—information that could tarnish your family's reputation. People like you always want something from people like me."

"We aren't that different, Helené. You're just from the Business District. We grew up with all the same things."

"No, I can promise you that we didn't."

"I don't want anything from you."

"You're lying. Don't lie to me." She spat. "Just tell me what you want and maybe we can strike up a deal."

"A deal?"

"I need something from you. You need something from me. So, tell me what you need, and I'll tell you what I need."

I thought for a second. "You're not who you say you are."

"Yes, I am." She answered almost immediately.

"What's your full name?"

"Helené Grace."

"Who was the King of Angeles before my father?"

She paused. Glanced around the rooftop like the answer would just magically appear somewhere. When she met my eyes again, I saw nothing but hate. The same hate that my father harbored, the kind of hate that festered inside of you for years. Anger pumped through her face. I should have been afraid of her—any sensible person would have—but I wasn't.

No, I felt no fear looking in her eyes.

"Who are you?" I insisted.

"Helené Grace."

"Do you realize what I can do? If I even suspect you of lying, I can call the guards right now and have you dragged down to the prison."

"Go ahead." She stood. "Do it."

I blinked, taken aback. "You—"

Helené stood. She started for the trapdoor that lead down to my mother's attic. I caught her by the wrist. She whirled around, twisted out of my grasp only to grab onto my forearm and pin it behind my back. I let out a cry of pain.

"You want to trade secrets, Prince Roman? How about this: I'm going to kill you. I'm going to kill you and make it look like an accident. I've always wanted to see royal blood spill and from such a pretty face nonetheless."

My stomach lurched in my throat as shocks of pain burst through my body. "Who are you?" I choked out.

"I don't let my victims live long enough to know."

Sirens began to blare. They always blared in the Royal District; always an emergency to attend to, always a problem to solve. Helené whipped her head around. It was enough of a distraction for me to ram into her. She fell to the ground, and I raced for the attic opening, leaving Helené trapped on the roof.

Chapter Seven
Ember

Fire raced through my body, burning every sense, singeing every defense until I didn't know who I was anymore.

My eyelids were crusted over. I had to fight to get them open. Wherever I was, I was held down in chains. My wrists and ankles were shackled, and something heavy wrapped over my waist to keep me in this sitting position. The room around me was damp and dark, the air rank with the smell of death. The rope around my waist burned into my skin whenever I twisted to get a better view of where I was.

My eyes adjusted.

I saw the walls.

I felt the walls, twisting around my body and suffocating me.

My throat began to close as I gasped for air, and the walls began to scream my name. Ember. Ember, Ember, Ember, who do you think you are? Child of the street, child of blood, child of murder, you've gone too far, you've dared too much. I could do nothing to fight against them. They pushed their way in my mind, tearing down every careful wall I've built. I couldn't cover my ears.

My mind raced, stuck between trying to find a way out of this prison cell and trying to find a way to stop the voices. The line between reality and fantasy turned to grey—was I back home? Were the guards standing at my door with their axes and swords? Was this pain even real? Were the guards dragging me out of bed and beating me senseless or was I just imagining all of this pain?

"Stop! Please, stop!" I cried. I knew it was useless. My voice didn't even sound like my own. This was the voice that belonged to the walls: the voice of a girl who tried to help her people, who tried to fight against a system that didn't care for its people, the voice of a girl who couldn't do it on her own but had nowhere to turn. This was not the voice of the once-great Bloodhound.

I shut my eyes tightly, as the memories came. Hitting the rooftop, pain sparking through my head. Stars danced in front of my eyes. I crawled over to the attic door, beating my fists against it, screaming curses at Prince Roman and at Angeles.

I did all that I knew to do. I scaled down the side of the palace, all forty-some feet, until I landed on the ground. I think I blacked out for a few seconds. Then, I ran. If my three years as the Bloodhound had taught me anything, it was that you never stopped running. Never.

And I almost made it, too. Some debilitating pain brought me to my knees, one that I'd never felt before. One that made me believe I was surely dying. It was a kind of pain that hit you all at once, hard, fast, and simply tore you to shreds. I fell face first, only a foot away from the gates. A measly twelve inches stood between me and safety.

Attacking the prince had been an afterthought. It was my anger that sparked it. I shouldn't have. I should have played the part of the quiet new girl, wide-eyed and afraid, but he caught me. Something about the prince sparked a sort of frustration in me that I can't say I've ever felt before.

My hands shook with the memory, tapping against the metal of the chair I sat in. This scene was all too familiar. The ceiling dripping with water; me, clawing at whatever I could get my hands on until my fingers bled, screaming incoherent words to a world that had gone deaf to my cries. The walls laughed at me. Their words snaked in my throat, choking, squeezing, pulling the life out of me.

The shackles I sat in were old and rusty—truly, they didn't think me to be this weak? Angelesans must really be as stupid as everyone said.

I pulled at the shackles, twisting and jerking until they snapped, leaving only the cuffs on my wrists. I pulled a bobby pin, somehow still twined in my hair, and stuck it in the lock around my leg. Mara had once taught me how to pick a lock when we were trying to get into Dad's safe because we were convinced he kept a treasure map in there.

To my surprise, both of the locks around my legs snapped open, and I was able to stand freely. Once I got to my feet, a voice from outside the door sent fear shooting through my veins.

"Now is not the time. Is Ian there with you? I'm fine. Tell him I'm fine. I know it was stupid, I got the speech from Ky alright. I know I should have left it alone." The lack of a response told me that someone was on their phone just outside my cell. The voice paused, waiting for an answer. "I'm coming home soon. I just have something I need to do. I'll be there in a minute, okay? Bye."

I backed away from the door when the footsteps came closer. Blinding light flooded in as the metal door slid open to reveal a tall figure. When my eyes adjusted, I recognized the person standing in front of me: a mess of curling brown hair, olive skin, and full lips drawn tightly into a frown. Prince Roman was dressed in a black t-shirt and khaki pants, a vast understatement from what I had last seen him in.

He looked from me, to the broken shackles on the ground, to the metal cuffs still around my wrists. He huffed, his stream of breath pushing a tendril of hair upwards. "I should make you pay for all of that."

"With what money?" I shot back.

He blinked, taken aback. "Cute." He set his hands on his hips, obviously deciding what to do with me. "So, are you going to explain yourself? Or should we start with the apology?"

"I'm not apologizing to you. I'm only sorry that I didn't kill you when I had the chance. I should now."

Prince Roman raised an eyebrow. "By all means, go ahead and try. You'll be dead before you can even reach me."

"And who's going to stop me?" He pulled at the chain around his neck. A little red button came from underneath his shirt. "Is that some kind of panic button?"

"The very second you overstep boundaries, I will press this and send in my men to execute you. I suggest that you do what I say."

"Cute," I mocked. "They can't even trust the pretty little prince to defend himself."

"I choose not to waste energy on monsters," he sneered. "After all, that's what they call you, right?" Roman kicked the door shut. It slammed with a damning thud, and he flicked a light switch that offered some sort of meager, buzzing fluorescent light from overhead.

"Why'd you come here? To make fun of me?"

"No, to give you a chance to confess."

"And you think I'd give that to you?"

"Yes. Because I'm being kind to you."

"It's not like I'm going to live either way."

"I might be able to work a plea bargain."

"Which means?"

"You can live, but you'll be stuck here. There's only one other prisoner in here for life, so it's not like it's completely off the table. If you don't want to confess, that's fine. I'll leave you to the guards, but I can promise that they aren't anywhere near as kind as I am. All the questions you refused to answer last night, I want an explanation for now."

"Wouldn't you like to know?"

"I would, actually, and it's in your best interest."

"You don't know what my best interest is. You don't know me."

Prince Roman ran an exhausted hand down his face and craned his head up to the musty ceiling. "I am trying to help."

I crossed my arms over my chest.

"Fine," Prince Roman threw his hands in the air. "I'll

just let them kill you." He started for the door.

My heart clenched. He had mentioned the prisoner—was it the prisoner I was supposed to save? I had to see my family again. I had to find out who killed my sister. I had to save the East Sector.

"Stop, Prince." I called. "I'll tell you."

Prince Roman turned around slowly. A smirk danced across his lips. I don't think I had seen him smile yet. There was something utterly infuriating about that smirk—about his face. It was the kind of face that made you believe you could tell him absolutely anything. I almost wanted to trust him.

Key word—almost. I knew that trusting a face like that would mean certain death. Still, I wanted to believe that people like him—good people—existed. But I don't like lying to myself, so I kept with the truth: this beautiful world of dashing princes and righteous kings was nothing but a facade.

I took a deep breath. "If I tell you, I won't die?"

Prince Roman nodded. "Right. I can try to work in a plea deal."

"But is there any way I could get home?"

Prince Roman started to shake his head, but then he stopped. He crossed his arms over his chest. "I think—there might be a way. It's dangerous. But something tells me you wouldn't mind that. Look, here, give me the answers I want, and I'll try to get you back to Kadjar."

"Trying is not good enough. Promise me."

Prince Roman rolled his eyes. My hands ached to slap

him. "Fine. I promise."

"Alright, then. My name is Ember. I come from Kadjar—the East Sector. I'm here on a mission from Empress Analita."

Prince Roman nodded. "And why are you here? More importantly, how did you get past the barrier?"

"I'm not telling you that."

He rolled his eyes. "You're stubborn, and you're making this harder than it needs to be. Do you want to get home or not?"

"Obviously."

"Alright, can you at least tell me why you were arrested? Do you know why my guards took you down?"

"Because I attacked you and threatened to kill you."

"And that is a capital offense in the nation of Angeles. You're aware that from here on out, you are property of His Majesty King Nero Stone and that you have no rights? You're aware that while you wait for exeuction, you must adhere to the word of the warden, and you may not resist, lest you be sentenced to immediate death?"

I nodded. "I guess."

Prince Roman lifted his shirt. There was some kind of little black box clipped to his belt. He ripped it off the waistband of his jeans and lifted it to his mouth. "There's your confession, warden. I'm turning the mic off. You need to turn the cameras off. I'll be out in a second."

Static burst through the box. "Yes, Your Highness." Prince Roman pressed a button at the top of the box and shoved it in his pocket.

"You were recording me?"

"We have to have physical evidence of a crime before we execute prisoners. The Senate insists on it. I'm not recording you now. I want to speak to you earnestly."

"And I'm supposed to just trust you now?"

"I don't give a shit if you do or don't. I'm giving you a mile when you only deserve an inch. Work with me here."

"So, what do you want? Or are you just staying to gloat?"

"What do I have to gloat about?"

"Why don't you tell me all about how you've evaded paying taxes while my family starves? Or how you're doing everything right by your citizens, but half of them are actually dying of malaria? Better yet, why don't you tell me a story about how you—"

Prince Roman held his hands up. "Kadjar is not Angeles. We have free healthcare, and my family has accessible tax records. I am not the person to take your vigilante anger out on."

"Oh, please. You nobility always have some skeletons in the closet. You are the perfect person to take my anger out on."

"I am not interested in your biased opinions. I want to know about you. What are you? Some sort of special agent? Why did you come to Angeles? To kill me?"

It was my turn to smirk. I ran my tongue over my top set of teeth as I thought. "They call me the Bloodhound of the

East Sector. I kill people like you. Thirty-six people like you, to be exact. They caught me trying to assassinate the empress and threw me in prison. On the day of my execution, I was offered a deal: sneak into Angeles and complete a mission in exchange for the change I was protesting for and my freedom."

The Prince of Angeles was as still as a statue. He didn't say anything, and I didn't expect him to. There was no way someone like him could relate or even sympathize with me. He was born with a silver spoon in his mouth while I had to dumpster dive for meals growing up. I've wanted the whole world, and he's never wanted for a thing in his entire life.

Roman blew out a long breath. "I knew something was up. I just—I don't know. I don't know what I was expecting."

"Well, this is what you get. You have your answers. Now, leave. I'd rather not spend my last few days looking at your face."

He started to move for the door but stopped. "You're too calm. Why are you so calm? You should be begging me for a way to leave."

"I'm not begging you for anything. I'll be killed before I'll beg a royal for anything."

"And you'd risk giving up your freedom? And the change you want?"

My stomach clenched. "What are you trying to do? Guilt trip me into breaking out of your prison? Have you lost your mind?"

"No, I just—I thought you'd put up more of a fight."

"Get out, Prince Roman."

"You can call me Roman."

"Fuck you."

"That's fair."

Prince Roman turned to leave, but I stopped him. "Wait, hold on. You...you said you could help me." He raised an eyebrow. "Would you help me get out of here?" I asked.

"Depends. What do I get out of it?"

"You want the king gone?"

Prince Roman blanched. "I never said that."

"You didn't have to. I put two and two together. I saw how you look at him. That, and you mentioned his outbursts. I heard Ivelisse talking about how she's afraid of what happens behind closed doors with you two. I'm not stupid. Do you want him gone?"

"You're not serious."

"I'm serious as the grave. You get me out of here, I'll kill him, and I'll go back to Kadjar. Just get me out of here."

"I—I can't...I can't do that."

"Think of Ian."

Prince Roman closed the distance between us. He jammed a finger into my chest, anger lighting in his eyes. "Don't you dare bring Ian into this. Don't speak of him. I'm not—I'm not like Ivelisse or Ky. I can't rule yet."

"You're going to have to eventually."

"I get that but—you can't kill him."

"Why?"

"Because I still...I can't let Ian lose a father and a

mother. I can't kill the king. No. I won't take that deal."

Chapter Eight
Roman

The prison was bigger than I had originally anticipated It was a maze of dimply lit hallways and empty cells with heavy metal doors separating me from some of the worst prisoners in Angeles. There was a total of four, three of them awaiting trial, one who was there for life. Yet, I didn't see a single sign of life while walking through the prison.

I bet they'd all kill for the chance to speak with the prince.

But no. I chose the Bloodhound of Kadjar, who tried to kill me only a day before. My father's advisors barely told me anything about her. I had to know the rest. It was going to eat at me—humans didn't simply kill just because. I had to know if a monster, a true, wicked monster had somehow infiltrated the barrier, and I had to figure out how to stop it from happening again.

I stopped in the threshold between two contrasting hallways. One was built of brick; whereas, the other was made of linoleum and concrete and doused in fluorescent light rather than dim bulbs swinging from the ceiling. The lighter of the two was the testing deck. This was where my father kept his prisoners contained before he killed them. This is where the experimentation took place.

There once were twelve prisoners of war here. I was eight when my father brought me down for the first time, so I could watch as he experimented with electroshock therapy in an attempt to brainwash the prisoners. They all died.

My father eventually stopped bringing me down here, around the time that he killed my mother. I always assumed that he stopped experimenting and just closed this part of the prison off. Only, it wasn't closed off. It was fully lit and smelled strongly of cleaning products, barely masking the smell of death that still lingered.

My phone buzzed. Ivelisse's contact name lit up my screen, her text message reading: *Where are you? Ian is getting worried and so am I.*

Did you seriously tell him where I was?

He asked, and I'm not going to lie to him.

After everything that happened last night, you told my twelve-year-old brother that I went to the most forbidden place in Angeles? Are you kidding me?

I only felt bad for my harsh words when her next text came through.

You, Roman Stone, are impossible.

The feeling's mutual. Tell Ian I'm coming upstairs in a second.

I shoved my phone back into my pocket and stepped onto the testing deck. All I could do now was find my way out of this maze and back to Ian. My thoughts were far too distracting to really focus on where I was going. I knew that this hall led to the warden's office, which would lead to the elevator that would take me to an underground bunker, which was used as a blockade to keep the prisoners trapped in case they ever escaped. A hidden elevator in that bunker would bring me to a small shed near the barrier. I'd have to walk to the palace from there.

Ember's deal was still swirling in my mind. The thought of having my father dead was undeniably tantalizing. There was no way I could trust her, though. She knew my most dangerous secret, and she hated me. I should want her dead.

But, still, I don't. I can't bring myself to want her dead. There are too many questions I have that she won't answer. Why? That question was going to drive me insane.

A world without my father was nice to think about. I couldn't possibly entertain the thought for any longer. It was ridiculous and would have to remain a fantasy.

I snapped myself out of my thoughts. There was a single door in the hallway with a long window stretching across. The glass was tinted, letting me know that whatever lies in there couldn't see me through it. Next to my head there was a clear bin pinned to the wall with a manila envelope slouched inside. The envelope was stamped with a bright red mark: PRISONER OF WAR.

A sheet of paper with a picture stapled to the side slid out of the envelope. The picture stapled to the top corner showed a scared face, tear stains carving down pale cheeks. Frizzy brown curls escaped from a knot at the top of the girl's head. Her piercing blue eyes were bloodshot.

I flipped the picture over to read the page:

PRISONER: MARA LEVIN

PRISONER #ID: 870458

AGE: 21

HAIR: brown

EYES: blue

CRIMES: assault on an officer, resisting arrest, treason

SENTENCE: life in prison

I shoved the paper back in the manila envelope and stuck it back in the bin. The bin itself fell from the pins that were holding it onto the wall, landing with a clatter. Immediately, a force slammed against the glass causing my insides to freeze.

Thud.

Thud.

Thud.

"I can hear you! I know you're out there!"

I reached for the door handle to get the hell out of here. Then, the broken voice cried out again. "Please! Please, don't leave me!" Despite hating my curiosity, I crept forward confident that whatever was beyond that glass couldn't hear cr see me.

A clean room drenched in awfully bright fluorescent lights lay behind the glass. A single metal table sat in the center, underneath a spotlight. There were black cameras that covered every corner of the confined space. A control panel sat next to me with a microphone and four buttons connected to each camera.

The prisoner, Mara Levin, came into view, pressing her palms flat against the glass. She sucked in a tight breath, and her small frame trembled as she released it.

"Please," she choked out. "Please don't leave me alone."

Questions tumbled through my mind. I had only ever seen these prisoners as huge men with long lists of crimes and scarred, troubled faces. There was no way in hell that this girl, this broken, feeble creature could have done something severe enough to serve life in prison. I guess, at first glance, one could have said the same thing about Ember.

I glanced down at the control panel sitting just below the window. One button to turn the microphones and cameras off. One button to unlock the doors. I turned the mics and cameras off before I unlocked the door.

Mara leaned her head against the glass. "Don't hurt me." She whimpered.

I opened the door. The second I walked in, I saw Mara back up against the wall, hands held high in surrender. "Who are you?" She asked, voice caught somewhere between a rasp of fear and a plea for help.

"Roman. My name is Roman."

"Prince Roman? The Prince Roman?"

I nodded. "And you're Mara. Mara Levin?"

"You don't know? He said you knew of me. He said the whole world knew of me." Mara swallowed. "Of all the evil things I've done. How wicked I am." Her dark hair, the color of tree bark, was neatly braided over one shoulder, tied together with a clear hair tie. Someone must have cared for her. Her skin was clean and so were her white scrubs.

"He?"

"I've committed three capital offenses." Mara continued. "He said he'd tell the world what I've done and how I don't deserve to live."

"All crimes in Angeles are capital offenses. Doesn't

matter if you steal a piece of bread or if you kill another human being. Who is he, and why did he say you're here?"

"King Nero. I—I was just looking for my little sister. I was in the middle of the woods and it was getting dark. I came to this clearing, and all of a sudden, these men swarmed me. I punched one of them in the face." Mara's voice cracked. She blinked furiously. "And then they brought me here."

"Your sister. Is she—are you Angelesan?"

"No. I'm Kadjarian. My sister, Ember, went missing before she was supposed to stand trial. I know she took off to avoid being put to death. I had to find her. I had to help her."

My stomach dropped at the mention of her name. "Ember," I echoed.

"Yes. My sister did some things and pissed off a lot of important people. She's never been the type to take things lying down. She's always fought back, but she crossed a line. She killed people. And she got caught."

"Did you ever find your sister?"

Mara shook her head. "I hope wherever she is, she's alive. I hope she hasn't been caught. I hope she's safe."

Guilt pounded through my mind. Ember didn't deserve my help. Mara, on the other hand, did nothing wrong. My father must've kept her imprisoned for this long simply because she survived all the experiments that the others died from.

I had to help her.

I had to prove to her and to myself that I was not my father. I wouldn't continue this tirade of killing wayward souls. I had to help.

"I'm going to figure something out. I'll get you out of here. I promise."

"How can I trust you?"

"I can't say anything to make you trust me, but I'll be back for you. I promise."

~

"Oh, hell no, dude. You've gone batshit." Ky had both elbows on the white cloth of the table, a meatball dangling from his fork. It was just Ky and I on the rooftop of the Auria. I had called an emergency meeting. Ivelisse said she couldn't get away from her parent's house—there were too many cousins for her to get away. Ky didn't have family outside the palace, aside from a sketchy uncle in the Agricultural District.

"C'mon. You didn't see her. She's innocent. I know she is."

"What happened to going down there to talk with Helené?"

"Her name's Ember."

"Oh, really? Talk about a plot twist." Ky turned his attention back to his fork, finishing off the meatball and swirling spaghetti onto the prongs of the fork.

"And, I did talk to her. She's not innocent, and what she did wasn't a mistake like I'd hoped. But I found Mara instead. My father forcefully took her, and her only charges are treason, assault on an officer, and trespassing. She was looking for her sister."

"Who's her sister?"

I glanced around the room like someone was going to

102

overhear even though there was no one here. Ky, Ivelisse, and I always rented out the back room when we wanted to go out to eat so no one bothered us. The Auria staff generally tried to keep this room empty for us.

"Ember."

Ky's eyes widened. He pointed his fork at me. "Now that's a plot twist."

"Be serious."

"That's like telling a fish to walk."

"Ky."

He held his hands up in defense. "Alright, fine. If we're being serious, why are you talking to me about this and not Ivelisse? She has more influence in the Court than I do. If you want something done—"

"I never said I wanted something done legally."

A smile grew across Ky's face. "Now we're talking."

"You and I both know that Ivelisse will do whatever it takes to stay in favor of the Court."

"And you realize that my morals are loose at best."

"Not exactly where I was going with that sentence but sure."

"What do you need done?"

"We're going to need Miles' help."

Ky blanched. "What do you know about Miles?" He set his fork down on his plate. A waiter came by to refill our cups of soda. Ky and I were silent. I studied my best friend's face. There was a faint white scar above his eyebrow and a cool undertone to his bronze skin. I remember that scar. I had one on my elbow from the exact same accident. We wiped out on the concrete while trying our new skateboards that we'd never ridden before. We were fourteen and thought we were dying after the fall. I caught myself with my arms. Ky caught the fall with his face.

I also remember the sting of my father telling me that Ky was not fit to be associated with me. The only reason I keep them around is in case Lori ever decides to take up my offer. They have no value to us—and in your world, son, friendship only means anything if there's value to it. If you're not getting anything out of the relationship, you don't need it. Remember that, Prince.

His offer to Lori being a lifetime of luxury—a penthouse in the Royal District, monthly stipend of more than enough to live on, all the gold and diamonds she could ever want, if only she became his mistress. Lori McKenna was the only woman to ever refuse my father. I knew it made his blood boil. Yet, he kept her close in case she ever changed her mind. He didn't care about the walls of degrees Lori had in her office. He didn't care about what Lori had to bring to his advisory council. He only cared about what she could give him. I hated him for it.

"I know that you spend every summer at his place," I said, bringing a spoonful of soup to my mouth.

Ky relaxed. "Right."

"Why? Is there anything else I should know?" I asked, only half joking. Ky shook his head. "Why didn't you go this summer?"

"No. Things have been a little, um, tense with my family. Rather not plunge myself into the middle of a cold war, ya' know?"

"I get it."

A silence rested over us, but it wasn't the same kind of aching silence that I hated. "So, what kind of plan do you have for this Mara chick? I'd rather not get Miles involved, but if we need to, I guess I can give him a call. Might take some convincing, if you know what I mean." Ky rubbed his fingers together to signify money.

"That's fine. I'm thinking if we disguise Mara and sneak her out of the prison, Miles can get her over the barrier with the rest of his—"

"Shut up!" Ky waved a hand at me.

"What?"

He leaned in and spoke through clenched teeth. "There are cameras here that don't need to know about the...refugees."

"Sorry. But—do you think Miles would take Mara?"

"With a little bit of convincing. Maybe some gold convincing or some monetary convincing."

"That doesn't matter. We'll do what it takes."

Ky leaned back in his chair, stretching his arms in the air, yawning. "Why do you even care about this chick, anyways?"

"Guilt."

He raised an eyebrow. "About?"

"Ember offered me a deal. She said she'd kill...him. I

105

couldn't do it. I can't rule yet. I—I love Angeles, and I love my people, but I can't lead them yet. I'm not ready. I guess this is how I can make it up to her. I'll get her cousin or sister or whatever out of Angeles."

"So, she knows about him? What he's done to you?"

"She doesn't know about Mom. She just knows that he's not what he should be. I told her he has outbursts."

"That's an understatement if I ever heard one."

I couldn't help but laugh, despite it all. Ky was the only person in the world who knew the full story—my mother's death, my father's anger. He helped me bury my mother. We were twelve. It was pouring rain. I had discovered her dead, asleep, only minutes before.

My father had found me, sitting in the corner of her dark room, holding my knees to my chest and sobbing. He smelled of beer and cologne as he bent down to my level, hell coursing through his eyes.

He'd said, "no one finds out about this. If they do, it's the end of us. Of our family. Got it?"

I called Ky the second my father left. I told him that no one could find out: for Ian's sake. We had to cover her body in a maid's cart and push her out in the rain, burying her next to her beloved rose gardens.

I held my breath, waiting for the pain of the memory to pass. Sometimes I think I'll go to my grave grieving for her, and for everything that I've lost.

"And Ivelisse? What's going on with you guys? You were getting the cold shoulder there for a while." Ky asked, as the waiter returned with our check. I pulled eighty notes out of my wallet and set it on the check. The waiter thanked me and took it.

"I don't know. I was kind of an ass to her the day before Ian's party. I asked her if I should order Killian to take a paternity test."

Ky's mouth went agape. "You did not."

"We were fighting, and it slipped out. I felt—I feel so bad. She forgave me at his party, but I don't know if that was actual forgiveness or the champagne talking. I'm going to hope it's the former."

Ky stood, and shouldered his jacket on. I did the same. "You know, once upon a time, I thought you guys were going to be something real. You know, the one arranged marriage that actually worked out. Guess not." He shrugged, like it was the simplest thing in the universe.

We set out, pushing our way through the door, down the steps, and through the actual restaurant. The waiters thanked us and waved as we pushed out the door into the busy street. A limousine was waiting just outside the Auria. We slid in, and Ky instructed the driver to take us back to the palace.

"Sometimes, you know," I started, leaning my head back on the leather headrest. "I think there's something wrong with me."

"What do you mean?"

"I mean, look at Ivelisse—she's perfect. She's beautiful, easily the smartest person in the room at any given time.

It's like she was born for this position. Yet, I don't love her. There has got to be something wrong with me."

"Are you just not attracted to girls?" Ky asked.

"I like girls," I said. "Just not her. I don't know why. I tried. I really did. I just want to feel something again. Anything. I feel like I'm skating on thin ice, and I'm just waiting for it to crack and pull me under."

Ky was silent for a second. "You're going to find your way out of this. It's all going to work out in the end."

I didn't answer him.

He continued when he realized I wasn't going to respond. "Shit sucks, especially when your father is the head asshole-in-charge, but you're going to get through it. You always have, and you always will." He paused. "Until then, maybe a little adventure wouldn't kill us."

I perked up. "Meaning...you'll help me?"

Ky pulled out his phone. "I'll call Miles. See what he can do."

Chapter Nine
Ember

I still remember the first time I asked my mother if we were poor.

She was doing laundry on the front porch when she accidentally ripped a hole in one of my father's shirts. She gasped, cursed, and set the shirt to the side. I noticed how she kept taking worried glances at the shirt. We had a box with scraps of fabric in it, but it was the thread that was expensive. She had to have been thinking of ways to pay for thread to fix the shirt.

I was sitting in our little tiny yard, between the tufts of green grass, bouncing a tattered soccer ball on the concrete foundation of our house. It would have been a school day, so I couldn't have been more than five. The memory was hazy in my mind, but somehow still stayed through the years.

"Do you want me to be honest with you, Em?" She didn't look up from the dress she was carefully washing in the metal bin.

"Yeah."

"We are."

"Is Mara going to get a job, too?"

"Soon, if things don't start looking up. But we'll be okay. The gods will provide. They always do."

"Will I have to get a job?"

"I don't think many places will hire a little girl. You go

to school first. But what you aren't going to do is let anyone tell you you're worth less than you are because of where you're from."

"Why would I do that?"

Mama shrugged. "If you keep your shoes and clothes clean, then they won't poke fun at you. No one has to know that you live in the East Sector. Only if you want them to."

I thought about this for a second as the ratty old soccer ball came rolling back to me. I held the muddy ball in my arms. "Why would I hide where I live?"

"I did when I was in school," my mother explained. "I didn't let them know that I was from the East Sector. I don't think it would have mattered now, looking back. I was just afraid of being picked on. You let me know if anyone picks on you. I'll send your sister and your father after them." She wiped a sheen of sweat off her forehead.

"And they'll beat 'em up for me?"

Mama laughed. "That's right. All three of us'll come after whoever messes with our Em."

Her words pounded through my brain, even in the dark of the Angelesan prison. Sleep was not coming easy to me.

I counted three hundred and forty-five sheep before I finally gave up. Sleep was a long-awaited wish that was not coming true. All I could think about was Mama's words. How I should have been there. How I shouldn't have ever tried to assassinate the empress. I would have been there for her. Mara might not be dead. Tears weren't coming, either. I guess I'd cried them all out.

There was nothing to occupy me in this prison cell. I had no way to tell if it was day or night. At least this cell was bigger than the one back home. It was six paces long and twelve paces wide. I counted over and over again. There was a small metal bed with a thin sheet thrown over it in the corner and a little bucket to be used as a bathroom.

Sometimes my memories weren't enough to block out the walls. I could do nothing but sit and stare at the dark walls. My chest tightened, knees weakened, and my head pounded All I could hear was a chorus of you are stuck you are stuck you are stuck you are stuck—

"Get OUT!" I pressed my hands to my ears, screaming as I slid down the wall in the corner of my cell. I screamed like somehow my own meager words would somehow make the bad thoughts go away, like my own pitiful voice could make my demons disappear.

What finally made them disappear was the light—small cracks peeked through the door when the prison warden turned on the light in the morning. My demons were forced to bow to the light. But, now, there was no light to save me, to protect me against the militia of walled demons marching toward me before any Angelesan executioner could touch me. The small amount coming through was not nearly enough to fight the armies of hell coming for me.

If I closed my eyes, I could almost picture the sky. The Angelesan sky was so much more beautiful than the Kadjarian sky. The stars were brighter, the clouds were puffier and whiter. I hadn't seen a sky like that before that night with Roman on the rooftop.

But that was hours ago. The lights have turned off, signifying that the day guards have gone home for the night. The night guards should be here soon, with their flashlights and loud, stomping boots. One of the guards had mentioned to his partner that in order to conserve energy, the lights in the hall were turned off at night.

The thought of never seeing the light again terrified me. For tomorrow morning, the prison doctor would make his way to my cell with his little syringe. He'd lay me down on the cot and inject a serum into me. I'd close my eyes for a final time. I already told myself that I wouldn't fight it. I've spent my entire life fighting. I told myself that it's time to accept what I can't change.

Tomorrow, the North Sector would finally be free of their sadistic little Robin Hood.

My people would still suffer. The people of the East Sector would die of diseases that the rich have long since eradicated because they could afford the vaccines. Mama would still have to walk two miles for water every morning. The potential of East Sector children would go untapped. All because I failed.

I could feel the walls creeping up my skin again, screaming Killer! Monster! Demon!

I ran my hands down my face, sitting on the floor of my cell. My body didn't feel like my own. It was the body of a killer, the body of a failed vigilante. God, why wouldn't the walls take me yet? These damning walls, these unforgiving reapers were going to murder me before the prison warden could even get the chance.

Worthless.

Worthless.

Worthless.

A worthless rebel championing for a worthless cause.

The words of the walls snaked in tendrils around my ears, sliding down my throat and choking me—finally, finally, finally I'd be free. Finally, this earth would be rid of the Bloodhound of the East Sector.

Please, Death, please welcome a monster like me—

I hadn't realized I was speaking—screaming, more like—until a voice from outside the door broke through my train of thought.

"Ember? Ember! I hear her!"

That voice. I knew that voice. I'd fought with that voice. Cried with that voice. Swore to protect that voice. I crawled, hands and knees, to my cell door. I knew there were two guards posted at my cell door. I pressed my ear to the door as their voices drifted inwards.

"…escaped? How? One—two? Three? You handle that. I'll stay here in case this one decides to make a break for it."

Feet pounded away from the door. A shuffle, a scream, and a thud all within the span of ten seconds caused me to tense. The other officer's voice cried out.

"Halt in the name of Angeles!

"Fuck that."

Another scuffle. A thud.

My sister. My sister. My sister. There was no way. It wasn't possible. My sister was dead, but still, unabashed hope rose in my chest. My heart pounded. Please, dear gods, let this be my sister. Let her be alive. My father said her body was fished from the East River, and I had believed that. But there was no way I could mistake Mara's voice.

I had to know.

Energy flooded my body. I could feel it pounding through me. This was my time, my chance. I kicked at the door, crying out my sister's name and clawing at the door until my fingers began to bleed.

With all the might I had left in me, I slammed my shoulder into the weak metal door until it fell to the ground.

I stood face-to-face with a young officer, who stared at me with fear pumping through his wide-eyes. Out of the corner of my eye, I saw a second officer lying in a pool of blood. The officer pulled a pistol from his belt.

"Move out of the way." I demanded.

"I—I'll kill you," he stuttered. "Get back in there."

"Really? You're going to kill me?"

Before he could react, I grabbed the pistol with both hands and shoved it back in his face. The butt of the gun made direct contact with his nose. He doubled over as blood began to spew from between his fingers. I caught the gun before it fell and pulled the trigger.

Once, in the head.

He crumpled.

Twice, just for good measure.

"Holy shit."

I glanced up to see three figures standing a few feet away from the second guard's body. Ky, Roman, and my sister.

My sister.

I ran to her, arms outstretched. Mara's tears bled into the fabric of my tattered dress, both of us crying out words that no one understood. She pulled away first, cradling my face in her hands.

"I told you—I promised you—" she hiccupped. "No matter where you go, I'll always find you. And I did."

There were no words I could say to that. I know. I'm here. All seemed too shallow for this moment. Mara was twenty-one years old, but in this moment, she looked like a child weeping.

Mara pulled me in once more. "Ember has to come with us."

"No," Ky and Prince Roman said simultaneously. I turned to look at the two of them. They were steel-faced and covered in what I could only assume was dirt and blood.

"My father is going to have a manhunt looking for her in a second. Taking her is a risk we can't afford," Prince Roman said. "Sorry."

"Don't say sorry," Mara stepped over the bleeding corpse. "Take her! You can't expect me to leave my sister to die."

Mara took my hand, bringing me forward as Ky spoke. "One more body isn't going to kill us, Roman. I'm sure Miles can make room."

"No!" Prince Roman protested. "If that manhunt finds either one of us, my father will bring hell down on our heads." He pointed in my direction. "I'm not getting killed because of her."

"Are you heartless? They're going to kill her." Mara interjected. Prince Roman shot her a deadly look.

"She threatened to kill me three days ago."

"But did you die?" Ky crossed his arms over his chest. "She comes."

"No!"

Ky, ignoring Roman, motioned for Mara and me to start down the long corridor while Prince Roman stayed put.

"What about—?" Mara asked, looking back at him.

"Give it a second." Ky sighed.

Footsteps pounded behind us, and Prince Roman broke through Ky and Mara, mumbling something about dying because of a traitor. My hands almost hurt with how much I wanted to punch him.

The corridor in front of us was narrow and empty, its few lightbulbs buzzing and cracking with electricity. Water dripped down from the ceiling, landing on my head and arms. Ky stopped just before a clean white hall, starkly contrasting from the one we'd just been walking through.

"Miles has a car ready to take us to the Agricultural District. He'll meet us there and take Ember and Mara. No

116

one should be around, but keep your heads down just in case," Ky ordered. "Got it?"

Mara and I nodded.

We went through the white hall into an elevator so small that I stood sandwiched between Prince Roman and Mara. Prince Roman kept his eyes trained straight ahead and a scowl plastered across his face.

Once the elevator let us off into a long, metal hallway, Prince Roman walked straight up to the metal walls and began beating his fists against them, producing a flat noise, until he reached the end of the hall where a hollow sound echoed. He scratched at the wall until what I thought was metal peeled back revealing another elevator.

Ky, Mara, and I got on, this one leading us to a gardening shed and out into the night sky.

The palace was oddly quiet during the night. It was so busy during the day that the silence of the night almost took me by surprise. The four of us made our way from the grass and dirt of the back of the palace, to the wrought iron gate where a beat-up blue pickup truck waited for us. Bales of hay stuck out of the bed of the truck. The clunker looked oddly out of place in the sleek Royal District.

Roman slid into the driver's seat and played around with the ignition for a few seconds as Mara and I got into the backseat and Ky in the passenger's. Mara's hand never left mine. It tightened as the truck lurched onto the empty and smooth Royal District road.

"We're going to have to go through checkpoints."

Prince Roman said, flatly.

"We're what?" Mara's head tore away from the window.

"Checkpoints. Guards will check our truck for any contraband or illegal things, I don't know. Just keep your heads down and pray my father hasn't already been alerted of your escape."

Minutes melted into hours as we traveled through the districts. The Business District was a gray monster of tall buildings and important-looking statues. The Common District was the most expansive and took the most time to go through. The roads were covered in potholes, houses were less nice than those that we'd seen in the Business and Royal districts, and the buildings were squatty, made of clay and stone.

And the sky—oh, the sky was beautiful no matter what district we were in. It morphed from the inky black of midnight to a bright array of pinks and oranges and yellows. It took my breath away.

The car stopped abruptly, just before a tunnel with a sign reading now entering the Agricultural District. Four guards, dressed in clunky black gear, holding assault rifles, walked up to the car. I stared intently at the ground.

"Prince Roman," the first guard greeted.

"In the flesh. And delivering hay to Miles McKenna."

The guard hummed, in the back of his throat. "Why did the McKenna farm ask the Prince of Angeles to deliver hay?"

"Are you questioning your prince?"

"I—no." The guard stammered.

Ky piped up. "He asked me to deliver the hay. I'm his nephew. Prince Roman was kind enough to come with me since it's so late. We have an early morning meeting after this."

The guard took a second to think and glanced down at his clipboard. "I'm going to need IDs of everyone in the truck."

A few seconds of silence fell over the truck. Those seconds felt like a goddamn eternity. Finally, Prince Roman spoke. "I wasn't expecting to need IDs. I don't have mine on me, neither does Ky. You know us though, right?" He forced a little laugh.

The guard laughed as well. "It's standard protocol, Prince. I can't let you through without IDs." The radio on his hip crackled to life—code red: escaped prisoners. Be on look-out for two white females, 17 and 21 years of age, blonde and brown hair, blue eyes, one wearing white prison scrubs, the other in a tattered black dress. APPROACH WITH EX-TREME CAUTION.

My blood froze in my veins. The guard set the radio back down on his hip. "Well, now I'm really going to need your IDs. Don't want to be caught breaking protocol with prisoners on the loose, am I right?" He chuckled.

Prince Roman did not chuckle.

Instead, I watched as his eyes trained on the empty tunnel in front of us. There was no gate, no barrier. So, Prince Roman gunned it through the tunnel, leaving the guard

119

screaming his name.

Mara held my hand so tightly, I was afraid she was going to draw blood. I held my head down lower, so I couldn't see anything, just could feel the jolts of the truck. I didn't dare look up until the truck stopped once more.

"Now what?" Roman asked as my eyes adjusted to the world around me. We were stopped at the end of a long street, surrounded by tall rows of green plants—what I thought to be corn.

"We wait." Ky answered.

"We what?"

"Wait."

"My father has search parties looking out for them right now, and Miles expects us to wait? We can't wait!"

Ky held two hands up in surrender. "You need to calm the hell down. No one is even awake yet, and they're probably still combing the palace. We're going to be fine. Miles is going be here with his van any minute now. He's just going to take them straight out of Angeles."

"Who's Miles?" I chimed in.

"My uncle," Ky clarified. "He takes refugees in and out of Angeles."

"And takes them to Kadjar?" Mara asked.

"Sometimes. Sometimes they go to Calais."

"Where's that?"

Ky didn't speak for a minute. "Far away from here. It's near the ocean—just a little seaside town. It's not that big, and it's—"

120

"Sound like you've been there." Prince Roman muttered.

"Why do you say that?"

Prince Roman mumbled something I couldn't hear and opened his door. He slid out of the truck door. Ky climbed out, and so did Mara and I.

Ky's phone began to buzz. He pulled it out of his pocket. "Hey, what's—what? No, we're here. Where are you? Wha—okay. Plan B? You barely told me Plan A. Okay. In the barn, keys on the porch. Alright, got it. Be there in five." Ky shoved his phone in his pocket.

"Miles needs us to meet him by the southern checkpoint. He got stuck while coming back from the outside and needs an alibi. I'll drive you two. We'll figure out disguises on the way. Roman, you just head back to the palace and cover our asses."

"Wh—" I started to speak, but was cut off by the hum of a car approaching. Mara and I joined Ky and Roman at the hood of the truck where we saw a sleek black limousine stop only a few feet away from our truck. A tall man stepped out, holding a smaller figure by the hair.

Prince Roman, obviously recognizing the figures before any of us did, lurched forward. He stopped just short of the man, who I now saw was King Nero, holding his youngest son by the top of his hair. He pressed a gun to Prince Ian's temple. The child, white as a sheet, stood stock-still.

"Let him go, you bastard." Prince Roman growled. He pointed a finger toward his father.

King Nero didn't falter. He didn't move his gaze from Prince Roman. "Ky, take Mara and leave."

Ky inched toward Mara, who pulled me close to her. "Not without my sister."

"Ky, take Mara and leave." The king repeated.

Ky put a hand on Mara's shoulder, nudging her toward the cornfield. "Go," he whispered. Mara didn't let go of my hand.

"Leave, Mara. I'll be with you soon."

"No—"

Ky pushed Mara once, harder. "We'll wait for her. Just go."

Mara, for once in her life, did as she was told. She and Ky took off and disappeared into the thick of the corn.

King Nero pushed Ian forward with a few steps. I could see the fear written across the young prince's face so clearly. Ian—his big eyes, the color of oak—flooded with tears. His skinny little arms wrapped around his body like he was trying to hold all of his pieces together.

"After everything I've done for you," the king started. "This is what I get? You betray me? You aid our greatest enemy? Do you realize what a bargaining chip Mara and Ember could have been? No, you were blinded by what you thought was right. Let me let you in on a little secret, Prince. What is righteous is not always what is right."

"Let Ian go." Prince Roman seethed. He inched toward his father with hands outstretched to Ian. King Nero yanked Ian back as Prince Roman came close. Ian let out a small cry.

"Please, Dad. Please take me instead. Kill me. Shoot me. Don't hurt my brother."

"You have always searched for what is righteous. You have always sought to be a better man than I, haven't you?"

"Let him go."

"But you have never realized that kings don't get to play by the rules. We play dirty to get what we need—what our nation needs. We kill. We injure. We invade, and we conquer. We do not follow any moral code. But you've always ignored that. You've always tried to be a better man than your dear old father."

"Don't hurt—"

"But don't think your efforts have gone unnoticed. I've seen you struggle with your own morality. That's why I sent you to the Healing Room in the first place. Because you couldn't handle ruling. You never could have. I should've seen it from the start. Your mother raised you to be a good man—she corrupted you."

"Please let Ian—"

"And what did that get you? A broken soul and a divided mind. I have searched high and low for an answer to this problem: what to do with my wayward prince? But your efforts of morality have found me my answer in the form of a bloodthirsty assassin."

I didn't move.

The king's eyes rested on me. "Let the prince go." I refused to let my voice waver. I have stared evil in the eyes too many times to falter in front of this man.

"Prince? Dear girl, call him by his name."

I looked at Ian. The shadow of a tear carved down his face as he kept his eyes trained on Prince Roman. King Nero couldn't kill this child. No, not even he was that cruel.

"Ian."

"What do you want with her?" Prince Roman interjected. "What about her?"

The king cocked his head. "Come here, Ember. I want to see the monster that's terrorized Kadjar for the past three years." The king nodded toward me, not daring to let the gun or Ian go.

I walked closer to him: five shaky steps toward the man holding a gun to a child's temple. Goosebumps raced up my arms as the king's eyes slowly grazed up and down my body, examining every inch of me.

"Beautiful girl, aren't you? Shame that your life has to end like this, what with the empress finding out that you failed and all."

I kept silent.

"Tell me, how is Empress Analita these days?"

No answer.

King Nero flicked the safety off the gun. Out of the corner of my eye, I saw Roman's knees buckle. He barely caught himself.

"Let Prince Ian go," I dared.

"How did it feel to kill all of those important people? Do you feel good about what you did? Would you do it again?"

"Let him go."

"Answer my questions."

My jaw twitched. A sick conglomeration of anger and fear thrummed through my veins as I spoke. "It felt like I was finally doing something right. I'd do it again in a heartbeat."

"How does a human being get so sick that murder feels right?" The king asked, wonder shooting through his voice.

"I had no choice. My people were dying. The rich had to feel the same pain we felt before anything was going to change."

A smile grew across the king's face—a smile I didn't trust. He shoved Ian away. Ian scrambled for Prince Roman, who held him close and whispered a few things I couldn't hear. In the flash of a second, King Nero's gun rose to my forehead. My breath hitched in my throat. The king took a step toward me, pressing the cool barrel against my skin.

"Would you die for what you believe in?"

"Ten times over," I said, unable to speak louder than a whisper.

He lowered the gun. King Nero looked from me, to Prince Roman, to Ian before he spoke in the same voice I'd heard at the party: the showman's voice. This was a game to him. Everything was a game, and he was relishing in the torture.

"No one dies tonight under one condition."

"Which is?" I asked.

"You stay in Angeles," he looked pointedly at me. "Work with me. Let me teach you how to rule. Let me teach you how to use that anger to lead a nation."

"No." My face betrayed me, my lip curling as disgust thrummed through my body.

The king continued. "You will be Roman's future queen. You will rule Angeles, or you will die tonight. If I can't use you, no one can. Are we clear?"

Roman was at my side in seconds. "No, we're not. Ivelisse is the future queen."

"Ivelisse is a yes-man. I don't need a yes-man on the throne. I want someone who is willing to hurt feelings and conquer nations to succeed me. I want someone with a backbone, and I obviously am not finding that in either of you. I want her."

"What makes you think I'd dare obey you? I bow to no man." I dared.

King Nero glowered. "What you couldn't change in Kadjar, you can change here. You are the culmination of generations of fed-up, underpaid, underfed people. There is an ocean of fury laying within you, and I want you to use that to better Angeles. I want Angeles to rule the world, and I need you to do it."

"Why would I work against Kadjar?"

King Nero lifted the gun to my forehead once more. "I'm not giving you a choice."

"You speak as though I fear death."

Three things happened in the next five seconds: One. Prince Roman Stone shoved me to the ground.

Two. When I flipped myself over and looked up, I saw

King Nero's gun fire into the early morning air. The sound ripped through my eardrums.

Three. I clambered to my feet.

King Nero's face was pale. His mouth was slightly agape, staring past Prince Roman and me. My ears rang as I watched the king wordlessly stumble back into his limousine. It sped off before I had the chance to see what he was staring at. I turned around when I saw Prince Roman fall to his knees.

The bullet that missed me had pierced Prince Ian Stone through the skull.

Chapter Ten
Roman

I always pictured that I'd die before Ian. Dreamed about it, even.

Although, my dreams were never of an old and gray version of me sitting in a rocking chair after having lived a full life. I always dreamed of being about to say goodbye to him, or leaving a note explaining why he'd be a much better ruler than I ever would have been, or how his big brother had demons he couldn't shake, and how he eventually had to bend to their will. I'd tell Ian to be brave and to be a kind ruler, better than our father ever was.

But in reality, I never even got to tell him that I loved him.

All I got to say was, "Don't be scared, okay? Dry your tears, alright? He can't hurt you anymore. We're going home."

My words were so hollow, so fake, after everything that had happened. I was a liar. I should have taken that bullet. I should have seen it coming.

I sat in my mother's old rocking chair, facing the window of my apartment. This apartment was the only one that had a window. It was one-sided, so outsiders couldn't see in, but I could see the gold roof of the front building glimmering in the sunlight. I could see beyond, into the Royal District, into Angeles.

There would be a mourning ceremony for my brother

in the coming days. Today, they'd announce his death. News had already been sent to the news stations, saying that Ian died after complications from a disease that went undetected by our palace doctors. By noon, I'd see the outrage. Calls would start rolling in. People would be standing outside the gate.

"Thought he had access to the best doctors in the nation?"

"How could this happen to our prince?"

"What does this mean for us?"

They had every right to be concerned, but their concern was directed at the wrong reasons. They'd make up rumors of a new plague sweeping through the nation, just like the one that had destroyed the world hundreds of years ago.

My father would televise Ian's funeral as people gathered in the streets, screaming, crying, mourning over the young prince.

And to think, I could have stopped it. I could have jumped in front of that bullet. I could have attacked my father, been bolder, been braver, and Ian wouldn't be dead.

Tomorrow, the sun would rise on a new day. It, and the days leading to Ian's funeral, would be declared national days of mourning. All the citizens of Angeles would begin preparing to either travel to the Royal District to pay their respects or mourn at home.

It would just be another day to them.

Not to me. Not to anyone who actually knew Ian.

A small yawn from behind me jerked me from my thoughts; I had forgotten that I wasn't alone.

Ember—I turned from the window to face her. She slept on my couch with a blue comforter thrown over her small frame. Her hair, still wet from the shower she'd taken hours before, bled into the gray couch, staining it black. She wore an old shirt and sweatpants I'd fished out of the bottom of my drawer. Ember had gone straight to sleep after her shower. I couldn't.

I shouldn't care what happened to her. I should have just left her for dead in that stupid prison. If she had just given up, or if she had just realized that you can't win in the face of a sick king, Ian might still be here asking for breakfast or running off to play with one of his friends. I wanted to throw every bit of blame and anger on her, but I couldn't bring myself to. She was a criminal—a killer. She belonged in that prison cell like the animal she was.

But last night, I saw something in her. Something that scared me: humanity.

I was paralyzed, kneeling in front of Ian's body. She walked to him, picked him up, and began running. I followed her blindly, running straight through the cornfield until we got to the McKenna farm.

Miles wasn't home, but his wife was, and she took one look at Ian and told me he was gone.

A sick, slow feeling washed over me. If I had just left Ember alone, she would be dead, yet Ian would be alive. Gods, why didn't I choose my brother?

Why was I so hellbent on seeing the assassin of Kadjar live? I owed her now. I owed her for everything she did last night. I'd never be able to repay her either, and I hated that thought.

She snored, slept in the same fetal position that I did when I was a kid. She looked so small, curled up like that. For the first time since I'd met her, she looked at peace. There was no anger like knives carving across her face. There was just blank peace.

My doorbell chimed.

I pushed myself out of the chair and went for the door. I found myself frozen, staring at the handle. More than anything, I wanted to open the door and find Ian there, like he'd never left, like he'd just been spending the night at a friend's apartment, and I had just forgot. I'd hug him and promise him a million things that I knew I'd never be able to see through, but that would be okay because at least he was here and alive.

King Nero stood behind the door.

I slammed it shut.

The doorbell rang once more. "Open the door, Roman." He ordered. I twisted the lock. He repeated himself.

"You have a key, asshole, use it."

I couldn't bring myself to walk away. I had to brace myself for the outcome of him having a key and his attack when he did open the door.

"You changed the scanner last week. My keycard doesn't work."

I breathed a sigh of relief.

"Open the door or I'm going to knock it down. Now is not the time to test me." His voice was rasping. I didn't trust it, so I did as I was told.

My father pushed his way past me into the living room. If he noticed Ember, he didn't say a word. The hardwood floor of the living room split off into our tiled kitchen. My father made his way for the coffee pot.

"I see you let the Bloodhound stay the night," he said, taking the pot off the burner and mug out of the cabinet. I wish I could take that mug and smash it over his head. I could slam his head into the counter and drag his body to the balcony before throwing him over it. My hands almost ached with the way I wanted to hurt this man. I needed him to feel the same pain that Ian did. I needed him to bleed like my brother.

I didn't trust myself to say anything—he was a walking landmine. One wrong move, one wrong word, and Ember and I would both be dead.

"You're not doing anything with her. Not now." I said carefully, calculated.

My father pulled a bottle of creamer from the fridge. "Why do you care?"

"I don't owe you an explanation."

He snorted. You're just going to ignore everything she's done? What happened to that little moral compass you care so much about?"

"I know what she's done, but I also know why she did it."

"And you're just going to excuse murder?"

"She killed for good reason. People who deserved to die. Rapists, murderers. All who were high up enough to get

132

away with their crimes. She needed the rich to feel the same pain she felt. I know that she's just as human as I am."

My father stirred his coffee and sighed. He waved a facetious hand. "Sadly, she is human. If I could create a robot to succeed me, I would. But she is as close to emotionless as we are going to get."

"What are you getting at?"

"I mean that when she does feel, she weaponizes it. All that anger turned into power, and that power changed her entire nation. Look at you, what have you been doing? Crying, that's what you've been doing."

"I haven't—"

"Don't lie to me. I'm not an idiot, boy. But that Bloodhound? She's going to change this nation. She's going to build Angeles up, and she's going to take over the world. There was a king in the land before named Charles the fifth. He conquered lands and took no survivors—they say that his was an empire on which the sun never set. That is what I want for Angeles. That is what Ember will bring us."

"She doesn't know the first thing about governing."

"But you do. So you two will work together. You will become the team Angeles has always needed—the team your mother and I couldn't be."

"You're insane."

He took a sip of his coffee. "Possibly." We stood there in silence. Normally, I would have walked away by this point. Walking away was always easier than facing my father-head on. The now-empty coffee pot was so close to my hands. If I could just reach a few more inches and slam it into his head, he'd be dead.

Please, God, if you're up there, just strike him down already.

"I wouldn't do that if I were you." My father said, like it was the simplest thing in the world. He took another drink of his coffee.

"Do what?"

"I see where your eyes are going. You're not as smart as you think yourself to be, Prince Roman. Hitting me with that coffee pot means that I could try you for an assassination attempt, which would make you a criminal. And you've seen firsthand what we do to criminals around here."

I turned on my heels, poised to walk straight out the door. His voice called me back. "Although, with your situation, I guess being a criminal wouldn't be all that bad."

Unable to stop myself, I let out a laugh. "Really?" I turned back him, arms crossed.

"Mmh. Being a criminal makes you a dead man. Being a dead man means you'd at least see your little brother again."

In a flash, I reached for the coffee pot. My father was faster. He dropped his mug, and it hit the floor and shattered. He grabbed my wrist and pulled me close, only inches from his face. I tensed. His eyes were wild, and now, so close to him, I smelled the whiskey on his breath.

"Don't do it, Roman." He growled. With his free hand, he freed the coffee pot from my grip and threw it to the ground, sending more glass scattering over the kitchen tiles.

My father brought my shaking hands between our heads. "Look at you—look at how scared you are, shaking like a leaf in the wind. How the hell did I raise such a spineless man?"

"I am not spineless." I rasped.

My father crossed his arms over his chest. "You are going to be your own downfall, aren't you? Forget the million other things that I tried to prepare you for. You can't block out the world like I tried to train you to do. Your own mind will be your achilles heel, Just like Ian's own blind trust was his—"

"What the hell is that supposed to mean?" I staggered back. "He was a child!"

"Ian got in that car with me and didn't question why there was a gun sitting in the backseat. Ian didn't run into the fields the second he had the chance. He waited for you to protect him, and that got him killed. I didn't kill him. His blind devotion to you did."

Anger coursed through my body. "You pulled the trigger."

"That bullet was meant for the Bloodhound. It's her fault that Ian is dead, not mine."

I turned away from him to keep from punching him. Instead, I kicked my foot into the cabinet. The wood splintered into my tennis shoes. I sent my foot through the cabinet once, twice. I only stopped when the splinters began to pierce my foot.

"Are you done?"

No. I wanted to say. I won't be until you're dead. Instead, I said nothing.

"Send the Bloodhound my best wishes. I'll begin training her soon."

"You're not—" I stopped myself when my foot began to throb. "Was it because of me? Did I do something? Are you trying to punish me?"

My father shook his head slowly. His voice dropped, almost to a whisper. "You think me to be that cruel?"

"I wouldn't put it past you."

He examined my face, and I saw something in my father that I can't say I'd never seen before. Humanity. Humanity tucked into sadness. "I've never—I've given you everything. Do you truly think I'd put a bullet in my own son just to punish you?"

"You've threatened it before."

"Threats are not actions. I only punish where it is warranted, and Ian did nothing to deserve the fate that he got. It was an accident." My father turned away from me for a second, like he was getting ready to leave, then he turned back. "I know you think that I'm not capable of the same love that the rest of the world is. But I am. And I love you, son. I loved Ian." My father's eyes welled with tears.

I was frozen.

No. I wanted to say. No, you don't get to make me feel bad for you. You don't get to make me want to apologize. You don't get to cry and make me forget everything you've ever done to me.

"Get out."

"What?" My father looked up at me.

"Get out. Sleep in your office. Don't come back. I won't let you in again." I pointed to the door.

He didn't fight me like I was expecting him to. I watched him walk away past the couch, where he didn't even look at Ember, and out the door.

Now, more than ever, I wished for that stupid cigarette. It hadn't ever occurred to me that someone like my father was capable of love. He never loved me. He just didn't want me to destroy him when I got on the throne—at least, that's the reason I had to tell myself now, so I could hold on to what shred of sanity I had left.

A scream coming from the couch jerked me away from all thoughts of my father and of whatever love he might have had for Ian and me. I looked over to find Ember reaching out into thin air like she was trying to grab onto whatever dream she had.

Ember's eyes found me standing in the threshold between the kitchen and the living room. I watched as she lowered her head into her hands.

"Bad dream?" I asked.

She didn't answer. After a few seconds of struggling to catch her breath, she lifted her head, not opening her eyes but rubbing her temples with her forefinger.

"Headache," she finally said. I retreated back into the kitchen and opened up the cluttered medicine cabinet. It was filled with old bottles of medication from past flu seasons and sinus infections. I grabbed a white bottle of pain pills and brought it over to the couch.

"Here—pain pills." I took a seat next to her and ran my hand down my face. She didn't take the bottle.

Ember looked from me to the bottle still in my outstretched hand. "Thank you, Prince."

I shook my head. "You don't have to call me prince. Just Roman. None of my friends call me prince."

"We aren't friends." She said, blankly.

"Ah, you're right. Being friends with a serial killer has never exactly been something I've been dying to cross off my bucket list, either." I shot back, words dripping with sarcasm.

She jerked the pill bottle from my hand and downed a pill. She set her elbows on her knees, staring straight into the coffee table for a second before turning her head to me. "I need a map to get to the Agricultural District."

"For?"

"I'm going back to Kadjar."

"You can't."

She raised an eyebrow. "Excuse me? Was that not the deal?"

"All deals were thrown out the window last night. You heard my father. He's planning on using you. There's no way you're getting out of the palace if he needs something from you. Every guard probably has you on their list."

She handed me the pill bottle. "You say that like guards have stopped me before."

"Weren't you captured?"

"I want to punch you so hard right now."

"Go ahead." I pushed myself up off the couch and went straight for the window.

My nation seemed so quiet in this window. It was like looking at everything through a snow globe, only without the snow. Everything was so still and so peaceful. Nothing hurt through this window.

But outside the apartment, the world was a loud, screaming array of people who needed everything from me. And I had nothing left to give.

Ian would have made such a good leader. So much better than I ever could have been. He wasn't broken like I was. Jesus, he was still a kid. My throat began to tighten. No, no, I couldn't cry now. Not while there was someone around.

I blinked fast, as if that would stop the tears. When it didn't, I wiped at my eyes with the palm of my hand.

The front door creaked. Fearing it was my father, I turned around. Ember stood with her hand on the doorknob.

"You can leave," I threw my hand in the air. "But you're not going to get far. They're going to catch you. You don't even know where the hell you're going."

"I'll figure it out."

"Fine. Go. Get yourself thrown back in solitary confinement."

I turned, and the door closed. Everything came flooding to me all at once. My little brother was dead. I held his bleeding body. His mouth was open like he was trying to finish a sentence that I'd never get to hear.

Roman, watch! I could see him in the reflection of the window jumping down from the couch, arms out like he was flying. I could see him running from wall to wall, toy car held in his little fist. I could see him waltzing through the door with a friend, exclaiming that they were going to his room to play video games. I could see him at every age, in every facet of life, calling my name, needing me for some reason or another.

And yet, last night, he was silenced by a man who claimed to love him.

His reflection danced around the living room in socked feet to the muffled beat of whatever played through his headphones. His reflection ran into my arms, already talking about whatever they had done in school that day. His reflection cried because he'd fallen and scraped his knee.

His reflection turned to look at me, mouth open, eyes wide with fear, and wavered.

"Don't—" Go. My words fell out of my mouth in a sigh. The rest of the sentence disappeared along with Ian.

"Don't what?"

I jumped. Ember was standing behind my shoulder. In the prison, she had been terrifying, like something straight out of a horror flick that Ky and I would rent just to watch at midnight and scare ourselves. But now that I saw her clearly, I saw that it wasn't just the lack of light in the prison that made her so haunting—it was the long white hair that fell down her shoulders, the sharp angles of her face and how they never seemed to smile or break from their permanently angry disposition. She reminded me of a siren, almost like she had jumped straight from the book of myths that was tucked neatly on the bookshelf in my bedroom.

"Nothing. Just...thinking aloud. If you really need a map, I can print one off for you later today. Just not now."

She didn't say anything for a while, and I didn't expect her to. I mean, what do you say after everything that's happened? I'd be fine if I never had to speak again.

"I'm sorry." She finally said. "About Ian. I'm really sorry. I feel like it's my fault. You pushed me out of the way."

"Yeah, I know. I don't...I don't know why I did that. I thought he was farther away. I thought he would've gotten out of the line of fire by then. But he was waiting for me. He wasn't thinking about himself. He was thinking about staying with his brother." I stopped myself from rambling as my chest tightened.

She shook her head. "I never meant for any of this to happen. I should've...I should've just stayed with Ivelisse. This is my fault. I'm sorry."

"Stop saying that, alright? I don't—I don't need you to say that."

"What?"

"Do you know how many times people are going to say that to me? 'I'm sorry' or 'My condolences'. I'm never going to get away from them, and every time I hear them it's going to be like—I don't know. I just want to be numb, for now. Say whatever, just don't say you're sorry."

"What do you want me to say?"

I shrugged, looked back out to the window. "There's

not much to say, is there?"

She shook her head. "I guess not."

A sick, slow feeling washed over my body. So, this is what it means to be alone. Alone staring out at my nation. My broken, hurting nation that was mourning the life of their lost prince while completely unaware to the fact that they were following his killer into a violent tailspin.

He was a reckless man, always had been. My mother once told me that reckless wasn't a bad thing to be, but it was what you were working for that mattered. My father was working for himself. He was working for a giant machine; trying to better and strengthen that machine without realizing that yes, he was still human and yes, he had to stop looking at the big picture long enough to see the world around him. Detached—I think that's a better word for him.

I hadn't realized that Ember was standing beside me until she sniffed.

She, in a way, was like an inverted version of him. In killing, she thought all too much of the end without thinking of the here and the now. All too much thought for the world around her and no thought for the smaller picture. She was just as reckless and detached as he was.

Look at me—the prince who lived his life as careful and calculated as he could, kept himself within his safe little box, only to be surrounded with people like this.

I guess you can't blame the reckless, though. They never stop to think about who they are hurting, do they?

Chapter Eleven
Ember

Ivelisse Grace's bedroom was probably the neatest place I'd ever been in my entire life. Her walls were pastel pink, the same color as the satin bow tying her hair away from her face.

My room back home was the size of Ivelisse's closet. My walls were made of brick and mortar, as was the rest of the house. Hidden in a shoebox tucked neatly under a pile of clothes I never wore, lay my knife, gun, and research from past kills. My mattress sat in the corner of my dirt room with a small dresser opposite of it.

Ivelisse, on the other hand, had a neat room with a desk full of carefully stacked papers, a tall dresser with perfume and loose change. A jewelry organizer sat on top of the dresser. A small, primitive part of me was aching to pocket a pearl necklace or two, or maybe the diamond earrings sitting in front of the organizer. I could find a way to send it back home. Gods above, rocks like that could feed Mara, Mama, and Papa for a few years.

No, no. You're here on business, not to steal. I told myself, bringing my attention away from the dresser. Ivelisse sat at her vanity on the back wall. I sat on the edge of her bed, toying with the ends of the skirt she'd let me borrow. I don't think such fine fabrics had ever touched my skin. I felt almost like one of the North Sector girls I used to see sitting outside the coffee shops in the marketplace.

The lights surrounding the vanity mirror illuminated Ivelisse's face. She wore a crown of purple and white flowers, the white a stark contrast against her dark, silken hair. She wore a dress of the same dark mulberry color as the flowers.

"Don't you think this dress is to *die* for?" She asked as she plucked a hair from between her eyebrows, wincing.

"Sure. I guess."

"You guess? I think it's to die for. I was supposed to wear it on the day that Roman and I announced our wedding—in a few months, on his eighteenth birthday. It's going to be the grandest gala that Angeles has seen in decades. I've had it picked out since last year. My mother never liked it though. She wanted me to wear white, but I'll only ever wear white on my wedding day." Her gaze fell to the countertop. She pushed a bottle of perfume back in line with the rest sitting against the mirror. "But now I don't even know if that'll happen."

"Can you still not get married to Roman?" I asked.

She shook her head. "No. I'm not the future queen anymore. The future queen marries the future king." She resumed plucking, whatever sadness that had found its way on her face now erased. "Besides, Roman wouldn't want to even if we could."

"Why?"

She set her tweezers down and turned around to face me. "We were *arranged* to be married, not because we loved each other or anything."

"You love him, don't you?"

Ivelisse paled. "No. Why do you say that?"

"I don't know. You look at him like he's worth all the gold in the world. I just thought that you two were in love or something."

"Well, we're not. We haven't ever been, so don't go thinking that you're breaking up some love story for the ages. Because you're not." She turned back around to finish plucking her eyebrows.

"You sound like you're trying to convince yourself more than me."

"You're getting annoying. No offense."

I shrugged. "Not the worst thing I've ever heard in my entire life." I watched her pluck at the stray hairs around her eyebrows, eyes watering as she did. I touched my own eyebrows, wondering if I should ask her to pluck mine. I'd never had them done before. I'd never thought the little hairs between my eyes had to be removed. But they were blonde and faint, so maybe they weren't that big of a deal. Maybe I could skip what looked like unnecessary pain.

"You didn't come home last night," she noted.

"What?"

"I couldn't sleep, so I went to go see if you were awake, but you weren't there. Where did you go?"

I sucked in my bottom lip. She must not have heard. Roman said all the news stations should have been relaying the news to the people, but Ivelisse hadn't left her apartment all day. Studying, she said. Studying old bills and making plans for the future. I don't think she truly believed that I was

145

really going to take her position. Truth be told, I didn't either.

How was I supposed to tell her? How could I tell her that I stood soundlessly as Roman held his brother's dead body? How could I tell her that I carried Ian through the corn-fields until we found the McKenna farm? How could I tell her that I held his hand all the way back to the palace? How could I tell her the horror that was watching Roman dry his tears in the seconds before we got to the palace, putting on a face of steel instead?

"I was at Roman's." Ivelisse dropped her tweezers, and I realized how my words must've sounded to her. "N-not like that! I just fell asleep on his couch."

She bent down to pick her tweezers off her white car-pet. "I'm surprised he even let you in. Why were you there?"

"I was just trying to gather answers about everything that had happened. You know, with the king's announcement and all."

"Right. Don't worry yourself about that announcement. If he hasn't said anything to the Court yet, I doubt he ever will. It was probably just a notion that he had. He gets those sometimes—ideas that can never happen. Bills and laws that'll never get through the Senate. Silly things, really."

"You don't think he's going to declare me as the future queen?"

"No. I've trained for this position since I was six. There's no logical reason for him to take that from me and give it to...you. No offense."

"Every time you say that I feel like offense is definitely

intended."

She shrugged. "Take it as you must." Ivelisse wiped the tweezers off on the hem of her cardigan and opened one of the drawers of the vanity to place them in. She pulled out a pencil the same raven color as her eyebrows and began filling in the bare spots of her eyebrows.

On the countertop, there was a line of glass perfume bottles and a picture of Roman and Ivelisse. She stopped behind him, her arms wrapped around his shoulders, her head leaning against his. They both smiled brightly at the camera.

She must've seen me staring at the picture because she stopped filling in her eyebrows and picked the picture up. A smile jerked at her lips. "He's a handsome devil, is he not?"

I nodded. She was right. Even with all the things going on, I still couldn't deny how attractive the Prince of Angeles was. No one alive could. He was like good art—something you had no choice but to notice, to stop and stare at.

The door opened. Li Grace stood behind it. She was a spitting image of Ivelisse, the picture of elegance, everything nobility should be. Her black hair was short-cropped to just below her chin, but her eyes, unlike Ivelisse's, were tired.

"Ivelisse," she spoke. "Your father and I are going to visit my parents this afternoon. Are you coming?"

"Are they coming here?" Ivelisse asked, not looking up from filling in her eyebrows.

"No."

"I'm not going to the Agricultural District."

"You're going to have to sometime soon. We move—"

"I don't want to think about it, Mother. We will cross that bridge when we get there, and right now, that bridge is still three days away."

Li took in a deep breath. "Fine. Have it your way. But I want this room ready to go by tomorrow evening. Okay?"

"Alright."

Li didn't say anything for a second. She stood in the doorway watching her daughter. Some kind of emotion that I couldn't quite figure out lingered in her eyes—something akin to sadness, I think.

"*Wǒ ài nǐ,*" she finally said.

Ivelisse didn't respond for a lot longer than I expected her to. She finally looked back at her mother and repeated, "*Wǒ ài nǐ,* Mom."

The ghost of a smile trailed across Li's face, and she left. "Did you hear that? What she said?" Ivelisse asked, the second the door had closed. "She said I love you. If she really loved me, she'd fight this."

"Fight what?"

"This stupid announcement!" Ivelisse threw her eyebrow pencil down on the vanity. It bounced off the wood and onto the floor. "You—he's kicking us out of the palace."

"He...?"

"King Nero! He had an assistant stop by to tell us that we had to be out in three days. My mother's been fired, and so has my father. Everything was riding on my becoming queen—our entire livelihood was resting on my shoulders."

"I'm sorry."

Ivelisse held a hand up. "You are the last person I need to hear *sorry* from." She took a deep breath and held it. Tears welled in her eyes. She released the breath and dabbed her waterline with her pads of her fingers. "Do you know what the worst part is?"

"What?"

"I'm sad about losing the position that I've trained so hard for, but...I am so in love with that stupid boy I think it's going to kill me."

"You just said you weren't in love with Roman."

"I lied, okay! I lied. I love him, and it's not the kind of love that I can just snap out of. It's the kind of love that I feel burning in the pit of my stomach just at the thought of him. But he's so oblivious. It's like he can only see what's two feet in front of him. And I know he doesn't feel the same about me. I get that."

"How do you know?"

"My mother looks at my father like he holds all the secrets to the universe. Roman looks at me like I'm just Ivelisse," she shrugged. "Just another one of the palace girls pining after him—no one to fall in love with."

"Anyone would be lucky to have you."

Ivelisse nodded. "I know that. I just never imagined that I'd find my 'one great love' only to find out that I'm not his. It just sucks that my life was so close to being perfect, and now it's all being ripped away by a king who thinks he's found the secret to saving a nation that doesn't need to be saved."

"Me," I finished. "I'm not—I'm not leader material. I don't know what King Nero is thinking."

"No one does. My mother says he works in mysterious ways. You never know his plans until they're already finished. He's deceptive, I think." She clapped a hand over her mouth. "God, I've never said anything bad about the king aloud before."

"Well, at least you have reason to now."

"I want him…I want him to feel what I feel. I *need* him to know what this feels like—to have your entire world ripped out from underneath you in a span of mere days. I need him to know how badly it hurts. This morning, I had everything, and now? Now I don't even know what I have."

"We can change this. We can fight this."

Ivelisse waved a dismissive hand. "Don't go saying things you know aren't true."

"No, I do know. We can find some way to reverse this, can't we?"

"There isn't a way to reverse it. King Nero has made up his mind. He thinks you're what Angeles needs. And, who knows, he may be right."

"He isn't. I need to get back to Kadjar. I don't want to be what Angeles needs. I'm what Kadjar needs."

"There's no getting out of Angeles now. You just need to suck it up and accept your fate. We'll all be better off if you do."

I'm not doing that. I almost said. Instead, I pushed myself up off the bed and out the door. Ivelisse's voice stopped

150

me just as I was closing the door behind me.

"Hold on," She called. I paused. "You're one of those world-shaking types, aren't you? A rebel, a vigilante, or whatever you want to call it. That's what you think of yourself as?"

"I guess."

"I don't care what anyone tries to do to stop you. Make King Nero feel the same pain he's put all of us through. And make sure it hurts."

Chapter Twelve
Roman

Advisory council meetings happened once a week, and I considered them to be among the worst three hours of my life.

They took place in one of the four bunkers beneath the palace. There was one for emergency Senate meetings, in case the palace came under attack and the Senate hall couldn't be used, two to be used as panic shelters for the royal family, and the last for these dumb advisory council meetings.

My father's council was made up of Li Grace, Lori McKenna, Mark Rowe, Joseph Clark, and Atticus Harper. These people have been plucked from the highest positions in the country: CEOs of major corporations, important activists, and politicians alike. Aside from Ky and Ivelisse's mothers, I didn't know the rest of the council personally. They'd always been there, amongst the rotating cast of politicians my father kept by his side.

"Your Highness," Mark Rowe started. "I just don't think that—"

My father, who sat at the head of the glossy table, held a hand up for silence. "Did I ask for your input, Senator Rowe?"

He closed his mouth.

There was an empty space beside me which belonged to Li Grace. I wondered where she was. I had half a mind to ask my father if he knew what happened to her, but he was in a mood. He had come into the advisory council meeting late, slamming doors and throwing his books down.

Come to think of it, I hadn't even seen Ivelisse today. I made a mental note to call her after this meeting was over.

News of Ian's death was all over Angeles by noon yesterday. My phone had been flooded with messages from unsaved numbers. People had been knocking at my apartment door like crazy. Eventually I took a seat on my balcony, waiting for nightfall so they'd all just go back to their apartments. They were able to return to normalcy. I wasn't.

I sat on my balcony well into the night staring at that little black cigarette. It sat across from me on a paper towel. Taunting me. My stomach churned, either with the weight of my decision or the utmost need to smoke.

My father cleared his throat. "This girl—no, this warrior—has shown the type of skills it takes to lead a nation that I have yet to see from either Ivelisse Grace or Prince Roman. It is within Angeles' best interest to accept her reign."

"Lest we forget where she comes from," Joseph Clark said. "Sir, she is an enemy assassin. She knows nothing of the ways of the Court, and we know nothing of her status back in Kadjar. How can we trust her?"

"You don't have to trust her. You have to trust me and trust my ability to assign a successor. I see what she is capable of. I can mold her into the ruler I know she can be." No one answered. My father let out a little laugh. "Do you all not trust me?"

"We trust you, Your Highness. But we don't trust her."

"She and I are one," My father said. That thought made my blood boil. "You deny her, you deny me." When no one spoke, he continued. "This can be a beautiful opportunity. Think of it—if we have a Kadjarian on the throne, we automatically have an alliance with Kadjar. We can open up trade routes once more, we can take down the barrier. That girl is intelligent, skilled, and cunning. You have no reason to deny her."

Mark Rowe spoke up. "A quick mind doesn't necessarily mean it's a mind wired to rule. Why spend time molding a girl who knows nothing of Angeles when your son has been brought up for this job?"

"He's right," Lori McKenna said. "And how can you just change the system of ruling? I mean, a queen ruling over a king? That's never been done before. How do you expect the people to take that?"

"They'll take it with grace because it's coming from the government that they trust. This girl can shake up our government, bring in new ideas and new things we haven't seen before. We need a change. We need someone who can strengthen our nation."

"She's not a politician. Prince Roman has grown up around politics. She hasn't. She doesn't know how governing works."

"That's the beauty of it!"

Atticus Harper sighed. "Forgive my lack of understanding, Your Highness. You want us to bring in someone with

154

absolutely zero political experience to lead our nation into an era of greatness, even though we already have someone lined up for the position with an entire lifetime of experience?"

My father nodded. "The Graces are gone. The wheels are in motion. Ember will rule."

"They're...gone?" Atticus Harper asked.

"As in, I sent them back to the Agricultural District. They weren't supposed to leave until after Prince Ian's funeral, but things need to be hurried along."

"You what?" My father made it very clear to me from the start that I was only supposed to observe in advisory council meetings, but I couldn't stop myself from speaking out now.

He jerked his head over to look at me, like he was just now noticing that I was here. "I sent them back home. Their services aren't needed." His eyes shot daggers at me.

I couldn't fight back. There were too many people in the room for us to get into an argument. So, instead, I slunk back into my chair and let him continue to speak.

"Ember and Prince Roman will marry on time, as Ivelisse and my son were to be married. She will rule over him, and there will be no questions about it."

I shut my eyes tightly, as if I could make the scene in front of me disappear. All of this happened because I pushed Ember out of the way of a bullet.

This is all my fault.

"Sir, how are we going to break this news to the people? They love Ivelisse. How are we going to introduce Ember to them?"

"Easily: talk shows, radio interviews, magazine shoots. Get them used to the idea of a new future queen. I'll have my publicists create a likable persona for her. I promise you all, this is what's best for Angeles. This is what we need."

Silence rested over the council. Mark Rowe spoke next. "Sir, are you well?"

My father, in one swift motion, stood and slammed his hands onto the table. I flinched. "I am fine. I am doing what's best for this nation. I am doing this, and no one can stop me because I am the king!"

"I'm sure you've made the right decision." Lori McKenna said. "Your council stands behind you."

With that, my father took one long look at the faces sitting around his council table and left the room.

We all sat there for a few seconds, waiting for his footsteps to go out of earshot. Atticus Harper stood bringing his briefcase to the table. He set his laptop and his cell phone in the case and slammed it shut.

"I don't care what they all say. Democracy is dead, and it died the second that bastard took the throne," he pointed an accusing finger at me. "And you can tell him I said that. I quit."

"You can't quit," Mark Rowe called out. "We're all under contract."

"I'm a lawyer for God's sake. I'm getting myself out of that goddamn contract. This is ridiculous. He calls a meeting just to parade around the new way he's conjured up to destroy

Angeles? He knows we can't do anything to stop him. He knows that the Senate is just a set up for the people to truly believe that they're still in charge, when he has the final say on every piece of legislation. He gets to decide what happens to Angeles. This isn't a democracy. It's a monarchy at the end of the day. He's sick in the head!"

No one said anything to contradict Atticus because he was right.

Slowly, one by one, they all drained out of the room leaving me by myself. Once alone, I pulled myself from my chair and made my way to the door. I ran smack into none other than Li Grace.

"Li—hi."

She didn't bother to greet me back. "Did he tell you? About us leaving."

I nodded. "I'm sorry, Mrs. Grace. I want to help you, I really do. If there's anything—"

The bunker adjacent to the one Li and I stopped outside of flung open. "Li! How very...brave of you to show your face after the events of the past few weeks. I thought you'd run home with your tail between your legs by now."

Li blinked. "What do you mean, Your Highness? All of our things are gone, yes, but we won't leave until this afternoon. That was the deal, was it not?"

My father moved to my side. He crossed his arms over his chest. "You don't think I know of everything that goes on within my palace? You think I don't have informants watching over this palace when I can't? You think I didn't hear of your husband's 3 AM rendezvous with mysterious strangers?"

Li didn't respond.

"I guess I should owe you some thanks. After all, you brought the Bloodhound to me. At the same time, you did deceive me. You made deals with my greatest enemy. You betrayed me and turned your back on your country."

"I'm sorry." Li kept her head bowed.

"If I weren't a better man, I would have you and Killian by firing squad. Get out of my palace and don't you dare return."

She turned on her heel and made her way to the elevator. I followed after her. "Hold on a second—"

Li Grace turned abruptly, just as the elevator door opened. "You want to be a good king, better than that man?" She asked, tears spilling onto her cheeks. "Fix this. Find a way to make things right."

"How?"

"You're the prince, not me. You find a way."

Before I could speak again, she retreated inside the elevator. I backed away as the doors closed. My father stood beside me, waiting for the elevator to return.

"We need this," he said, more to himself than to me. "This is what Angeles needs."

Your son has died. His funeral is tomorrow. And yet, all you can think about is your nation. All you can think about is growing and conquering.

The elevator opened once more, and my father stepped

inside. He looked at me, as if asking if I was going to get on with him. Finally, I stepped into the elevator. We'd ridden this ride in silence so many times before, but none felt quite like this. There hadn't been a sense of dread like there was now.

One more day.

One more day, and the world would have to face my reality.

But then they could return to their lives. They could forget Ian's death. They could go back to their nine to five jobs and their own families, and he'd fade from their minds as nothing but the young prince who was robbed of life by some unknown disease.

Only three people alive would know the truth: me, my father, and Ember.

The elevator emptied, and my father and I walked back to the palace, side by side. He went to the front building and I, to the back. I walked in a daze to my apartment. It stood on the top, the only apartment on the floor.

The figure at the end of my hallway stopped me dead my tracks. "Hello?" I called out. It turned around, and I saw her—Ember.

"I didn't know where else to go." She looked at me with stern, gunmetal blue eyes. I pushed past her and slid the keycard into the scanner. My door clicked, and I opened it. Ember followed me inside.

"So you decided to come here?" I asked. She stopped in the middle of my living room while I made my way to the kitchen, going straight for the coffee pot.

"I just—the Graces are leaving." She said like I didn't already know. "It's my fault."

"It's not your fault. None of this is your fault." I grabbed two mugs from the cabinet. "It's all his fault. He's got this notion in his head that you're some kind of savior. He's projecting everything on you. You just need to lay low." I poured the coffee into the mugs and reached into the fridge for creamer. I paused. "Do you want cream in your coffee?"

"I've never had it."

"Cream?"

"Coffee."

I raised an eyebrow.

"It's not a necessity. If we can afford to live without it, we do afford to live without it." I poured a bit of creamer in her mug and brought it out to the living room. She held the mug between her hands, staring down at the brown liquid.

I took a seat in the rocking chair adjacent to the couch and pulled out one of the binders sitting on the coffee table. This one was filled with Senate documents that must've been dropped off for my father—meaning he didn't attend the Senate meeting. I picked up the documents to see what he missed out on and what I could do to pick up where he lacked.

The papers consisted of bill proposals—one for new paved roads for the Common District, another for the construction of a schoolhouse in the Agricultural District. Things that shouldn't have trouble passing, but still needed my father's signature. Nothing ever got through the Senate without the king's approval.

Out of the corner of my eye, I saw Ember take a seat on the couch. I watched her continue to stare into her mug like it had every answer in the world.

"I can't stay here, Roman." She finally said. "I need to know if Mara got home alright. I need to be with my family. Gods only know what the empress is doing to them because of me—because I'm not home to protect them."

"Well, you've got another enemy now—the paparazzi. They're starting to crowd the palace in preparation for. . .his funeral. We've tripled military presence around the gates just so they don't break through."

"I still need that map."

I looked up from the papers. "I can't force you to stay, but I'd hate to see you die out there."

"If they think that I'm their future queen, no one's going to lay a hand on me."

"They don't know that yet. My father wants to announce your reign right after the funeral. He wants to cancel out a negative with a positive."

"I don't know why you're so against me leaving. It seems like it's a plus for the both of us. I get out of your hair, you can rule, and I get to go home."

I tossed the papers back down on the coffee table. "I don't know either, okay? It's stupid. I want you to stay for a stupid, selfish reason, so if you really want that map, I'll go print it off now." I pushed myself off the wicker rocking chair and started for my bedroom where I had a printer sitting on my desk.

"Hold on," she called. "Why do you want me to stay?"

I stopped in my doorway. My words came out slow, like molasses, almost as if I knew they were a bad choice, but I couldn't stop myself from saying them. "Because I hate you. I hate you more than I ever thought possible to hate another person. I hate you so much that I think this singular feeling is going to destroy me, but at the same time, I owe you."

"Owe me?"

"You stayed with me. You carried Ian when I thought I could barely move. I screamed at you and I told you to go back where you came from so many times that night. You could have run after Miles and Mara, but you didn't. You lost what might've been your last chance to go home for me and Ian."

Ember didn't speak. "You would have done the same thing, wouldn't you?"

"No." I crossed my arms over my chest trying to mask the unbridled anger that was pumping through my veins. "No, I don't think I would have. I think after the fifth time of being told to fuck off, I would have done just that."

"You can't pay me back for something like that."

"Oh, I've realized. But I don't want to go to my grave owing someone like you."

"Someone like me?" She rose up from the couch, matching my pose.

"A killer."

"You don't know jack shit about me or who I am."

"I think I know enough. You parade around like some

162

vigilante, but at the end of the day, you've killed people. You took away human life. No matter the reason, how does that make you any different than any other serial killer?"

"You don't get to play gods with me, Prince Roman. Your family is just as corrupt as you think I am."

"Do you think you're not corrupt?"

"I did what I had to do to save my people." I scoffed at her words. She threw her hands in the air. "Gods, you are infuriating!"

"So I've been told, Bloodhound."

"Oh, don't you dare use that prince-voice on me."

"That what?"

"That 'holier-than-thou' voice of yours. You think your shit doesn't stink? You think you're not guilty of your own list of crimes? You can take that voice and shove it up your—"

"I am—" I stopped myself short. Your prince. But I had no jurisdiction over this girl. She was in and of her own free will.

Admittedly, that thought made me wickedly jealous. I wanted what she had. I wanted to be free. I wanted to be able to belong to myself and not to the throne of Angeles. As much as she was free, I was still the prince.

I wanted what she had, the good and the bad. She was a storm in the middle of my calm beach, and a small, primitive part of me was attracted to whatever danger she brought with her.

She stepped up to me. "You are what? My prince?" She

raised an eyebrow, leaning in so close to my face that I could see flecks of gold dancing around her blue eyes. "Let me tell you something, Prince, since you think I'm so despicable. I killed for everything you were born into. Don't think that just because we saw the same horror, I won't send you to meet your maker. I've killed men far better than you for far less."

My blood boiled. "Do it." I said through clenched teeth. "Kill me. Kill me in the most inhumane way and watch how the people of Angeles crucify you before you even have the chance to blink."

She leaned away. "You are just like him, aren't you?"

"I am nothing like him. You know it, but you can't stand it. You don't want me to be different than the rest of them—those people that you killed back in Kadjar. It scares you, that someone like me can exist in the midst of all of this, doesn't it?"

"I fear nothing. No man, and certainly no prince."

"Oh, you fear too many things. That's what drove you to start killing in the first place. I know you, Ember Levin. I know you better than you think I do."

Ember didn't say anything to that. She just watched my face like there was going to be some damning answer in there that would justify her killing me.

There was none.

I ran my tongue over my teeth, trying to grasp at an answer for her. "You and I are working on different sides of the same cause."

"What is that supposed to mean?"

164

"Means that we both want to see two leaders die. You want the empress gone, and I want my father gone, but we both have yet to face that we aren't going to win against them unless some omnipotent force steps in."

She thought about this for a second. "You'd think for someone like yourself, you'd be a bit more optimistic. You're going to be king in a few years, aren't you? Why don't you just wait before you make your move?"

"God, please, let's be real here. He has no plans of ever leaving the throne, at least not until he's dead. He'll find a way to get me out of line."

She shook her head. "You sound...calm. Like you're okay with the idea."

"I guess I am. I've had quite a while to think about it. At this point, I don't care what happens to me. I just want all of this to be over. I don't care if I rule or not."

"You should care."

"Why?"

"You're the only one who can fix your problems. Nothing is going to get better unless you make it better."

I stared at her for a second as the words sank in. Then, I turned on my heel and retreated into my room. I went straight for my desk that sat next to the glass door to my balcony. She stood beside me as I searched for a map of Angeles on my computer. I found one detailed enough that would lead her right to the Agricultural District.

My mouse hovered over the print button.

Nothing is going to get better unless you make it better.

All of the events of the last two weeks flooded through my head. Meeting Ivelisse in the rose gardens that afternoon where I told her the truth about what I felt seemed like ages ago. That memory melted into Ian's gala, which melted into his death, and…my memories went gray after that, like nothing else mattered.

But now, I could make things matter. I could change everything—maybe I couldn't take back his death, but I could make everything right once more.

I closed out of the tab. "What was that?" She asked.

"You can't leave Angeles. Not yet." I pushed myself out of my computer chair. "I need something from you."

"Which is?"

"Kill him. Kill him, and I'll help you take the empress down."

She blinked. "You've lost it."

"Killing him was your idea."

"That was before I knew what he was capable of. I don't—I don't know if I can kill him now. I don't know if I can get close enough to him."

"Don't worry about that. Let me set everything up. I just need you to pull the trigger. I can't. I need you to do this for Ian. For Angeles. For me."

She looked at me, badly hidden fear crossing through her eyes. "I was caught assassinating the empress. I can't be caught again. I have to get back home."

"If they catch you, I'll be there. I won't let them take you. I'll go with you to Kadjar. I'll make sure you get home."

Ember swallowed. "No matter what, this ends with me getting home. Are we clear?

"We're clear."

Alright." She held a hand out. "It's a deal."

I took her hand. "Deal."

Chapter Thirteen
Ember

On the day of Ian's funeral, I was woken early by one of
the king's assistants saying that I'd been summoned to the
king's office.

And, so I got dressed in the apartment that once belonged to the Graces. While they'd left all their furniture, the
apartment still seemed barren, without a single trace of life.
The clothes that I wore were ones that Ivelisse left behind,
those she said she didn't need.

I stopped in front of the mirror by the door. I ran a hand
along the silk shirt I wore. It was a dark purple—Mara's favorite color. My stomach churned at the very thought of my
family. It'd been too long. I was so close to getting them back,
and I let them slip through my fingers.

Now, though, I stood in front of the king's door unable
to think about the knife that was sitting in the purse I clutched
between my hands. I knocked on the door, waiting for a response. I counted the seconds that ticked by. Thirty-four seconds had elapsed before he opened the door.

"Come in," he said, walking back to his desk.

I didn't move.

"Why did you call me here?" I asked.

King Nero relaxed into the office chair. "You needed
to speak to me." I furrowed my eyebrows. "At least, that's
what Prince Roman told me."

"Oh! Yes. I do."

"Well?"

"I—can it wait until after Ian's funeral?"

"No. If you have something to say, say it now. I'm not going to be in the Royal District after the funeral. Actually, I'm leaving in about an hour."

"Where are you going?"

King Nero picked up a pen and began writing as we spoke, obviously only half interested in the conversation before him. "I'm going to the barrier checkpoints. I'll be staying with a few trusted advisors at the south and north checkpoints. I'm closing them down."

"What? I thought that's how Angeles traded with the outside world."

"It is—or, rather, was—how Angeles was dependent on the very people you are going to conquer. I'm only doing you a favor. Now, what was it you needed? I don't know how long I'll be gone for. Might be a few days, might be a few weeks."

"You...hold on, you're not even going to be in the district for your son's funeral?"

King Nero stopped writing. He set his pen down and looked around the room as if he was trying to think of a socially acceptable response to that question. "Funerals are extraneous. Ian is dead. That's the end of the story. Why drag things out?"

All empathy that I would have expected to hear in his voice wasn't there. "You sound apathetic."

"I am. Ian shared my DNA. That was it. I don't understand why I have to mourn the death of someone who didn't do anything for me. That's how the world works—people should only matter to you if they're worth something. Ian wasn't worth anything to me, so I don't have to mourn. That's how any good leader would protect himself."

"He's your son."

King Nero shrugged. "Roman only has to believe that I love him and Prince Ian, so he doesn't obliterate me when he takes the throne—if that even happens. That's as far as my love for my sons go."

"You're a monster." The words left my mouth before I could stop them. I clapped a hand over my mouth.

To my surprise, King Nero only chuckled. "Please, if you're trying to insult me, at least come up with something original. Monster is highly overused. Now, why did you need to speak to me? I'm a busy man, Ember."

"I—um, I wanted your advice. About ruling."

He picked up his pen once more, the ghost of a smile tracing across his lips. It was almost unnerving how much King Nero looked like his son. "What about it?"

"Everything. I don't know what I'm doing."

"You will, soon. I will train you. Once the checkpoints are shut down and life at the palace has returned to normal, I'll train you. I'll tell you everything I know."

"But...what about now? Is there anything I can do now?"

The king thought about this and stood. He went for the

bookshelf beside the window, turning his back to me. The knife in my clutch slid out the second I opened the bag. I caught it. The piece of silver felt as though it weighed a thousand pounds.

I crept over to him.

He bent down to examine the last shelf on the bookcase. I thought my heart was going to beat out of my chest. Inches away from the King of Angeles, I reared back ready to strike the knife into his neck.

"If you dare kill me," he said. "There will be a small army of guards on you and the prince within seconds."

"Leave Roman out of this."

King Nero stood and turned to me. He wrapped his hand around my wrist and lowered the knife, then ripped it from my hand. He set it down on his desk.

"Why? That boy stands for everything you hate. Why protect him?"

"He—" my words dissolved in a sigh. I had no reason to protect Roman. I should want to throw him under the bus, but I couldn't. I could stab Nero and make a run for it, leave Roman to deal with the repercussions, but I couldn't make myself do it.

"You've fallen into his trap, haven't you? He's put on that troubled, distant persona and you've fallen for it. You care about what happens to the wayward prince, don't you? You care for the very thing you hate."

My stomach churned. "I don't. I hate Roman, and I hate you."

King Nero took three careful steps, and he was in my face. So close that I could smell mint toothpaste on his breath. "And you can cry those words all you want, but at the end of the day, you're mine. You belong to me, and you belong to the throne."

"I belong to no man."

"I'm not a man, remember? I'm a monster."

My hands began to shake. "I just want to go home. That's all I'm trying to do. I want to go home in peace."

He leaned back. "There is no peace for the wicked. You of all people should have learned that by now."

"I'm not your savior. I'm not a queen. I destroy. That's what I do. If you let me on the throne, I'm going to destroy Angeles."

"No, no, dear girl. How can you not see the power that you have? You are going to save Angeles, just like you wanted to save Kadjar. I believe in you."

"You're putting your beliefs in the wrong person. Try putting them in your son before a stranger."

"Roman can't rule. That's said and done. He's weak and spineless and it's all my fault, so now I have to fix it. I have to find another successor. I ruined my own son in pursuit of what I thought was best. You fix things. You almost fixed a third of Kadjar, and I need you to fix Angeles."

"I can't! I'm not an empress, I'm not a queen."

King Nero retreated back to his desk. He ran a hand down his face. "I don't need this. Not now. I have too much to focus on. Just—get out of my office. When I come back

172

from the checkpoints, you will be ready to start training. You will accept the throne. I don't care what I have to do to you."

I almost started to protest, but I stopped. There was no winning with this man. It was only mind games with him. So, instead, I turned on my heel and left. Down the hall, to the elevator, to the foyer, and out the front doors, almost as if I was floating through a dream. It was completely silent. All activities had been canceled in observation of Ian's funeral.

Seeing the Royal District so silent was a little disconcerting. The last time I'd seen it this quiet was the night of Ian's actual death. I stared out at the courtyard in front of me: cherry blossom trees lining the path to the wrought iron gates, scattering petals in their wake. Lush green grass aside from the path covered every inch of the ground. A fountain sat at the end of the steps leading down from the palace.

A car, baby blue and patched with rust, stopped in front of the gate. The guards at the till took the ID from the driver, and the gates opened. Ivelisse stepped out of the car. She said something to the driver in a language I couldn't understand, and the car sped off.

"Ivelisse?" I called her name as she brushed off her skirts.

She looked up, like she wasn't expecting to be greeted by anyone. "It's six in the morning. What are you doing up?"

"I had a meeting with the king."

"And?" She met me at the base of the steps.

"I tried to kill him." Her jaw fell open. "I couldn't do it. Roman asked me to, but I—I couldn't. I can't. I just have to find a way home."

"You know you can't leave."

"I'm going to find a way to kill him, and then I'm getting the hell out of here. I don't care how—I'll walk if I have to. I'll leave the queen work up to you."

She let out a pitiful laugh. "That's just wishful thinking. He'll track you down. Once the king has his mind focused on something, he won't let go. You can't escape him, Ember. You can't leave Roman to shoulder all of this by himself."

"I don't care about Roman."

Ivelisse crossed her arms over her chest. "God, of course you don't. You know what? Do you really want a way out? Do you really want to go home?"

I nodded.

She set her hands on her hips. "Fine. If you think that you can escape King Nero's armies, I'll get you out."

"Are you serious?"

"Serious as the grave. Meet me outside the Royal District checkpoint by midnight. I'll be waiting."

Chapter Fourteen
Roman

Frozen pizzas were the only thing I had consumed for the past week.

Tonight, however, I stood in my kitchen chopping up carrots. Carrots were healthy. Carrots meant I didn't have to sit in front of an oven watching pizza cook while ignoring the piling responsibilities. There were reporters who wanted interviews. Magazines that wanted photoshoots. Newspapers that wanted to write editorials. They all needed something from me. Something that I didn't have the energy to give them. I wasn't sure I was ever going to have the energy to deliver.

Carrots gave me something to do. I didn't even like carrots, but they were the only thing in the fridge that wasn't microwavable. I'd figure out what I was going to put them in later.

It was 11 PM. I hadn't eaten all day. I wasn't really hungry, but the damning thoughts and the memories were threatening to drown me. I had to do something to distract myself, and that happened to come in the form of carrots.

The door to my apartment swung open so hard that I flinched when it slammed against the wall. I hoped for Ember but got my father instead.

A strange feeling washed over me. *Ember.* I hadn't seen her in four days. It had been four days of utter silence. Four days of wondering where she was, if she was alright, if she had killed him and escaped. Four days of silently hoping she'd come find me before I found her.

My father walked into the kitchen. "I'm back from the checkpoints, if you were wondering where I was."

"How'd you get in?"

"I asked the secretary for the master keycard. Said I lost mine."

"Of course you did."

"I figured something out before I left for the checkpoints," he said, leaning against the counter. I didn't respond to him, just pulled another carrot from the grocery bag and kept chopping.

He reached over me and grabbed a chopped carrot, popping it into his mouth, then reached for another. "You tried to have me killed." A hint of a laugh played its way into his words. I stopped chopping.

"No, I didn't."

"Don't lie to me."

"I'm not lying." I couldn't bring myself to look at him.

My father only scoffed. He grabbed the full carrot I was chopping from my hands and bit into it. "It's funny, you know. My own son tried to have me killed, like he really believed that he could somehow outsmart me. Me!"

"I didn't try to have you killed."

"I told you not to lie to me. You should know not to deceive me by now. I *always* win, don't I, Roman?" He set his carrot down.

I didn't respond to him. I pulled another carrot from the bag and kept chopping. My father's face came close to mine. "*Don't I, Roman?*" He repeated.

"Yes." I choked out. "You do."

He leaned back. "I thought the girl was going to be easy to control. Kadjarian prison is quite effective in breaking its subjects down to their very core. You walk into that prison and you don't walk out the same. She's looking for something to cling onto, so she can gather up her sense of humanity again, and for a second," he picked up the half-eaten carrot and took another bite. He pointed the carrot at me. "I thought it was going to be you."

I stopped. "What are you getting at?"

"I don't know. Just…something about the way she looks at you. Like she has everything in the world figured out but you. Oh, what's the word I'm looking for? *Wonder. She* looks at you with wonder." Goosebumps pricked at my arms, and I couldn't figure out why. "It's a crying shame that things played out the way they did."

"Why?"

My father shrugged. "You two could have been unstoppable. With her fire and your intelligence, I don't doubt that you could have conquered the world."

"Stop it," I said. "Don't talk like that—like this was ever going to work out."

"Oh, what happened to the optimism, son?"

"You burned it out of me."

My father's face drained of emotion. He continued, ignoring me. "I thought that a distraction like her might ease the pain."

"She's not a distraction, she's a person. Unlike you, I don't view women as objects to use and throw away." I continued chopping the carrot. "And I'm not in pain."

My father groaned. "Don't act like this doesn't hurt. I know it does. His death is killing you."

"Don't talk about Ian."

"Why? You act like he wasn't my son. The only good thing your mother ever did was create that boy."

"You killed him." I slammed the knife down on the cutting board. Anxiety pumped through my veins. I had never spoken to my father like this before.

"It was a mistake. How many times do I have to say that? Do you think I wanted to kill one of the only pure things in this godforsaken world? I never touched Ian, not once. I tried to keep him safe."

"If you had all this love for Ian, why did you bring him to the fields in the first place? Why threaten his life?"

"It's all for show! Anything I ever do is for show—to be a good leader is to establish dominance. Have you not learned this yet? I never meant to kill Ian. I only meant to make Angeles great. That's all I've ever meant to do."

"But you meant to kill Mom, didn't you?"

My father tensed. "I did. She was stopping me, and she was going to stop you. She loved too much. She felt too much, and it made her weak. Any weak link in the royal family must be terminated."

"My mother was not weak. She was the woman who hid me when she thought you were going to kill me. She was the one who stood up for me when I didn't have a voice of my own yet. That is *far* from weak."

King Nero studied my face—studied how agonizingly similar we looked. Same green eyes. Same brown hair. Same sloping button nose and same long eyelashes framed against tan cheeks. I had spent the last seventeen years making sure that that's where the similarities stopped.

"Where did I go wrong with you?" He asked, voice not rising above a whisper.

"You broke me," came my reply, with a quieter voice than I cared to admit.

For the first time since I could remember, my father fell quiet. There were no beautiful words or grandiose gestures, just simple silence as his eyes skated over his son's face like he was really seeing me for the first time.

"I was making you strong, Roman. That's all I've ever done."

"No, you just screwed with my head."

My father crossed his arms over his chest, leaning against the counter. He thought for a second, then spoke. "I'm sorry." He said, strong and assured.

For a shining, glimmering moment, I wanted to accept his apology. Maybe it was the confession of his love for his sons or how I saw myself reflected in his eyes. Maybe it was

my secret aching for the approval of the man who was supposed to have raised me.

All of that was soon shoved down by the anger of past
years. The hurt. The grief. The pain. "No. No, stop." My father knit his eyebrows together. "You don't get this redemp-
tion arc. You don't get to pretend like you're the victim here.
Every shitty thing that's ever happened has been your fault.
You will *always* be the villain of my story."

He snorted and went to leave the kitchen. "I'll always
be the victim from the jaded perspective. You have always
been perfect with semantics, haven't you? Every time I think
we are so different, you do something, and I see my teachings
reflected in you."

I leapt into action. My father turned back around to
meet my raised knife, pointed directly at him. "Liar. You have
done nothing for me."

King Nero slowly held his hands up. "Don't do this,
Roman. I told you I was sorry. I've said my piece." There
were no guards here to save the king.

"If you really think apologies are what I care about at
this point, then you're more of an idiot than I thought." I adjusted my aim.

Four words passed through my mind as my knife sunk
into his chest.

Long live the king.

And then, I ran.

I had planned everything except for this. This can't be
happening. No. It wasn't supposed to go down like this. My

mind swirled as I barreled out of my penthouse while my father's broken voice screamed my name.

"Roman! Stop!"

I sprinted into the elevator and slammed my finger into the button for the foyer. I leaned back against the chrome wall, hands twined in my hair, breaths coming in short, sharp gasps. This wasn't supposed to happen. Not yet.

The world around me moved like molasses. The clock on my wrist moved at a snail's pace, and all I could do was pray to make it to the foyer without guards set on killing me finding me.

When the doors opened, I barreled out. The secretary sitting at her desk greeted me with a smile. I interrupted her greeting. "I need the key to the Grace's apartment."

"Alright, do you—"

"G-gimme the key. I need—I need the key now."

She blinked, and I nearly shouted out another *come on*, practically bouncing in my sneakers. She knit her brows together and grabbed the key off the rack. I jerked it from her hand and headed back into the elevator.

The fiftieth floor couldn't get here fast enough. Seconds dragged into minutes until the familiar ding of the elevator overpowered the music and the doors slid open.

I unlocked their door before throwing it open. The Grace's penthouse was devoid of everything except for the furniture belonging to the palace. None of Li Grace's paintings hung on the walls, nor the sticky note reminders that Killian Grace slapped on the walls near the door to remind himself of the things he had to do. It would have been sad had it not been for the adrenaline pumping through my veins.

Everything was empty because the person now living here had nothing to her name.

"Ember!" I cried out, my voice coming out broken and cracked. I prayed that she was here. This was the penthouse assigned to her after the Grace's move. Every time I'd checked, the penthouse was empty, and the security guard said he'd seen her leave that morning. When I check the next morning, he'd say that she came back for a few hours only to leave once again. Avoiding me, I'd assume.

Her head poked out of one of the rooms. "Roman? What are you—"

I ran to her, pulling her by the wrists toward the door. She was completely dressed in a white t-shirt and jeans with a backpack on her shoulders. My eyes trailed down to the gun tucked into a holster wrapped around her waist. I should have asked questions, but I didn't. Too much was happening—too much was going through my mind to worry about why this assassin was armed and where the hell she got a gun from.

"Come with me. We need to go *now*. Before they find us." I kept tugging, and she resisted, finally jerking herself out of my grip.

"Wait, who? What's going on with you? Stop pulling me!"

"I've just stabbed my father."

"Is he dead?"

"I don't want to stay long enough to find out."

182

Her eyes widened. "Roman," she whispered my name like it was caught somewhere between a prayer and a curse. "What have you done?"

"I don't know...I don't know what's going to happen, but I know that I'm getting out of Angeles and I want—I *need* you to come with me."

I met her gaze. She knew what I meant. She knew the kind of burning need that I couldn't fully understand. I needed her, and I don't know why. I needed to see her, I needed her with me. I couldn't have explained any of it if I tried, but I didn't need to. I didn't need to explain anything. She just knew.

"Where are we going to go?"

"Kadjar. I guess."

"Good," she set a hand on the holster of her gun. "That's where I was headed."

"You—what?"

"Ivelisse has had me on standby for four days. I've been waiting to get out of Angeles with her help, and tonight's the night we were supposed to get out. That's why I'm dressed like this at midnight. I'm leaving."

"No, we can't get Ivelisse in on this. It has to be just us."

She studied my face for a second, eyes searching for answers I knew they weren't going to find. "Why did you come for me? You could have been out of the palace five minutes ago if you hadn't stopped."

"I didn't want to leave you here. If he lives, he's going

to crucify you. If he doesn't, you'd going to be the next in line for the throne if I'm gone."

She nodded. "Good. Yeah. That's what I thought."

Ember and I went for the door. "Do you know how we're getting out?"

"I think, yeah. It's a shot in the dark, but it's the best shot we have."

~

The moonlight filtered between the forest leaves onto the mulch beneath our feet. Ember and I walked silently side-by-side. The second we reached the edge of the forest, she pulled her hood down, slid off her jacket, and took a look at the night sky. I wanted to run straight for our exit, but she stopped, dead in her tracks.

"I'll never see this sky again," she said. I couldn't hear the sadness in her voice like one would expect.

"Me either," I walked to her side.

"No," she shook her head. "You're the prince. You have to come back. You have to rule."

"I know I do." I said for the first time in my life, and I meant it. "I'll wait for the dust to settle. I'll collect myself, and I'll come back. I'll lead my people."

I started to walk from the edge of the forest to the checkpoint, where guards swarmed the tall, square-shaped hole in the barrier. It was just big enough for a semi-truck to fit through. The guards were all armed with clunky black battle gear and guns the size of my arm. Faintly, I could hear their voices, but none of them spotted me yet.

184

"Roman, hold on." Ember's voice called me back to the forest. "Are you sure about this? About leaving?"

"I don't exactly have another choice. I'm not staying for the investigation. I can't."

She nodded. "When we get to the East Sector, we need to have a story. We'll say I kidnapped you. The empress will let you stay for a few nights. She's still scared of Angeles, I know she is. Then, you leave. Get to Calais or wherever the next stop for you is."

"Why can't we know each other?"

"We need to be separated. The first thing the empress is going to do is kill me."

"You don't know that."

"I do. I failed our deal, and she's going to be looking for any excuse she can to execute me. This is the perfect opportunity."

"She can't do that. She can't kill you. The courts won't let it happen."

"There are no courts in Kadjar. What she says goes. You know it's the same way in Angeles, but King Nero at least had the decency to pretend like there was some form of democracy still alive."

I shook my head. "I'm not getting into an argument with you now. She's not going to kill you. I won't let it happen."

"Like you have any power over her." I shut my mouth at her words. The hint of a smile jerked at the corner of her mouth. "Thank you for the sentiment, at least. It's nice to

185

know that for the time being, I'm not fighting alone."

I wanted to take her hand or something, but I wasn't sure she'd let me touch her. So, instead, I nodded toward the checkpoint. "Yeah. Let's head out."

Just as we started to head onto the grass leading to the checkpoint, a twig behind us snapped. I jumped as Ember pulled the gun from her holster. Ivelisse walked from the shadows still dressed as though she never left the palace.

"How did I know that this is where I'd find the two of you?"

"How did you find us?"

"Roman has his location shared with me on his phone. I tracked him. I've been waiting for Ember for the past hour and a half. Somehow, I knew wherever I found her, I'd find you. Not that I wanted to, anyways."

"I—" I started towards her, hands out like there was any possible way that she'd accept me after everything that's happened.

Ember stepped between us before I could get to Ivelisse. "Why are you here?"

"I can't let Roman leave. I can't let him do that to Angeles—to me."

"This isn't about you or Angeles. This is about Roman escaping what he's done."

Ivelisse ignored her. She stepped aside, so I could fully see her in the dim light filtering through the leaves of the forest. "Come back with me, Roman." She held her hands out. I wanted to take her hands and promise her that I'd do whatever as long as it meant she wouldn't be hurt.

Just like always. Just like the past eleven years.

But now I couldn't. Now I had to think about more than Angeles and more than Ivelisse and more than the sum of my entire seventeen—almost eighteen—years.

I had to think about Ember. And I had to think about myself.

With my silence, she hung her head. Set her hands on her hips, and when she looked up again, she looked Ember square in the eyes. "Every life that's lost from here on out, whether it be his or yours or mine, is because of you. And when they arrest me for attempting to help, my blood will be on your hands."

"Don't blame her." I said.

Ivelisse's laugh, a symphony of a soprano tremor, filled the forest. "That's like not blaming a hurricane for destruction. All she's done, all she will ever do, is destroy. Don't you think, Ember? Do you not feel guilty for what you're doing?"

I watched her face, but Ember's expression never faltered. Silver curls of hair framed her jaw, escaping from her ponytail. Her steely blue eyes went blank. "I've done nothing wrong."

"You, the assassin, didn't convince him that he was ready to take over a nation? You didn't convince him that he could kill his father?"

"I did that on my own." I interjected.

"Oh, dear God, Roman. Let's stop kidding ourselves. You've never done anything on your own in your entire life.

187

You've been coddled since *birth*. Let's stop pretending that you've ever had the gall to kill a man, let alone your own father."

Her words hit me like a slap. My face must've betrayed me because she reached out to touch me. I turned away from her hands.

"Roman, I—" she started coming closer.

"Don't touch me."

"I didn't mean it."

"No, you did. But I think, in a sense, you're right, and it's time that ended. It's time I found my gall, and I think that's going to start with this."

I took Ember's hand.

Turned toward the checkpoint.

And ran.

We stopped just short of the guards who were pointing their rifles at us. They hollered orders and threats in our direction. I put my hands behind my head and got down on my knees. Two guards with smaller guns moved to pat us down. The first guard took Ember's gun and flung it to the side, eliciting a cry of protest from her that was ignored.

A third guard, carrying a bigger gun and wearing a riot mask, made his way over to us. "Why are you—Prince Roman?"

"Yes. I…" I only realized that I was woefully unprepared when no excuses as to what the hell I was doing at the barrier exit came to mind.

"—am greeting foreign dignitaries with me. His…"

Ember's eyes met mine as she searched for another word.

"Future queen, Ember Levin." I filled in. "Ivelisse Grace has since stepped down. News has yet to break, but that doesn't mean business has to stop. The king has other...things to attend to so he sent me and Ember."

The guard blinked, taken aback. "Ivelisse has stepped down? I didn't think you could do that. Is she—"

"She's fine. Alive and well. Court life was not for her, and this decision has been a long time coming. Are we cleared to pass?"

He nodded once, curtly. "I—I guess. You'll have to forgive me, Your Highness, but news like that is a bit of a shock. Let me raise the gate."

The guard began walking toward the till sitting next to the barrier, motioning for the man inside to raise the chain-link gate that covered the hole.

All of the guards parted, waiting for us to step through. Ember started but I held back. "Hold on. We need a car."

"A car?" One of the guards repeated.

"How do you expect the prince and future queen of Angeles to travel in the middle of uncharted territory if not by car?"

I watched the guards, faces covered in riot masks, exchange glances with each other. No one answered my question until the man in the till popped his head open. "Sir, there is the one patrol car outside the barrier. The keys are right here." He nodded to the third guard who had been talking to us.

"But the night patrols are going to need that car."

"It's not like they can't get another identical car at the armory."

The third guard mulled this over, and then motioned for the man in the till to toss the keys over. He did, and the third guard handed them to me. "Next time, Prince, a little heads up? We'll have a better car waiting for you."

I nodded. Ember and I walked through the gate and out to the other side.

I'd never been outside the barrier before in my life. I don't know what I was expecting, but I was met with a wide expanse of desert—sand, rocks, and tumbleweeds. It didn't exactly live up to what I'd imagined while playing in the schoolyard with my friends all those years ago. There was a serious lack of quicksand and black lagoons. I didn't see any witches or flaming lakes, either.

Huh. A little disappointing. I thought.

"If you're done staring out at the sand, I'd like to get this show on the road." Ember's voice came from the car, which was parked next to the barrier and emblazoned with the symbol of Angeles across the side of the black vehicle. I made my way toward her at the hood of the car.

"Do you know how to drive?" I asked.

"No. I assumed you did."

"You assumed wrong. I've never even touched a steering wheel before."

"What? Did you always have drivers?"

I furrowed my eyebrows wanting to prove her wrong

but knowing she was right. So, instead, I said the first thing that came to mind, "Maybe." The answer I settled on proved to be worse because she just smiled.

"Looks like we're both going to have to figure it out." She took the keys from my hand and unlocked the car. I hopped into the passenger side.

She jammed the key into the ignition four times before throwing the keys on the dashboard. "The car isn't working. We need to get a new one." I took the keys from the dashboard and slid them into the ignition. The car burst to life. "I'm denying that that ever happened." She said, flatly.

Ember fumbled around with the gear shift, eliciting a scream from the both of us when the car burst into reverse until it was finally put into drive once more.

"Do you know the way to Kadjar?" I asked.

"Do I look like a human map?"

I sighed and unbuckled my seatbelt. "You know, if I were the empress," I said, opening my door and jumping out. "I would have jailed you too."

"Too soon, Roman." She mumbled.

I walked to the back of the truck and pulled open the hatch. Sure enough, there was a black duffle bag sitting, untouched. After a car of soldiers got lost in the desert a few years back, my father implemented a survival kit into each military truck. I rummaged around in the bag until I found a small tablet.

As soon as I picked it up, it burst to life, a detailed map of the valley surrounding us spreading across the screen. I double tapped the search bar in the upper righthand corner and typed in *Kadjar*. The map zoomed in on a 3D recreation of one of the only pictures of Kadjar that Angeles still had.

The directions to Kadjar split down the opposite side of the screen. I got back into the passenger's seat and set the tablet down on the dashboard. Ember picked it up, staring at the screen.

"Let's go home, then." She said and began driving.

~

The clock in the car said we had been traveling for three hours and fifty-five minutes before Ember stopped the car. Just in the horizon, I could see buildings rising in the distance.

"Why'd you stop?"

She nodded toward the buildings. "That's my home."

"Yeah. Go fast."

Ember shook her head. "I—give me a second. I need you to promise me one thing." She turned to me.

"What?"

"When this is all over, and you go back to Angeles and when you're on that throne, I need you to remember this. Remember me. Remember everything that I fought for."

"You say that like I could ever forget."

Her eyes met mine. I saw the steel melt, and for the first time, they were soft. They weren't made of hard edges and burning metal. They were made of soft down and understanding. They took me by surprise.

"I'm serious. I used to dream of being so close to a leader like you because that meant I'd finally have my chance to change your mind. Before I die, I need to know that there's going to be someone to continue my legacy—to do what I couldn't."

"You're not going to die. Stop talking like that."

"You and I both know that my execution is inevitable. I don't know why you refuse to see that."

"Because I don't want to lose you."

"Why?"

No answer came. After what felt like years, she slowly reached over and took my hand, lacing her fingers through mine. Her skin was rough, callous against my hands, clear of blemishes and bruises.

"It's strange to see someone like you afraid of losing someone like me." Her voice didn't dare go above a whisper.

Still, I didn't speak.

Ember continued. "But I need you to get over that fear. I need you to understand that when I die, you have a whole nation ahead of you that needs to be changed. I need you to see that change through. Change Angeles where I couldn't change Kadjar."

The moment between us disintegrated when a faint, humming noise roamed over our heads. "What was that?" I asked.

Ember shrugged and opened the door. I followed her to the hood of the car, both of us staring up at the wide expanse of dull blue sky.

"Look," she pointed her finger toward a white streak barreling through the sky. "What the hell is that?"

My heart began to beat wildly in my chest. "Oh, God. No."

"What?"

"Please, no," I breathed, mind racing back to the advisory council meetings on war tactics. I was barely old enough to understand what war was, but my nation was still reeling from the aftermath of the Kadjarian war.

Napalm bombs. My father had said. *I want napalm and thermobaric bombs used for war, and I want the two bombs combined into one saved just for Kadjar. If they ever cross us again, I want them destroyed for good, are we clear?*

"What, Roman, what is it?"

"A bomb. A napalm and thermobaric bomb." Ember and I watched in dumbfounded silence as the jet plane carrying the bomb flew past us. The thin plane, barely visible from so far away, hovered over Kadjar, deposited the black bomb, and left.

The bomb, only a dot against the blue sky from so far away, crashed into the city.

Ember fell to her knees.

And I froze.

A plume of smoke billowed up from the city, gray and black. *No. No, this couldn't be happening. This couldn't be true—the only man that had those launch codes was dead. I killed him. I thought I killed him.*

No, King Nero was not dead. This was his message to me, to my defiance. I had failed, and I had destroyed Kadjar and every person within the city.

I jumped into action—pulling myself into the driver's seat as Ember barely clambered in. She sat in shell-shocked silence as we drove the rest of the five minutes to Kadjar.

By the time we arrived, Kadjar was a steaming wasteland. Plumes of black smoke billowed up from where a mighty city once stood. Ember sat in the passenger's seat as I parked in front of the melting black gates. She gripped the dashboard so hard I was afraid that she was going to pierce the leather.

"What do we do?"

In a flash, she had the door open and was running for the gates. I followed in after her, just barely catching her before she could throw herself onto the gates that were now bending and glowing with the fire that was raging around us. Heat from the flames piled out of the city, pounding against my face. My eyes watered. The thick black smoke made its way into my throat, choking me.

"Ember, stop!" I screamed as she struggled in my arms.

"They're in there! My family is in there!"

She twisted and turned, reaching out for the bars that were glowing orange and bending like noodles. "You're going to kill yourself!"

Ember turned to look at me, eyes bloodshot and face strewn with ash. "I don't care. They're in there. I need to find them."

"We'll both go. J-just hold on." I reached over and ripped the sleeve off her shirt, and then did the same to mine. I didn't let go of her hand as I made my way back to the car to pull a water bottle from the back seat. I wet both of the cloths. "Here—put this over your nose and mouth so you can breathe."

She took the mask and plunged into the city, and I went after her.

A wall of fire engulfed me on either side. I could barely see her through the smoke and through the tears pricking at my waterline, due to the rough air around me. All I could make out was a white banner of hair streaking in front of me.

This world didn't even look like a city. It was nothing except orange flames masking what once might have been buildings. I saw bleeding bodies in front of me, reaching out to me or reaching out to other charred bodies. I saw people rushing past me, almost knocking me to the ground as they tried to flee.

Faces stained with blood and ash and tears barreled past me as I followed Ember deeper into the fire.

We rounded a corner, faced with a wall of fire taller than the barrier ever was, and Ember slowly backed up as the screaming flames crept toward us. Her hand was slick with sweat, but she wrapped it around mine.

"This is the entrance to the East Sector. What do we do?" Her voice was muffled through the cloth.

"Turn back. We can't keep going like this."

"They're in there. They—" Her head shot over to a building made of sandstone and concrete that hadn't been touched by the flames yet. I watched in awe as she began to scale the building, one foot on jagged stone and one foot on a

196

windowsill.

And still, I followed her.

When we got to the top, my legs felt like they were going to fall off. My hands shook, and I collapsed to my hands and knees, the cloth dropping and a mouthful of smoke snaking inside my lungs. Around me, the burning nation roared like a giant that was eventually going to swallow me whole.

"Ember—I can't—stop!"

She dropped to her knees beside me. "No! No, Roman, come on. You can't do this to me now. We have to keep going."

"You…you go. You go find them and come back to me. I can't keep going. I'm not—" I choked out a cough. "I'm not like you. I can't do this."

"I promise you can. They've all lied to you in the worst way—you are strong, Roman. I need you to keep going."

I looked up to find tears on the Bloodhound's face. Her chin quivered as she wiped the ash and sweat from my forehead.

She wiped at her cheeks with the palm of her hand, mixing soot and tears. "I need you with me. I can't do any of this without you." Her voice cracked, and her breath came out in a choking sob. "And I don't know why."

I shook my head, pulling myself to a sitting position. "You don't have to know. Neither of us do. We just need to get the hell out of here."

I clambered to my still-shaking feet. "I think I can get

us out," she said. "Stay by my side."

As I looked down upon the raging fires beneath us, I thought, *I will. I always will.*

Chapter Fifteen
Roman

The night patrol guards traveled light. There was nothing in the car except for two water bottles hidden under the seat.

By the fourth day after the bomb, we hadn't found any signs of life. It was like all those people I had ran into on the street were gone.

Or dead.

Ember and I spent the next four days stumbling around the wreckage. I think she spoke to me once, maybe twice. The citadel, I came to find out, must've been a grand place before the fire. Now, all that was left of it was a skeleton of melted beams, concrete rubble, and marble strewn across the perimeter. The worst part about it were the bloody handprints and footprints on the sides of the broken debris where people had tried to get out.

This was a land of nightmares.

On the fourth night, I found myself standing at the road that led to the North Sector. Ember had once told me that these were my people—the affluent, the wealthy, the ones with more money than they even knew what to do with.

Now, the North Sector was nothing. Where tall mansions once stood, there was nothing but black, charred roads and skeletons of drooping steel beams and crumbled concrete. There were no signs of life. There were no signs of wealth.

Just destruction.

Look at them, the people who were once hunted by the Bloodhound, now without a single thing to their names because it was I destroyed by the King of Angeles.

Anger flourished in my veins. Actually, maybe it was hunger. Could've been both.

My head pounded as I near the marketplace. Ember and I had promised to meet in this strip of charred land when night fell, and the sky was beginning to bleed from blue to orange as the sun set on the horizon.

Small fires crackled at my feet, and I had to sidestep to avoid the burning embers. In the very distance, I could still see smoke trailing up into the sky. The crater where the bomb had hit was too far away to clearly see.

I had singlehandedly destroyed this land because of my stupid, blind faith. Faith that I was strong enough to defy him. Faith in the Bloodhound of the East Sector. I should have kept my head down. I should have just done what he wanted me to do until the law forced him to step down. I was stupid for thinking that I could do anything other than what fate has lined out. Look where it got me.

He'd come for me, soon enough. He'd come and drag me back to Kadjar. He'd find a new queen, I'm sure, and he'd force me to marry her. He'd force me to become the king, and if he didn't like what he saw, he'd do away with me and find a new prince to take over.

The thought sent a sick feeling washing through my body. This cycle of power was never going to end.

"Who's there?"

I jerked toward the source of the voice: an old woman stepped out from one of the less destroyed buildings down the block. She made her way to me. I froze staring at the ash-stained woman with jeans torn at the knees and what once must've been a white shirt, now stained with red and black.

"Who are you?" I asked. She stopped a full foot away from me. I smelled her before I even fully saw her face. Fish and sweat—just enough to make me want to gag.

"Could ask you the same." She retorted. I backed away from her, turning to run, but she caught my wrist. "Are you one of 'em?"

"One of what?"

"The aliens!" She exclaimed. The woman's accent condensed the word to two syllables, rather than three.

"I am no alien," I said, flatly—even though technically, I was. She let go of my hands.

"You aren't from here, that's for damn sure. You ain't one of us."

"Us," I echoed.

"The survivors."

"There's more of you? Where? I—my friend, she's been combing the city trying to find her friends, but neither of us can cover enough space fast enough."

The woman shook her head. "If they're East Sectors, they're dead. There ain't nothing left. If they're South Sectors like me, they might've gotten lucky. All a 'em goddamn North Sectors is fine, though. They're up in the camps like they own the place and—"

"Please. I just need you to take me back to your camp. I need to find out if her family is alive. She's supposed to be meeting me here soon, so if you could just wait, we can all go back together."

"There's only about a hundred of us. If they weren't North Sectors I can probably tell you if they're alive or not."

"I—I don't know any names."

"Sounds like a shit friendship if you don't even know the names 'a her kin. What's their last name? Do you even know that?" The woman scowled.

"Her last name is Levin."

She paled. The woman's mouth opened slightly and closed again like she didn't want to say what she was thinking. A crooked finger rose to point in my direction. "Them Levins ain't welcome around here no more."

"What?"

"She's what brought this. The empress said she brought the aliens, and the second she gets back, we're going to take her down. Her and the rest of her bloodline."

The woman began to back away, but I followed her. "No. No, you don't understand." *It's my fault.* I wanted to say. *Everything is my fault. Don't touch Ember or her family.*

"I ain't bringing that curse back. I ain't going to die alongside the Levins. That ain't my problem, and, boy, if you had any lick of sense in you, you'd get far away from the Levins. They bring nothing but trouble, and that's a damn fact."

I watched the woman back away far enough to where

202

she turned on her heel and began to run. I followed her. It was only when a familiar voice rang out that I stopped.

"Roman?"

She stood at the head of the street. She was completely covered in soot, just like I was, but there were dried bloodstains on her shirt. Dried blood coated her hands and nails from where she had been digging in the debris. A thick sheen of sweat covered her face.

Somehow, still in the midst of this mess and broken, burning world, she was beautiful.

"Hey," I began walking to her. "I think—I think we need to go."

"What?" When I didn't offer an explanation, she continued. "No, Roman. Leaving is insane. We still have the entire East Sector to cover still. We have to find them. They're here, I know they are. We just have to keep looking."

"No, I'm serious. This place isn't safe."

"Well, yeah, obviously. But we have to find them. They're *here*. I can feel it. Don't you feel it too?"

No. I feel the pain of the world I destroyed, and it's going to kill me. This search is going to kill you, too, because you know they're dead, but you don't want to believe it.

Of course, I didn't say that. I opted for silence.

Ember watched my face, searching for my answer that didn't come. "Even if we did leave, where is there to go?"

"We'll figure that out later. I just—I don't think now is the best time to search. Let the smoke die. Let the survivors come out themselves."

"What if they're trapped? Or hurt?"

"Then we would have heard screaming by now. We would have heard cries of help. Have you heard anything at all?"

She crossed her arms over her chest. "I just...I have to keep looking. We have to look for them."

"Right now, I'm telling you—promising you—that I will find a place for the both of us. But it's not here. We have to get out of here." I took her hands.

She jerked out of my grip. "And *I* am telling *you* that there is no home for me outside of Kadjar. I have to keep looking for them. For the survivors. I owe it to Kadjar, and I owe it to my family. After everything that I've done, everything that I've destroyed, I need to do this."

"You fought for your people. You made things even."

"No, I didn't! Stop kidding yourself. You know what I did just as much as I know what I did. There is no justifying what I've done. I'm a monster. A monster trying to repay, somehow,the debts that she owes to her society."

"You're not a monster."

She shook her head. "You—"

"You've shown me more humanity in the last month that I've known you than I've seen in all of my seventeen years. You care all too much, Ember Levin, and that is where your fault lies. You are not a monster. You are not a beast. You are fatally human."

Ember stopped. She didn't speak. The only noises audible were the snapping crackle of fire and the soft heave of her breaths. "I…You're lying. You're a liar."

"You can deny the truth all you want, but that doesn't change its authenticity. You know what I'm saying is true. You're just afraid to believe any different. And, you know, maybe if you believed, maybe if you had a shred of hope about your own resilience, the empress wouldn't be having a manhunt for you right now."

"I—what?"

"The empress isn't dead. There's a camp of survivors, and the woman I found told me that no East Sectors survived. But she said that the empress is waiting for you and so are the survivors."

"If they want to find me, they might as well. But I'm not going to stop looking for them."

"I don't want you to. I just want you to pause. Just until you're safe."

"I don't care about safety!"

"But I do! I don't know how it happened much less why, but somehow your wellbeing became intertwined with mine. I don't know how much clearer I have to make that for you. I can't let you go. I can't just watch you die. You said it yourself. We need each other."

"That was a moment of weakness. I don't need anyone but myself, alright? Let's make that clear right here and now. I don't need you."

"You think I believe that bullshit? You need me just as much as I need you, and it scares you. You care about some-one, and it *terrifies* you."

Anger brought a brick red color to her cheeks. "Fuck you."

"Look me in the eyes and tell me you don't care about me."

Her hands flexed at her sides. She held my gaze for a full ten seconds before she turned away from me, craning her neck toward the smoky sky. "So what if you're right? So what if I care about you? What's it going to matter when the empress kills me?"

"What matters is that you're still human, and you still have a fighting chance. You don't have to subscribe to the fate that's laid out for you. You can *fight*."

Ember shut her eyes. "I'm sick of fighting. I'm sick of waking up only to face another day that I have to fight against. I just want the world to work in my favor for once."

"Unfortunately, neither of us can make that happen. But fighting with someone is better than fighting alone, don't you think?"

I knew she wanted nothing more than for me to just forget her, to leave her alone, but I couldn't. There was no way in hell I could forget her, and that thought was unnerving. I couldn't forget the way she looked at me like I wasn't the prince. She only ever saw Roman. I couldn't forget the way I *felt* when I was with her.

So long I'd been walking around like a numb shell of a man, and she brought out the best and worst that I had trapped inside of me. There was life outside of those black cigarettes, and she made me believe it.

Somewhere in my mind, there was a speech made for her. There was a speech of beautiful and eloquent words that would make her believe everything I was saying, something that would make her fall into my arms at a moment's notice. I decided that I was still writing that speech, so I wouldn't say it. Not now. For now, I just had the truth. Maybe one day after all of this was over.

"And if I go with you, if I leave and come back," she took a shaking breath, "I won't be fighting alone."

"No. I swear. Give me a week to figure everything out, and we'll come back for them. We will look until we've searched all of Kadjar. I promise."

"If I find out that you're lying to me, I will break you, Roman Stone."

"I'm not lying to you."

She crossed her arms over her chest. "Fine."

The sky was fully encompassed by oranges and pinks, now encased in a sunset portrait rather than a late afternoon sky. "Tomorrow, we'll leave. We'll find a place." Ember nodded.

One more night.

Then we'd be free.

Chapter Sixteen
Ember

Roman and I made a makeshift bed inside one of the only buildings with a roof in the main strip. It was a tailor's shop with a floor covered in spools of needles and baskets. Fabric lay scattered amongst the broken pieces of plastic sewing machines and split tables. Roman and I halved the salvageable blankets, so we could put the bed in the corner that had the least debris to clear out.

He had left for an hour or two while trying to find something salvageable to eat or drink. No such luck. It had been a full day and a half since the last time either of us had consumed anything—the last thing being a can of beans found in the middle of a pile of debris and the last water bottle kept in the patrol truck.

I tried not to let those worries or hunger bother me too much. Roman didn't seem to have any trouble with that. He was asleep the second his head hit the floor.

Sleep was a far-off goal that I couldn't quite reach. So, I watched Roman instead.

Thick brown eyebrows drew themselves close together as he slept, like something was confusing him deep within his dream. A frown crossed his face. There was a bit of soot over his forehead. I reached out and gently wiped it away.

Somehow, some way, this beautiful, broken prince saw past the facade that I put out for the rest of the world. He saw the girl that I had spent the last month clambering to find. He didn't see a criminal like the rest of the world did.

This prince sparked something in me, and I was still trying to figure out whether or not it was enough reason to run far, far away from him.

But, then again, when I saw myself reflected in his eyes, I *liked* the person I saw. I saw a girl trying her best, and for once in my entire life, trying was enough. I saw myself happy. I saw myself okay. I never wanted to lose that feeling—I never wanted to lose him.

What a terrifying thing, to find your happiness intertwined in someone else.

"You're staring at me," he said, without opening his eyes. "It's weird. Very weird."

"What? No, I'm not. Shut up."

He snorted, and opened one eye. "It'd be a lot less weird if you had a good reason, though. Like there was something on my face. Or in my hair."

"A lot of dust." I said. Roman sat up and shook his head. A cloud of dust and ash rained down to his lap. He wiped at his face, but all that did was send a long streak of grease down his cheek. I tapped my face. "Grease."

He lifted up the hem of his shirt and wiped at his face. "Still there." I said. Roman wiped harder. His cheek burned red with the friction. "You're fine." I lied.

"Really?" He asked.

"No."

Roman huffed, and wiped once more. The grease was

just beginning to fade as he stopped wiping. "I think looking for a bathroom around here would be a fruitless search."

"Yeah, probably. Sorry, I should've told the empress to get her nicest bomb shelter ready for His Highness."

"While you're at it, I would've asked you to get a bottle of sparkling water, too. Maybe a fruit basket or two. Only the best for visiting royalty."

I scoffed. "She would've killed us both before I even had the chance to get the words out of my mouth."

"Hey," he said. "At least we'd go down together, right?"

I rolled my eyes. "Oh, yes, there's *no one* I'd rather die with." Sarcasm dripped from my words. The corner of his lip quirked up.

Roman leaned his head back against the wall, staring up at the cracked ceiling. "Can I tell you a secret?"

"Sure."

"I think I'm afraid to die. After everything that's happened, I think the idea scares me more than it used to."

"Most of us are. You were too out of touch to fear something like that."

"Out of touch?"

"Before everything, you were just some little prince without a worry in the world, weren't you? Now—look at you. Look at the weight you've got on your shoulders. Of course you'd realize your own mortality now."

Roman frowned. He shook his head. "I might've been out of touch on most other things, but I knew about death. I met death when I was a child. I just didn't realize that my own was looming closer than I'd ever thought."

"You met death when you were a child? What does that mean?"

"Nothing."

"You can tell me the truth."

"No, I can't."

I sat up a little straight and turned to him. He didn't turn back to me. "I'm not under your rule or anyone else's. You can tell me."

Roman took a shaking breath inward. "Do you know why you never met my mother?"

"Ivelisse said she was in the Common District."

"She's dead." I froze, unsure of what to say next. Thankfully, Roman filled the silence. "She's dead and Ky and I had to bury her when we were twelve. He killed her."

"Your father killed her?"

"She was sick for a long time. Could barely walk, and never spoke. She just laid in bed, but my father brought her all of her meals. I should have known. I should've known that he was poisoning her. It wasn't fast enough for him, though. I found her, sick and frail as she was, with a bullet in the side of her head."

"I had no idea."

"Of course you didn't. That's what I mean when I say that I've known death for a long, long time. All my father wants is total, ultimate power. He doesn't care who he has to kill or maim to get it. I know, in your eyes, I may be out of

touch, but I'm not. I know that people in Angeles are struggling, just like they are in Kadjar. I know now that I have to
rule to fix what my mother wanted to and what my father
won't."

"Rule? I thought you didn't want to?"

"This—you—have changed my mind. I know what I
was born to do. This is what I've been training to do for the
past seventeen years. I'm the prince, whether I like it or not,
and there's a whole nation looking up to me."

"You're right." I said.

Roman laid back down. "I'm going back to sleep.
Goodnight, Ember.'

"Right. Me too. Goodnight, Roman."

Without anything left to say, I lay back down, covering
myself with the thin blanket and rolled over. Next to my head,
a strip of moonlight fell through the air, illuminating the floor
by my head—glass, plastic, cut fabric and all. I stared into the
glass reflecting the moonlight, mind finally empty. Eventually, my eyes grew heavy and slammed shut. I hunched down
in the blankets, waiting for it to fully embrace me.

A rustle by my side shook me awake. What I first
thought to just be Roman moving in his sleep proved to be
Roman standing up and walking out the door. The voices
coming from the outside were what brought me to my knees,
caught in fear.

"…think she'd listen to me?"

"Doubt it. Might cut your head off for even mentioning
her name."

"Well then why the hell'd you say you'd help me? This information is useless, Mary."

Mary. Mary. I racked my brain. I didn't know a Mary. Then again, there were over ten thousand people living in Kadjar, and I had just spent the last year isolated from them all. I might've known a Mary once upon a time.

Footsteps pounded away from the tailor shop. I waited until they were nothing but a small thud in the distance before I popped my head out the broken window. Mary and Roman were shadows in the night, almost disappearing from my sight.

I found myself frozen, staring out the window of a tailor shop on what used to be the main strip. Surrounded by what once was my home, I found myself frozen in fear. All I've ever known—gone. Gone because King Nero saw fit to destroy my home. Gone because of me and because of Roman. Gone because of a stupid infatuation with a beautiful prince. Gone because every time I saw him, I was left wondering what his lips would feel like against mine.

Propelled by my own anger, I found the courage to follow them. I left the tailor shop in pursuit of Roman and Mary, trying to ignore my simmering home. At the end of the main strip, the dirt road belled out into a circular cul-de-sac that had once been the marketplace, filled with goods straight from the fields. The marketplace divided into three streets: the North Sector, the South Sector, and the East Sector.

My stomach sunk as I saw the destruction of my home. There was nothing left. It was all flat, charred land. All of it.

The Sectors. The fields behind the Sectors. Everything was gone. All that stood to identify the Sectors were the broken, half-melted signs dangling from their posts.

Roman and Mary walked straight into the East Sector.

I kept my head down and made sure to stay as far away from them as I could. I tried not think about what I did to my own home. What I've done and what hell I've brought here. Maybe Ivelisse was right, and Roman was wrong. All I do is wreck things. All I will ever do is wreck things.

Roman and Mary stopped suddenly, and I crouched in front of a metal can labelled *waste.*

"We've got ourselves camps set up by the military academy. They ain't much, but they're all we've got. She does rounds like this now, so she can survey the damage. Oh, look, I think that's her."

"Hold on, don't—"

"Over here!"

Roman shushed Mary, until approaching footsteps quieted him. "Prince Roman Stone? What gall you have, showing up in my nation after everything that you've done." Empress Analita spoke.

Roman, you idiot.

He ignored her. "This kind woman says you would be open to a deal of some sorts." A professional air rose in Roman's voice. I could practically see him straightening his posture, letting a small smile play across his face and clasping his hands behind his back—a stature of his I've learned to see straight through.

"This woman doesn't speak for me or my city. What were you thinking?"

Mary cleared her throat. "Well, I was thinking that we ain't in no position to turn down some help, even if it comes from Angeles."

The empress sighed. "Help from the enemy is nothing but a wolf in sheep's clothing. But I guess you couldn't have known better. Leave. Let Prince Roman and I speak alone."

Silence. Then, Empress Analita said, "Where is my Bloodhound? What has your father done with her?"

"Why should you care?" Roman didn't give her time to answer. "I'm not here to talk about Ember. I'm here because I need your help."

She scoffed. "And you assume that I have help to give you? Or have you forgotten your title or your lineage? Have you forgotten what evil your father is?

"Trust me, I met that evil when I was a mere child, and I continue to see it every day. I'm coming to you, shedding all of that—title, lineage, everything. My father is dead. I killed him, and now I am the king."

Liar. I wanted to say. *King Nero dropped this bomb.*

He was working an angle, he had to be. There had to be some method to this madness. The Roman I know wouldn't make deals with the woman who wanted me dead. No, I had to trust him.

The word *trust* was a word I hadn't ever used. The word *trust* left a sour taste in my mouth. All I had to do was *trust* Roman.

A sharp gasp left someone's mouth—the empress, I assumed. "No King of Angeles is welcome here. There's barely ninety survivors because of what your father did—"

"Exactly. I am not my father."

"I don't care who you think yourself to be. His evil blood runs through your veins. You're lucky that I haven't killed you on the spot."

I could practically hear the cocky smile lacing through his words. "You and what army would kill the King of Angeles?"

His words hung in the tense air. "Why are you here, King Roman?" The empress' voice was coated in ice.

"I'd like to offer you a deal."

"Go on."

"I know where the Bloodhound is."

My breath hitched in my throat. The world felt all too real and all too fake at the same time. I stood, not bothering to care if they were far enough away to hear me run. I fled, through my home, through the marketplace and back to the main strip.

All I had to do was trust Roman.

And my trust was going to kill me.

Chapter Seventeen
Roman

"Of course you know where she is. She's in Angeles."

"No, she fled with me."

Empress Analita's honey eyes lit with interest. "She's here?"

"She's hiding. From you."

"I don't care for your semantics, King. I can't afford to have the Bloodhound walking this earth any longer. Where is she?"

"I'll tell you under one condition."

"Which is?"

"Ember gets to live. She gets to see her family." I took a step closer to the empress, lowering my voice. "I'll tell you right now that if this deal is put in place, but harm does come to her, the armies of Angeles will wipe out every single Kadjarian on the face of this earth, including your beloved sister "

The empress paled. "How do you—"

"You think me to be stupid? I've done my research. I know about the sister and the life you abandoned on the outside. I know that you're not actually Kadjarian. And don't think I won't use that against you if the need should arise."

Empress Analita blinked. "You are exactly like him, aren't you? But you are more of a king than he ever dared to be."

"And I will be your worst nightmare. So, what do you

say, Empress? Do we have a deal?"

She took a deep breath and looked around, surveying the destruction of her city. She set her hands on her hips. "No."

"No?" I echoed.

"The only reason I want her back in Kadjarian custody is so that I can kill her. What makes you think I'd ever keep her safe?"

"Because you need a force like her."

Empress Analita craned her neck back and let out a laugh from deep within her, hard and sharp like glass. "You think I need her? The only good Bloodhound is a dead one. She's terrorized my country for far too long."

"Everything about her makes you wonder: what would have happened if she was working for me? What would have happened if she wouldn't have defied me? I'm giving you the chance. Keep her alive. Don't harm her, and you can learn from her. She is the sum of all of the anger in your nation. Don't you want to fix that?"

The empress crossed her arms over her chest. "You don't know anything about me or my nation."

"I might not know anything about your nation, but I know everything about raising a nation back from the dead. I watched my father do exactly that after Kadjar destroyed us. You are going to need someone like Ember as you bring Kadjar back. Keep her safe. Keep her beside you, and maybe you'll stand a fighting chance."

She paused, and, for a second, I thought my words were

getting through to her. "Let me think about this. I will send correspondence to Angeles when I've made up my mind."

"Alright, I look forward to hearing from you."

The empress nodded, and I left. It didn't take me long to get from the East Sector to the little circle of burnt debris that Mary said was once the marketplace and to the main strip.

A faint figure in the distance caught my eye. A figure staring into the broken window of one of the half-obliterated buildings. A figure with long, white hair. A figure hugging itself, breathing like it had just run a marathon.

"Ember?" I called out.

She turned to me and pointed something at me. I came closer and saw a jagged piece of glass in her hand. "Don't take another step." Her voice shook.

"What's going on?"

"I—I heard you. You're a traitor." I took another step toward her. "I'll cut you. I'll kill you. You *lied*. And to think I was stupid enough to believe you."

"What are you talking about?" I held my hands up in surrender as she backed away, still wielding the piece of glass in her hand. Faint drops of blood dripped to the concrete below as the glass cut into her skin. "Put the glass down. You're hurting yourself."

She ignored me. "I heard you talking to the empress. I heard everything. You lied. You lied, and I trusted you."

"Did you not hear the full story? Ember, c'mon—" I reached forward and grabbed her wrist, pulling the glass from

219

her hand and slicing my palm in the process. The glass shattered the second it hit the ground. Ember reeled back like she was going to punch or hit me. I braced for the impact, but it didn't come.

"All I'm trying to do is *survive*," she growled. "I won't have you getting in the way of that." Her hands flexed at her sides.

"Would you just listen to me? I thought you trusted me. I thought—I thought we were past this." I motioned up and down to her body that was practically shaking with anger.

"Past what?"

"This anger. I would've thought by now that I've proven myself to you. I'm not going to lie to you. I'm not going to hurt you. Not now. Not ever. I'd rather lose the world than lose you."

She sucked in a breath. "I'm trying, Roman. I'm trying to trust your words, but I keep going back to all the times I've been burned by people like you."

"Just listen to me. That's all I'm asking. Listen to the truth."

Ember raised an eyebrow as if to ask *what?*

"I struck up a deal with the empress. A deal so you can stay in Kadjar and live." I shook my wrist out like that would somehow get the sharp pain in my palm to disappear.

"She wants me dead. There's no way she'd agree to a deal like that."

"And she hasn't, yet. But I think she will."

"What did you give her?"

"I told her that if she hurt you, my armies would wipe the rest of Kadjar cut and finish what the war didn't."

"You said that?" I nodded. "For me?" Again, I nodded. "What about you? She's not going to let you stay here?"

I took a deep breath. "So, I'll go back to Angeles. I'll try to fix what I've broken. You'll stay here and find your family."

Silence fell between us. "No," she said. "I'm going back with you."

"No, you're not."

"He's going to kill you, Roman."

"I can withstand him. I've done it for seventeen years. He needs me, after all. It's not easy to find another heir to the throne. You'll stay here, and I'll go back. That's…the end. This is the end." Those four words burned in the back of my throat.

She swallowed a breath of air like she was trying not to cry. "This can't. It can't be the end. Not after everything we've fought for."

"It has to be. This isn't about us anymore. It's about something bigger—it's about you finding your family again, and me ruling my nation."

"I want it to be about us. I want—I want you." Her words came out in a breath of rushed air like she had been holding them in for far too long.

I had no words left that could offer her comfort. I had promised her honesty, and I had no honest words left. Sure, I had sentences stolen from past speeches and books I'd read, but there were no beautifully honest words that I could say to take away her pain.

Oddly enough, I didn't need to speak. I felt peace with silence, and as the Bloodhound of Kadjar wrapped her arms around me, I found peace within her fire. I held her fiercely, as if I were going to lose her the second I let go.

"I can't lose you, Roman." She confessed. "Like you said: I'd rather lose the world than lose you."

I pulled away from her. "We have to fight this. We have to find a way to fight this, to fight him." I said and meant it. Looking into the eyes of one of the most dangerous people while standing in the ruins of an obliterated city, I found my gall. I found my courage.

Before I could talk myself out of the idea, I pressed my lips to hers. I let my hands rest at the small of her back, holding her against me. First, it was slow. Slow like I couldn't get enough of her and how the girl who's spent her entire life festering in anger fit so well against my body, like the puzzle piece I hadn't known I was missing.

I pulled away. "Are you sure—is this—am I—"

Ember answered by deepening the kiss. I cupped her face in my hands. Her cheeks were warm. She kissed like she'd just won a war. Desperate. Breathless. Hungry. *Electric.* She kissed like she finally knew feelings were a fleeting thing, a shout into a black void that didn't care about you or your love. She kissed like she was okay with that.

Then, all at once, the kiss grew faster. More desperate. Fast like knowing that all the fear I've ever felt in my entire life couldn't compare to the thought of having to give her up. Desperate like realizing that I couldn't let the throne take her from me. Fast like I knew that this love, this kiss, was going to be thing to destroy me. Desperate like I finally knew that I was okay with that.

The kiss was fire. The kiss was desperation. The kiss was a cacophony of all the unexplained emotions I've felt for her coming to a hot, confusing climax. The kiss was the sum of my dreams and the answer to my questions.

She pulled away first. In that moment, all the beauty in the world lay inside of her blue eyes.

My entire life I had either cared too much or not at all. I couldn't let myself care about what's going to happen. All I could let myself care about is the love that I was willing to let destroy me.

On that night, all I cared about was the Bloodhound of the East Sector.

Chapter Eighteen
Ember

The walls

I awoke with a jolt, my chest heaving and my face sweating. The weight of the walls in my dream still rested on my shoulders.

His face came to mind next, obliterating every single thought of those damning walls. "Roman," I breathed.

The tips of my fingers danced across my bottom lip. I let out a long breath of air. It was almost as if I could still taste him—salt and the bare remnants of toothpaste. I could still feel him and how he held me like I was the most fragile thing on this earth. His hands had raced up and down my skin like he was trying to memorize a map of my body.

He had smiled into the kiss like I was everything he wanted.

The fluorescent lights around me pounded against my head. I let it drop into my palms, a second's relief from the harsh light. Though, the down comforter on my lap was like heaven after having slept on the broken tile floor of the tailor shop.

Ice crackled through my bones when I stretched my arms above my head.

There was something I had to be doing—somewhere I had to be going. Something rested on the tip of my tongue. The room around me was barren, offering no clues as to what it was. Stark white walls and a white ceiling drowned in the bright lights. The only semblance of another color came from the black marbling twisted in the white tile floor.

An IV drip rested next to my bed. I followed the cord down to my hand where a needle lay nestled under my skin. The world around me was nothing but a hazy dream.

Drugs, I thought, fixating on the IV cord. *This must be drugs.*

Roman's face felt like a distant memory and something that happened only yesterday at the same time. What was happening to me? Was I sick?

This room smelled of perfume. Fancy perfume, like the kind that the North Sector ladies wore on their way to their churches. This room, this expensive perfume, and this world weren't meant for me. These were meant for a ruler.

I was going to be a ruler, I thought with a laugh. *I was going to rule with Roman. I was going to rule* over *Roman.* Imagine me, once the feared Bloodhound, hanging up my dagger in exchange for a crown. I fell back against the plethora of white pillows, thankful for the warmth they brought.

The door opened, creaking ever so slightly. A man's blurred frame came closer to my bedside. I made out short-cropped brown hair. Dark, forest-green eyes. Tan skin with the hint of a wrinkle crossing his forehead. It was him: The King of Angeles.

This man, this terrifyingly wicked man who trapped me within Angeles and promised to mold me into something I didn't want to be, was standing stock-still watching me. I should want to run, but I'm so tired. So cold.

"Hello again, Ember." His voice was quiet. Strange to hear such softness from such a vile man.

So many words raced through my mind. So many questions. Was this all a dream? Had it all been a dream?

"How do you feel?" He asked.

"Dizzy."

"Do you know what happened?"

I shook my head, swallowing back a wave of nausea. King Nero pulled the chair next to the nightstand over to my bedside. The chair was completely white, and I hadn't even noticed it was there until he sat down.

"Do you remember *anything*?" He continued.

My mouth was dry. I swallowed, trying to think. How did I get here?

The sun. I remember the sun. A hot, burning devil piercing into my skin. Roman holding me. Days were passing, and I didn't know if we were going to make it out alive. I made the choice to follow him back, and that choice almost killed me.

That's when I started thinking that maybe it wasn't my smartest decision.

"I remember...I told Roman that I chose him. I'd follow him to the ends of the earth, and I meant it. It was hot, I think, and he was running a fever. He was delirious, and I was barely hanging on. We ran out of gas and...I don't know from there."

"You were found by the barrier patrols. My son was

226

hardly breathing, and you were drifting in and out of consciousness. Roman knows the repercussions that his actions have. He and I have since discussed them. I'm here to deliver you yours."

"Repercussions?" I echoed, trying to get into a comfortable sitting position. My hip was killing me.

"You defied me. All those who defy the face of the throne will die. But, alas, I can't kill you. There are, however, things much worse than death. I will find each of those ways, and I will make you suffer. Are we clear?"

I nodded my head.

King Nero continued. "Starting with Roman's birthday party," He stood and walked to the foot of my bed. "What, didn't you know? His eighteenth birthday is in a week. It's such a glorious time for young princes. He will be inducted as a full fledged member of the Senate and his training will begin. You will also be announced as the future queen."

"No."

He let out the smallest laugh, like he couldn't believe that I still had the guts left in me to deny him. "You've been asleep for quite some time, so I'm afraid you don't have much longer to waste. Roman and I have been preparing this ceremony for the past week while you've been resting. The party will be held in two days' time. The rehearsal dinner is tonight, as the next night, Roman will be busy with other preparations. Once you're ready, your team will be waiting for you."

"I've been asleep for a week?"

King Nero nodded. "Your injuries were severe. Dehydration, malnourishment, heat stroke, and, well, I may've slipped you some other…narcotics just so we all could make sure that you were fully rested and ready to take on the task of preparing for the throne."

"I don't want to be your queen."

"Too bad. You'd better start getting used to the idea. Remember, dear girl," the king moved to leave my room. "You have nothing left because of *me*. I've taken everything from you, except for one thing—my son. But don't doubt that I won't take him from you too."

He slammed the door shut so hard that I flinched.

After a few seconds of boiling in my own anger and fear, I sat up. A small spark of pain burst through my hand when I ripped the IV out. I slid my legs over the side of the bed. It was almost as if the floor was moving underneath me, waving like the ocean that I'd seen in movies and ads in the Royal District.

You've been through a hell of a lot worse, I told myself. A wave of nausea knocked me back down the second I stood. My heart began to beat wildly, like a trapped bird against its cage. I ran my fingers over the white comforter trying to slow my heartbeat.

Maybe this is all just a fever dream. Maybe I'll wake up back in Kadjar any time now. Maybe…

I'm not in the business of kidding myself, so I didn't even bother finishing that thought. I got up once more and took a step. Set all my weight on both feet. Left foot in front of the right.

And I hit the ground almost as soon as I had stood. My vision blurred, swirling in and out of focus. An array of drowning white lights pounded through my head. I turned on my back as rounds of pain burst all throughout my body. My chest heaved.

Was I going to be stuck here forever?

No—no, I couldn't be stuck here any longer. I had to find Roman. I had to get out of here and back home. I had spent too goddamn long being a slave to these walls, these damning, unforgiving reapers, and I refused to spend another second at their service. I had to break out of this hell. I had to save Roman and my family.

I had to get out of here.

I pulled myself to my hands and knees. My stomach lurched with the nausea from the leftover painkillers. This pain was going to make me lose whatever I had left in my stomach, but I had to do this. Only a few more steps, and I'd be at the door.

A dull throb washed over my body as I reached the foot of my bed and pulled myself to my feet. Cold sweat drenched my body as I let my eyes flutter shut.

Deep breath in. Let it out.

My heart slowed, and some of the dizziness left. I opened my eyes once more to find the room at a standstill. Five slow steps got me to the door. I stood in front of it staring at my hand sitting on the golden knob. My skin was a pale yellow. Even if there was a mirror within this small room, I couldn't bear to look in it, fearing what I'd find staring back at me.

These walls had been my only friend for the past year. I had listened to them sing to me in the dark depths of hell, telling me that I'd be theirs until the moment I died. They hissed at me and clawed at what little sanity I had left.

Now that was all stripped away. I couldn't think about the walls anymore. All I could think about was getting out of here, finding Roman, and getting the hell out of Angeles. I made a mistake coming back here. I was blinded by the kiss and what love I might've felt for him. Now there was no time for that love. There was only time for escape. We could think about that kiss later.

I pushed the door open. The hallway in front of me was just as white as the room behind me. A doctor walked past in blue scrubs, barely glancing at me as he fastened a mask over his mouth and nose.

"Ember?" A woman with rhinestones glued to the corner of her eyes caught my attention. Well, given the fact that she was wearing a hot pink jumper in the middle of all this white would've caught my attention anyways.

"Who're you?"

"Hazel."

I blinked. "And you're here because..."

"I'm getting you ready for the rehearsal dinner. We were supposed to have four days to plan your outfit, but I'm afraid your team and I had to go ahead and get ready despite your comatose state. I do hope your dress fits."

"I—I'm not going to the rehearsal dinner."

"Well, you'd have to take that up with the king, not with me. He's expecting you," Hazel looped her arm through mine and led me down the hallway. I followed her into an empty elevator. "And I wouldn't want to be the person to let King Nero down. Especially with all he's been through in the past two weeks."

"All *he's* been through?"

"Yes! The rebels sneaking into the palace and kidnapping the prince, stabbing King Nero in the process. Oh, I can't believe we serve such a resilient king. Just the thought makes me so joyful I can hardly speak. Don't you feel the same? I mean, he'll be your father-in-law soon enough."

My stomach clenched and flipped. I grappled for an acceptable response as the elevator started its ride downward. "Yeah," was all I managed to push out. Hazel seemed to accept this. She patted my arm.

The doors slid open revealing a busy foyer grander than any building within the gates of Kadjar. It had a high, golden ceiling and marble tiles, with cushioned chairs sitting in the corner, a gift shop to my left, and another set of elevators to my right. The secretary sat behind a desk next to the elevator we came out of. Hazel waved to the man sitting behind the desk, and I followed her out the set of revolving doors.

The sunlight was blinding. Hazel got in the black car waiting for us. I stopped, taking in the sun. All that mattered in this moment was that I was alive. I was standing underneath a vibrant blue sky. That's all I needed.

"Are you coming?"

I nodded and got into the car after Hazel. She instructed the driver to head to the palace. I watched as the Royal District flew past us: people in business suits hailing taxis so they could head to the Business District, Senators and regular people alike strolling along the sidewalk. The little television screen above my head told me that it was Saturday, September 21st. It was sunny with a mild wind, and it was 2:03 PM.

"So, what happened?"

"What?" I questioned.

"The king's assistant told me that you collapsed a few days ago, just after the news of your stepping up to the throne was announced. I was afraid we'd have to postpone Roman's birthday party. How tragic would that've been?"

"Yeah. Tragic."

"So what was it? Dehydration?"

"Ye—"

"Or was it stress? Stress can really do a number on a person. I swear I almost passed out from stress when we were sewing your dress. Oh, I just can't wait for you to see it. It's gorgeous. You'll look like a true queen in it."

I nodded, trying to swallow back the fear. I wondered how long it would take to get from here to the checkpoint outside the barrier.

The car came to a halt just in front of the palace. The door was opened for me, and I got out into the afternoon light. Cameras clicked in my face, blinding me with their flashes. Voices called out my name, asking questions I barely had time to process. I shielded my eyes as Hazel met me on my side of the car, leading me into the palace. I looked back for a second to see a wave of people holding pads of paper, recorders, and cameras.

Hazel and I walked side-by-side into the lobby, stepping into the first elevator. "You'll have to get used to that. And you can't clam up like you just did. King Nero wouldn't like seeing pictures of you looking confused all over the papers."

"What was I supposed to do?"

"Smile. Wave. But don't speak. You never speak without a publicist present. That's what Prince Roman and the king do, and that's what you'll have to do soon enough."

"How do you know so much about this?"

"My father is on King Nero's advisory council. I've heard my fair share of things and have seen more than enough political scandals."

The doors opened to a marble hallway that I didn't recognize. It was dressed in golden walls and painted ceilings, pictures of cherub babies floating over gardens danced above our heads. Men and women wearing uniformed clothes, carrying plates and trays, vases of flowers and table cloths moved past Hazel and I.

"What is this?" I asked.

She snorted. "King Nero really did pluck you out of the backwoods, didn't he?"

"I—what?"

"This is the grand hall. Right there," she pointed to a

tall, black door at the very end of the hall. "Is the ballroom. That's where all parties and galas take place. We aren't getting you ready here. I wish, though. Isn't it beautiful?"

"Yeah,"

A set of gold stairs led straight to the tall black door. This hall was nicer than the empress' entire citadel. This entire palace was so beautiful it left me breathless. I wished, more than anything, that I lived in a world where I could stay.

The plaque above the doors read *ballroom* in swirling calligraphy. Workers drained from the room out of one door and filed in through the other. They jogged up and down the stairs with their arms full.

Was Roman through those doors? Did he remember what had happened? I almost ached with the way I needed to see him. Realizing that, I felt sick. Who was I now that I needed someone like this? The Bloodhound had never needed anyone.

Then again, I doubt I could even call myself the Bloodhound anymore. No, the Bloodhound didn't need anyone, but Ember Levin did.

"Alright, are you done gawking? We're through this door." Hazel pulled me by the hand through the crowd of workers and into one of the smaller side doors.

"This is...?" I asked as I took a look around the wide room that surrounded me. There was a small couch pushed up underneath a painting of a bowl of fruit hanging on the beige walls. A balcony sat across from me next to the vanity mirror.

"Your dressing room. Get into the dress and call me

back when you're ready." Hazel nodded toward the mannequin on the other side of the vanity, and before I could ask her to stay, she left.

And I was alone. Alone, with the perfect escape.

The door to the balcony was unlocked. Soft wind blew inside, barely pushing my hair back behind my shoulders. Beneath the balcony, a little forest covered the space between the palace and the barrier. Faintly, I could see the rose gardens at the side of the palace.

If I was careful, I could scale the building. I could leave. I could find my way back to Kadjar—I'd take my chances if it meant getting home.

But I'd have to leave Roman. I swallowed against my dry throat, the very thought of him and me out in the desert surrounded by tumbleweeds and the burning sun, thinking that we were going to die out there. Thinking that I was going to die without ever having kissed him one more time.

I had long since accepted that love was not meant for someone like me. The girl I was before Angeles would've laughed in my face for even thinking that I could fall in love with a prince. She would've told me to get home and get back to what I do best: fighting. Fighting for my people. Fighting for my life.

But I'm tired. I would've said to her. *I'm tired of fighting. I'm tired of screaming when there is no one to hear my cries. I've finally found someone who I don't need to fight for. Don't I get to have that?*

The girl I was before would've scoffed and said, *are*

you really that selfish? Do you think yourself to be more important than the hundreds of people dying because of the empress?

I shut the balcony door.

The person who stood in the vanity mirror looking back at me, was not the same as that girl who accepted the empress' deal all those weeks ago. I'm not too sure who the girl in the mirror was.

Maybe following Roman was a mistake. Becoming queen was a hellscape that I didn't want to venture into. I couldn't do it—not for Roman, not for all the jewels and riches in the world. I wouldn't become queen.

Just how I was planning on avoiding the throne, though, was still a mystery.

I turned to face the girl in the mirror. Sure enough, there was a monster staring back at me. Sallow skin. Sunken eyes. My hands were burnt, covered in scars from the fire and bruised at the knuckles. This broken body was not the body of a queen. This was the body of a criminal. There was no way a dress could hide who I was.

But it was beautiful. I ran my hands along the baby blue tulle skirt resting on the mannequin. Jewels and lavender flowers peppered the bodice. The thick straps had been dipped in the same shimmering silver that sparkled along the hem. This was a dress fit for someone like Ivelisse—fit for a queen. I was no queen. I was barely human.

Just for tonight. Maybe you can trick a few people into believing that you were born for this.

I shed the white hospital clothes and unzipped the dress, pulling it from the mannequin. The fabric was smooth across my skin—a stark change from the scratchy clothes I taken off. I managed to zip the dress up all the way.

"Maybe you are a queen," I whispered. "If not, at least it's a good costume."

The door opened. "Are you—" Hazel stopped. I turned to see her standing in the threshold, mouth open. "Oh, Ember, you're simply beautiful." She crossed the room to me, fluffing the tulle and fixing my straps.

"Thank you."

She pulled the chair in front of the vanity out, motioning for me to sit down. I took a seat, and she reached over me for one of the flat jars. She coated my face in the pale powder, then reached down to apply it to my neck.

"What's this?" I looked up to see her holding my hair back, revealing a long scar I'd acquired in prison.

"Nothing." I said quickly. "It's nothing." I pulled my hair back down.

Hazel continued, slowly. "Is it the prince?" She asked quietly, grabbing a vial of brown powder. She dipped a brush in it and brought the powder to my eyelids, carefully coating them. I shut my eyes as she did.

"No. It's not Roman. I did this to myself." I lied.

"You hurt yourself like that?" I opened my eyes once I felt the brush leave my skin. "Do you need help?"

"No. I don't. It's all in my past. I'm not bothering with it anymore. Can we just leave my hair down for tonight? So no one sees?"

Hazel nodded. When she was finished with my makeup, I was a blank canvas once again. She'd done her best to cover my scarred, bruised hands, but there wasn't much she could do about those.

After braiding sections of my hair to twine through the rest, she stepped back. "Alright, we're done. Tomorrow the rest of my team and I will get you ready. That should take a little bit longer than tonight did."

I stood. "Thank you, Hazel."

She beamed. "You're welcome. If you need anything— ever—come find me in the tailor shop. We're right on the edge of the Royal District. Ask for me personally."

"I'll do that," I said, even though I knew there was no kind of help that she could give me.

Hazel squeezed my shoulder. "Your prince should be waiting for you in the grand hall whenever you're ready."

I gave her a nod of thanks and watched as she left the room. I waited long enough so that I was sure she'd be gone, and then I stepped out into the grand hall.

It was completely empty where it had been filled to the brim with people only a half hour ago. I craned my head up, eyes trained on the domed ceiling. I watched the painting before me unfold, angels and men. There must be some meaning to it—why would angels walk among men when they have all the heavens to themselves?

"Thank you, Senators, for catching me up," I turned around upon hearing the voice I've been waiting for mixed in with the pounding of footsteps against the tile. "I assure you all that I am fine. The hate groups are strong, but the might of the throne is stronger. I assume my father has gone over the events of tonight's dress rehearsal with you all?" A chorus of agreement rose up from the group. Roman stood at the helm of the group of suited men fixing the cuffs of his shirt. He wore a sleek navy blue dress suit, almost exactly the same as the suit he'd worn the night of Ian's party.

"Good," Roman continued. "You all are dismissed. I'll see you in the ballroom."

He glanced up at me as the Senators left the hall the same way they'd accompanied him in. "Looks like we're back in the same place we started." I said as he came close, still trying to fix the buttons on his cuffs.

"Apparently so."

"What's going to happen tonight?"

He didn't meet my eyes. "Tonight we'll go through what's going to happen tomorrow. My father will give a bull-shit speech. I'll give a bullshit speech. We'll eat dinner. After dinner, the servants will take the tables and chairs out of the ballroom, and the religious leaders will come, bless me and Angeles, and we'll dance until we're too drunk to walk. At least, the rest of the Court will. You and I aren't allowed to drink."

"Got it."

"And after tonight, my father will announce a wedding date."

"I'm not marrying you."

239

Roman shrugged, finishing his right cuff and moving to his left. "Maybe you'll get lucky and he'll decide that you're just as expendable as Ivelisse before he sets a date."

"Here," I reached for him. "Do you want me to fix them."

He jerked away from me. "No. I'm fine. Don't—don't touch me." He brushed past me, making his way to the staircase. I followed after him, questions along with a twinge of anger blowing through my mind. There wasn't time to worry about that, though, because trumpets blared from within the ballroom.

"What's wrong with you?"

"Nothing," he insisted, voice angrier than I was expecting. "Just…whatever happened between us in Kadjar, needs to stay in Kadjar."

"Why?"

Roman stopped as we reached the top set of stairs. He set his gaze on the doors before us. "He has us trapped, Ember. We just have to play the game until the law forces him to step down off the throne. I don't need you to screw anything up with your questions. I'm just trying to survive until tomorrow."

"What do you mean 'my questions'?"

"You always ask *why*. You can't question him. I thought you would've learned that by now, but I guess you haven't. I don't need this vigilante shit ruining my chances of survival, alright?"

"You are being such an ass."

"Yeah? I've heard worse." He clasped his hands behind his back. "This is my country. I was stupid to even try to run away with you, and you were stupid to follow me back. There is no world where we can exist together, and that's since been made very clear to me."

"By him? By the same man who killed your brother?"

Roman's cheeks grew a dull, brick red. "Don't bring Ian into this. Please, dear God, Ember, don't bring him into this. I just need you to forget about it all—about us, about Kadjar, about your life before—and obey him. It'll make the descent so much easier."

"The descent to what? Hell?"

"No, to the throne."

"Lately those are starting to sound more and more like synonyms."

More fanfare blazed from inside the ballroom. Roman straightened his back, and I did the same, matching his posture. The doors flew open. Roman plastered on a wide smile, and walked inside the doors with arms wide open like he could hug the entire Court before him.

Like this, Prince Roman looked so much like his father.

Chapter Nineteen
Roman

The wind whistled around me, blowing loose curls of brown hair in my line of sight. The trees beneath my balcony bent and swayed to the wind's every whim. They seemed so weak compared to the strength of the wind.

I sat with my legs in between the gray columns underneath the railing and rested my weight on my arms behind me. The weatherman on the TV that morning had said it was going to rain overnight. The stars had disappeared, making way for the dark clouds. I had yet to change out of my tuxedo from the rehearsal dinner. I didn't care if it got ruined by the rain. I didn't care if the rain washed all of Angeles away.

"Found your stash." The sliding door closed as Ky came out to the balcony. He sat down next to me.

"Of?"

"The black cigarettes. You have another stash I should know about?"

I shook my head. "What're you going to do? Destroy them?"

"I could. But you'll just go get more. You lied to me, Roman. You told me you threw the third one away. You told me you hadn't even thought about using it."

"Sorry." Even I knew that my words were a pitiful excuse for what I'd done.

Ky shook his head. He shifted his weight so he could

sit down with his legs crossed. I looked over at him. Something had changed—Ky looked tired. Worn. Beaten. His clothes hung off of his thin frame in a way that they hadn't before, like he'd either lost weight or hadn't bothered to look in the mirror this morning. Something deep within him was gone, or changed, I couldn't tell which. While I was so worried about myself and everything that I had going on, I hadn't ever stopped to think about him, my best friend.

"You lied to *me*, of all people. You broke our promise."

My breath hitched in my throat at the mention of the promise. When we'd buried my mother, Ky had set the last shovel of dirt on the grave. He looked up at me through the tears and the pouring rain and said, "Swear to me that you'll tell me the truth, no matter who it hurts." I had spent the past twelve years of my life lying to him about what my father was putting my mother and Ian and me through. Those lies, and every lie I'd ever told Ky, were supposed to end that night.

"I'm sorry," I said, and this time I meant it. "But it's not like you don't have your own secrets, too."

"I don't keep secrets from you."

"You and I both know that you don't go to Miles' house in the summer. You come back every summer a little bit more serious and a little bit angrier than you left. It feels like I'm the only person in the world that notices."

"This conversation isn't about me."

"But it needs to be. Where do you go, Ky?"

He hung his head. "You'd hate me if I told you the truth."

"It's going to take a lot for me to hate you."

Ky took a breath. "My father...I know him. That's where I go. I live with him every summer, but last summer, things changed. *Everything* changed. Something—someone happened. I don't want to talk about what happened."

"Someone as in a girl?"

He shook his head. "I'm not talking about it now. I'm not ready to talk about it. That's why I stayed here this summer. I don't want to face him."

"Your father?"

"No. Just—forget about it, alright? The point is, my father wanted me to stay with him for good. He told me he'd get me a job in the marina, but I just couldn't accept it. That's what I've been hiding. That's what I've been wrestling with for the past year."

"Where does he live?"

"Calais."

"Why didn't you go?"

Ky shrugged. "Because. You and me, we're all we've got. All those times when I had my back up against the wall with the Court wanting me gone, you stepped in. And I figured that you're going to need me in the next couple of years. You and I have got to stick together."

I smiled despite everything, and I looked over at Ky. He had spent so long being a man divided: divided between the life he lived in Calais and the life in the Court. No one had ever wanted him around his entire life. He was a bastard, and that was the last thing you wanted to be in high society.

"What's his name?"

"Matthew. He sent me a letter the other day, and he asked me again. I got to thinking that if you really wanted a way out, this is it. You and I could leave for Calais—Miles would take us. You know Miles, my cousin who's been waiting this whole time to take Ember out of Angeles? He has had a seat open for her for the past few weeks. I'm sure he can make room for the two of us. I'd be okay with facing Calais again if you came with me."

I focused on my hands in my lap like they were going to give me the answers that I needed. "I can't."

"What? Why?"

"I have to rule, Ky. The person that I was before all this, the person who didn't want to rule, was a child. I know my place now, and I can't disrupt the order. I have to rule. I'm sick of living in fear of the crown."

Ky blew out a slow breath of air. "You're an idiot, Roman Stone, a real, true idiot. You're backing yourself in a corner."

"No, I've realized who I am."

"And that's a dangerous thing for someone like you to realize. You know once you begin your training, he will have complete control over you? You think it's bad now? Once you and Ember start learning from him, he'll have you under a microscope twenty-four seven. This is your last chance. I am giving you your last chance."

"I can't abandon Angeles."

"Roman, you look sick. You can't save the world if the

245

world kills you first. Ever since you came back from God knows where, you've looked like you're two seconds away from death. You can't take the throne. It's going to kill you. Why did you leave in the first place?"

"I went to Kadjar."

"What? Why?"

"I went for Ember. I went because I was afraid, but while I was over there, I realized that I can't let what happened to those Kadjarians happen here. I have to save Angeles from my father."

"You can't save the world."

"But I can try."

Ky leaned his head back, staring at the overcast sky. "He's going to take you down, and all of us are going to go with you. Me. Ember. Ivelisse."

"I'm not asking you to go with me."

"You don't have to. I'm your best friend, you idiot. I go with you no matter what dark and twisted path you get led down. Alright? Bottom line, end of story."

"It can't…it can't be like that anymore?"

Ky furrowed his eyebrows.

"My father has this list of rules—it's been passed down through generations of men in my family, and he gave them to me a while back. I've tried to ignore them, but after next week and after my birthday, I can't anymore. The first rule is to isolate myself, so I can focus on the crown and the crown only."

"That's a death sentence."

"Not to him. And right now, I have to obey him. I broke things off with Ember today before the rehearsal dinner. I was such an ass to her. The look on her face—the way she—God, I don't know. I've never felt like this before. He's watching me, Ky, and he's making sure I cut everyone off."

He went silent. It was starting to rain. Pinpricks of water fell on my face and hands. I couldn't tell Ky to leave. I couldn't put eighteen years of him and me on the back-burner and say that it was either our friendship or my life. It was Ky I was talking to. My big, beautiful empathetic idiot of a best friend who rarely ever thought about himself. My best friend gave up the life he'd always dreamed of for me, and here I was telling him he would have been better off if he had taken it.

"Did you love her?" He asked, quietly.

"No. Jesus, no. I can't even think about what would have happened if I loved her. We kissed for the first time when we were over in Kadjar. Something about her tells me that I'm not going to get over her that easy. There's been this dull pain in my chest ever since I told her to let us go. I can't explain it."

He crossed his arms over his chest and stepped inside the doors of my room. "If it makes you feel any better, I did hear about a rave going on tonight in the Business District. You know those are the best ones. You in?"

The corners of my mouth tugged upwards. "Always."

One more night without my father's stupid rules. One more night.

247

Ky shouted a goodbye before he left. I returned to my bedroom, closing the door behind me. My sheets were tangled from yesterday's restless night. I ran a hand down my face. Every single time I closed my eyes, all I could see was her. My father refused to tell me if she was alive or not after we'd been captured by Angelesan patrols. Seeing her in the grand hall, feeling how the very sight of her made my heart race, was enough to drive me mad.

All I could think of was the way she'd kissed me, like she knew the world was ending but that didn't matter to her. Yet, I still had to throw what could have been away in favor of the throne. She was the one spark of flame I'd found in a dark, dark world. She was a hurricane in my calm beach, but danger has never been mine to entertain.

"I trust that you've been putting the rules into place?" My father's voice echoed from my bedroom doorway.

I nodded.

"Excuse me?" His voice came closer from the other side of my bed. I turned to face him.

"Yes, sir."

King Nero took a seat on my bed. "I promise, son, this is all for your own good. This is for the betterment of Angeles."

"Yes, sir."

"After I step down, you will handle domestic affairs, and Ember will handle foreign affairs. She will conquer the world. Though, she still isn't keen on the idea of the throne. Any other girl would be jumping at the chance to marry a prince. With some…discipline, though, I don't think she'll be too difficult to manage."

I winced.

"So, Roman, tell me what you've learned in the week since you've been home."

"Everything I do from here on out must be for the glory of Angeles." My voice came out rough, like I'd just swallowed a handful of rocks.

"And the rules?"

I began to recite the list, every syllable burning like fire racing up my throat. "One. Isolate yourself. Focus on nothing but the crown ahead. Two. Assert your authority over the people. A good leader is fair, but stern. Three. Take the throne."

"And what will happen if you disregard any of these rules?"

I kept silent.

My father's hand clamped down on my shoulder, fingernails digging into my skin. I shrugged from underneath his hand.

"Ember dies." I choked.

Chapter Twenty
Ember

I think it was the night terrors that brought me to Roman. Burning, aching nightmares that morphed into the walls that would whisper words in my ear, the same words I heard in prison.

I had always been able to fight the nightmares on my own before. This time, though, I sat in bed for about an hour, wiping away my tears and steadying my breathing, before I gave up. I thought, maybe, he knew what they were like. We'd lived two completely different lives, but we both knew the same fear all too well.

I guess I was wrong, because he refused to speak to me. I leaned against the chest at the end of his bed while he sat motionless on the balcony. It was almost morning. The world outside was soaked with rain, but the awning above his balcony shielded Roman from the wet.

"Did I do something?" I asked while playing with one of the white curls of the shag carpet underneath me.

"No."

"Would you tell me if I did?"

"Probably." Roman said, still not looking at me. "You should go to sleep, you know. You're not going to get any tonight."

"Here?"

"Either you sleep on my bed, and I'll take the couch, or

vice versa. I really don't care. I just don't...I don't want to talk."

"Why?"

"There's nothing to talk about." He shrugged. I pushed myself off the chest. When I came closer, he barely turned his head toward me, then whipped it back around when I sat down next to him.

"You promised me honesty." I said, but he didn't respond. Roman rested his head on one of the columns underneath the railing as I continued. "Why did you kiss me like that? Why did you hold me like that if this is how you were going to treat me in the very end? How is that fair?"

Roman lifted his head. "It's not."

"So why treat me like that in the first place?"

"Because, Ember, there are rules that I have to follow. Rules that keep me in line, and if I step out of line—I can't even think about what will happen. I can't. Alright? Just, respect that, please, and go to bed."

"No! No. I'm not going to let you treat me like I'm some paramour. You owe me honesty. I let you in. I let you kiss me. I let you *hold me*. You don't get to throw all that away just because you feel like it."

"You think I don't want you? You think I haven't dreamt about you every night? Every time I close my eyes I see you. You are the very breath in my lungs, and all I want to do is tell the world about you, but I can't. Do you know why?"

An angry, frustrated string of incoherent words and

half-baked sentences had formed on the tip of my tongue. I didn't say them, though.

"Because he's threatened your life," Roman's voice sounded so pitiful. So defeated. So unlike how I was used to hearing it.

"Death threats have never stopped me before."

"But they're enough to stop me. He could've threatened my life, and I wouldn't have blinked. But he threatened you. And I can't live with myself if I'm the reason he kills you."

"I'd rather love you for as long as I have left than live the rest of my life away from you." ·

Roman shook his head. He ran a hand through his hair, trying to gather his thoughts together. "You don't understand. I am bound to the throne of Angeles before I can be bound to any person. Your chains were destroyed along with Kadjar. As long as the throne stands, mine remain linked together holding me back from what I want most: you."

I let out a long breath. "I know. I know, Roman, I know." I stepped away from him, breaking a little bit of the tension between us.

"You do?"

I nodded, scoffed a little. "Don't you think I haven't seen it—seen the chains? I see how you look at your father. I see how you look at the outside world. You are not the same person you are in here than you are out there. I ignored it. The looks. The facade that you've so carefully made yourself. I just...I guess I wanted to live in a world where we could be for as long as it could last."

He took a step towards me, obviously against his better judgement, and crossed his arms over his chest. I wanted to reach out with every fiber of my being. I wanted to run my hand up his arms, down his chest until there wasn't an inch of the Prince of Angeles that I did not know. I wasn't ready to let go. I wasn't read to face the world and fight once more.

Slowly, ever so slowly, I reached over to take his hand. Roman inhaled a sharp breath, and he shook. I twined my fingers in his. Just as I thought he was going to accept my touch, he ripped away.

I tried to step towards him. He held a hand up and winced like my very presence was hurting him. "No. Don't do this to me. Don't touch me. Don't look at me like that." More softly he added, "Please. I can't let you destroy me."

"I'm not trying to hurt you. I'm just—I'm just trying to figure out a way that this could work."

"It can't, okay? I was foolish in trying to think that I could rule my people and make us work in the same breath. It doesn't work like that. It didn't work like that for my father or my grandfather before him, so it won't work like that for me. I can't let my people down."

"You think I can let mine down? I don't know who's alive and who's dead. I was supposed to save them. I *failed*. And now I have to fix this. My people were counting on me and I let them die."

"You could leave, you know. You could find Miles like you originally planned. Now that you're the future queen, no one can really say no to you. Miles could take you to Kadjar."

"Alone," I said.

Roman hung his head. He stared down at the ground underneath his feet before looking up at me. "I can't leave Angeles. You have to leave Angeles."

"So we're stuck."

"No. I'm stuck. You have a way out."

"Not if that way out means leaving you."

One second, Roman's eyes narrowed. The next, he stood, walking through the balcony doors. "No, no, stop. You don't get to do that to me."

"Do what?" I asked, following him.

"Look at me like that. It's not fair."

"Like what?"

"Like you *love* me." His words hung in the air for ten seconds longer than they should have. His wild-eyed look made my heart beat faster. Roman took a step toward me, taking both of my hands in his. It wasn't enough. These touches, so simple and so bare, would never be enough. They were just safe enough to not get us in trouble and just dangerous enough to get my heart beating a little bit faster.

I do. I wanted to say. *I love you.*

I held myself back. I didn't wrap myself in his arms like I wanted to. Roman held my hands tightly, like he'd lose me if he let go. "In a perfect world," he said. "You and I could belong to each other without the threat of the throne, but we don't live in such a world. You know that. We can't do this." He dropped his hands from mine, leaving me cold and aching.

"My father has taken away everything I've ever loved.

254

So I can't love you. I can't even think about letting him take you from me." He said.

"King Nero won't touch me. He needs something from me."

"In his eyes, everyone is replaceable. I know he's testing me by using you, Ember. If I screw up, he'll kill you because he believes that emotions do nothing other than weaken a man."

All I wanted to do in this moment was kiss him. I wanted to kiss him so badly that goosebumps rose on my arms. I wanted nothing but him. I knew he could see it too, my desire written so clearly across my face. Roman took a quiet step toward me, pressing his forehead against my own.

His lips lingered above mine as his fingers danced below my chin. "One last time." His voice shook. "And then it's over. Let me hold you one more time. Alright?"

I nodded, not trusting myself to speak without crying.

Roman took over. For the first time in my life, I let another person take control without worrying about my own safety. I trusted him. More than I've ever trusted another person, I trusted him.

This kiss spoke a thousand words that neither of us had ever had the gall to say. This one said *I-miss-the-way-you-feel-against-me* and *I-never-want-this-to-end*. This kiss was as fiery and demanding as we were. In this moment, I could no longer think straight. All of my thoughts had been replaced with his hands on my body and his mouth pressed to mine.

If I could bottle up a single moment to keep forever, it

would be this one. It would be of him, holding me like he was going to lose me. Because he was. This would be a moment to recall if I ever made it to being old and gray. I would think of the way that his hands scoured my body, as if I were a photograph he was eager to memorize. Those hands that finally finding a home at the small of my back, pressing me even closer.

I knew this couldn't be. I knew this was all a temporary thing, and the very thought killed me. I wanted this moment forever.

He pulled away first. Our foreheads leaned against each other. "I don't think I've ever told you this," he said, taking a deep breath. "You have shaken and replaced every thought in my mind, Ember. You make me want to forsake every damn rule I've ever been taught."

I didn't say anything back. *I want to fight for this. I want to fight for you, just as much as I want to fight for my nation.* I wanted to say. But, like always, was silent instead.

"So that's it, then?" I asked.

He nodded. I took a few steps toward the door, still seeking solid ground. And, we just stared at each other. A helpless, silent stare. My stomach churned as I stepped into the hallway. A lump formed in my throat.

"Guess that's it." He finally said.

"Yeah."

"I'll see you around, Ember."

I turned outside of the penthouse and down the hall with angry, frustrated tears finally boiling over and burning down my cheeks.

~

I remember the kill all too well.

I remember the smell of blood, the feel of its stickiness oozing down my arms, the sound of screams echoing through my ears. And the fight. Oh, how I miss the fight. I miss the aftermath—feeling like I was finally doing something to fix my broken nation. Feeling like, no matter what happened when the sun came up, I would have done something to fix the world I was born into. Change only ever came to those who fought for it.

The one thing I don't miss, however, was the body itself. Faint regret singing in my ear, telling me that I've just killed someone's son or daughter, someone's parent, someone's lover. I've just taken a life, no matter how wicked that life was.

I don't know why I ended up walking down the road of the Royal District. I do know that the tee shirt and dress pants Ivelisse had left behind were a weak protector from the chill of the night air. I didn't stop long enough to truly feel the cold seep into my bones, though.

The palace was only a glimmer in the corner of my eye. Streetlights buzzed above me. All I could focus on was the pulsating nightclub in the second story of the skyscraper ahead of me. Colored lights bled from darkened windows, reflecting green and red and purple and blue onto the dark concrete around me. Disembodied shadows pushed up from the array of people, dancing, jumping on the floor.

I had to do something to distract myself, and this was easiest. I couldn't keep thinking about Roman, about the kill, about taking the throne. I hadn't meant to stumble upon the nightclub, but it just happened. Ivelisse had said something about the nightclubs in the Royal District and how they were no place for a lady of the Court.

The very last thing I wanted to be was a lady of the Court.

In a different life, I might've been. I might have been someone like Ivelisse, beautifully cordial with a proper smile, someone who never tired of shaking hands and was content with staying by Roman's side until the world ends. But I'll never be that girl.

I was not fit to be quiet. I was not fit to be queen.

For tonight, though, I would push every single self-deprecating and condescending thought out of my mind. I would deal with my demons in the morning. Tonight, I'd dance with them. I'd shed the name of the Bloodhound and the throne to become someone who didn't belong to either. For tonight, I'd be the kind of girl who let strangers dance close to her body and kiss her scars. I'd be the kind of girl without a care in the world, at least until the sun came back up.

I stepped up to the front door. Through the glass, I could see a girl in a tight black dress puking in a fake plant while another was holding back her hair. Stragglers from the nightclub sat on the ground near the elevators. A janitor swept the floor where the party debris lay. I paused. Wind from the few taxis and cars racing through the streets blew my hair around my head.

My hand barely touched the cold golden handle of the door when a voice from the alleyway beside me came bursting through the air.

"Stop it! Let go!"

My hand fell from the door as the rustling from the alley grew louder. I stopped, staring at the door handle, listening to the voice.

Angry scuffles, grunts, and shouts resonated from the alley beside the building. "Oh—shit, is that a knife? Okay, look, just put the bag down, and I won't tell anyone. Alright? Just let me go. No one has to know. I swear, I won't tell."

"It's *mine*." The other voice was low, dangerous, and raspy. "I didn't travel all the way from the fucking Common District to not leave with a bag of coke. You honestly think I'm that stupid, Michael? I'm not leaving without that bag."

"The deal was twelve hundred notes. You gave me eight hundred. You know I need that twelve hundred—my rent is due next week and I—"

"I don't care! You told me eight hundred!" The second voice screamed.

My hands fell from the door as a rustling grew from the alley. I took a few steps toward the noise. Grunting. Angry huffs. "Dude, get off of me! Toby, put the knife down!"

I had to do something. The words of their conversation and Michael's angry cries became fuel for me to run into the alleyway. The man, Toby, was twice my size and wider than two of me put together. He barely glanced at me. Michael,

259

who I now saw to be a scrawny man drowning in a ratty coat, pushed Toby off and backed up towards me.

"Go away," he rasped. "Run. Get the cops."

"He has—"

"A knife, I know, I—"

"Both of you! Shut up! Listen to me," Toby screamed, wielding the knife at Michael. "You, give me the bag. And *you*, leave." He pointed the knife in my direction. In the dim light, I could just barely make out a cut bleeding across his cheek. I hoped it was from the keys held between Michael's fingers.

Memory rushed through me. I had killed a man in Kadjar over a drug ring. Someone he'd crossed had told me about it, said that the drug ring was happening from within the citadel and was comprised of some of Kadjar's best. It had taken me a month to bust that ring and kill the head of it.

Toby jerked his head toward the street. "Go, kid, I'm giving you a chance. Go before I change my mind." The knife in his hand gleamed in the dim moonlight.

Cold fear washed over me in tidal waves. It was the same kind of cold fear that I'd sworn off the second I came to Angeles, the same kind of cold fear that stopped me from killing the empress and stopped me from saving my home. If I couldn't save them, maybe I could save Michael.

Hot anger replaced that fear, scalding me from the inside out. My fingers thrummed with energy and anticipation. I was shaking. If I could just get one good jump in, one good distraction, I could wrap my fingers around his neck harder,

harder, harder, harder, and then—

Snap.

I could kill him.

But something told me that he was going to kill Michael before I had the chance. Michael stepped in front of me as Toby got closer, still holding that silver pocket knife.

"She's just a kid, dude. What's wrong with you?"

"I gave her a chance to leave. She's deaf or something, 'cause she's still here, and she has to pay for not listening to me just like you do."

Michael sputtered for a second. "The hell are you talking about? This isn't about her. This is about the drugs. Just— fuckin' take the coke. I'll find the rest of the money somehow. Put the knife down."

"No! This was never about the drugs, and you know it!" He stomped his foot like a child deprived of their way.

"What is it about, then?"

Toby's voice was on the verge of tears. He took a deep, shaking breath. "I don't know! I don't….I—" He threw the knife down on the ground. Michael stepped to the side, just enough for me to see Toby pull a gun from his pocket. "You know what this is about. You know that that knife, those drugs, were just a coverup."

I watched Michael swallow. "You're going to kill me?" He whispered like if he spoke any louder he'd be speaking truth into those words.

"Ever since you stole from me—don't think I don't know about the money—I've been planning this, and now you have to pay. You don't know what you destroyed that night you took all those notes from me."

Michael let out a long breath of air. He held his hands up in defense. "Shit, dude, I didn't think you noticed. It was barely twenty notes."

"When you live like we do, twenty notes can make or break a man."

"You think I deserve to pay for it with my life? What about her? Does she deserve to pay for twenty notes?"

He shook his head. "No. But she has to now that she's seen what she has. Stand still, Michael. It'll make this all go a lot easier."

My heart thumped so loud I thought it was going to break through my ribcage and fly out of my body. He flicked the safety off of the gun and aimed directly at Michael's face.

I launched into attack. Gunshots pounded off the side of the building as I brought the man to the ground. I wrestled the gun from his hands, twisting his wrist until I heard a crack and a scream leave his mouth.

Barely, out of the corner of my eye, I saw Michael run off. I prayed that he'd go get help. I stumbled back, scooting on my bottom until I was far enough away from the man. "You don't want to do this. You don't want to kill anyone."

"You don't know me."

"I know that you don't want to kill someone. I've been where you're standing." I got to my hands and knees, still holding the gun underneath my hand. "I promise you, you don't want to do this."

"Why? How do you know?"

My throat went dry. "I promise you, no matter what, you will never stop thinking about death once you've brought it upon someone. You don't want that weighing on you."

He laughed, dryly, like he couldn't believe the sight in front of him. "Who the hell are you to tell me about death? You're just some rich little palace girl, aren't you? What family do you belong to?"

"I don't belong to anyone." Toby got to his knees, eyes on the gun in my hand. I continued, "It doesn't matter what difference you're making, no matter who those kills are going to help, you won't ever stop thinking about what you've done, and you won't ever stop hating yourself for it. I should know. I wake up every day thinking about my kills."

Toby stopped. "You've killed? You're..." His eyes left my face trailing down to the ground where my burned, scarred hands gripped onto the gun. "What are you?" He whispered.

"You don't need to know. Toby, I promise you, once you take a life, you won't ever stop thinking about it."

He shook his head. "If you're such a killer why didn't you kill me when you had the chance?" He nodded toward the gun. "Why don't you kill me now?"

I rose to my feet. "I swore to myself that I'd never take another life. You need to go. Go back to the Common District."

And he did.

I watched as Toby stumbled out of the alleyway, barely glancing back at the girl who convinced him not to take a life.

I stared at the gun in my hands for a second. It was heavy, the gray metal still warm from the weight of Toby's hand wrapped around it.

I could take a life with this. I'd never used a gun before, only knives and swords. Once, in a pinch, I had used glass from a beer bottle. Civilians rarely had access to guns, and the finer weapons Kadjar had to offer were saved for the military.

But this gun held a world of opportunities for the Bloodhound. She could kill as many people as the ammunition inside allowed. I'll bet she could get away with it, too. I'll bet she could go on a spree right now, killing at least half of the nightclub next to her. She could waltz back into that palace just in time for the morning news. No one would be none the wiser.

The girl holding the gun was not the Bloodhound. The Bloodhound lay dead in the ruins of the East Sector. This was a girl who was trying to save her home when she could barely save herself and trying to love a broken prince who didn't know how to be loved. This girl was not a murderer.

But maybe you can't change a monster. Maybe you can't change the call of the kill no matter how many times you curl its hair or wash the blood from its hands. Maybe this girl will always be a murderer. I don't think there's a perfume strong enough to cover up a soul devoid of grace.

I stood, not daring to take my eyes off the gun that lay between my hands and walked to the sidewalk closer to the street. I leaned against the wall of the nightclub. The faint thud of music still beat through the walls. The stragglers who were leaving didn't pay me any mind. They didn't bother to notice the girl with the gun in her hands, staring up at the sky like it could somehow give her all the answers in the world.

What would happen if the Bloodhound came back while I was on the throne? Roman wouldn't know what to do. I wouldn't know what to do. If an Angelesan found out that their precious queen was a murderer, it would ruin everything that generations of kings and queens had fought for. It would ruin Roman. But, why should I care? I'm not one of them. I will never be one of them.

I don't have any time to ponder on that thought be-cause—

"Ember?" A familiar voice called out to me.

Just barely a few feet away from me, I found Ky. "What is—h-holy shit." He held his hands in the air up like I was going to shoot him.

"No. No, it's not what it looks like. I'm not…" *A killer.* I trailed off unable to finish the lie. Ky shook his head and put his hands down.

"What, you're holding a gun in front of one of the most packed nightclubs in Angeles? Roman said you were—"

"He told you?"

"Yeah. After I forced it out of him, he did. Don't worry, though, your secret is safe with me as long as you promise not to, like, kill anybody while you're over here. Not my circus, not my monkeys, not my problem, you know?"

"No. I don't know what any of that means."

Ky let out a long breath of air. "Of course you don't.

Okay, hey, let's just put the gun down and walk away. How about that? There's this house party in the Business District that Roman and I are going to. I was supposed to meet him at the gas station by the house like thirty minutes ago. You wanna come?"

I shook my head. "No. I really just want to go lay down."

"I'll walk back to the palace with you. Let me just text Roman and tell him I'm going to be late." Ky pulled his phone from his pocket. "I probably should have done that thirty minutes—" His eyes widened. Ky opened his mouth, like he was getting ready to say something, but only a small gasp came out.

He crumpled to the ground.

Michael stood just behind Ky, the knife dripping with blood. He looked up at me, and back down to Ky. "I thought—I thought that was Toby."

"No. No!" I fell to my knees before Ky. "Call an ambulance." I looked up at Michael, who was still holding the knife in wild-eyed terror. "Now!"

"They're going to arrest me!" He cried out.

"And I'm going to kill you! Call the goddamn ambulance!" Michael fumbled with his phone before dialing the number and crying to the poor dispatcher over the phone.

I pulled Ky into my lap. The blood—gods, the blood was everywhere. It poured from his back, down my pants and pooled on the gray sidewalk around us. His face was pale. A light sheen of sweat covered his brow-line.

266

"Jude," he whispered.

"What? Who?"

"Call Jude."

"Who's that?"

Ky blinked, taking a heaving breath that dissolved into a fit of bloody coughs. The knife dropped by my side, and when I looked up, I saw Michael standing there. "I gotta go. Ambulance is on their way, but I can't get arrested. I can't leave my family. I'm sorry. I really—"

"Go!" I choked out. "Just go."

He left, this time I knew he wasn't coming back. Ky let out another round of rattling coughs. I didn't know what to do. I'd never tried to patch up a wound before. I tried to wipe the sweat off his face, but only smeared blood on his forehead. He was warm, still, at least.

"Please call Jude," Ky tried to sit up. The blood came pouring out of the wound, and I eased him back down on my lap. "I need him."

"Who is Jude?"

"I can't—I can't die without him."

"I'll call him, I'll get him. Who is he? Is he in your phone?" I reached over and took Ky's phone from his hand. I hadn't the slightest clue how to work a cell phone. The buttons were bright, and names of people I didn't know popped out at me.

"N-no. Get Jude. I need to see him." He took a shaking breath.

"I don't know who that is! Is he in your phone?"

Sirens wailed faintly in the distance.

Ky took another breath, labored and slow. "Ky, don't do this to me." His eyes fluttered shut. I shook his shoulders. "Please, come on, Ky. Wake up!"

The sirens turned onto our street, flashing red and blue against the buildings. I don't remember much of what happened next. I remember an emergency medical personnel wrapping a blanket around my shoulders as they lifted Ky onto a gurney. I remember crying into her shoulder. She told me that everything was going to be all right.

I didn't have the heart to tell her that that was a lie.

~

The first time I killed someone was the first time I truly felt like I knew where I belonged in the world. That's too crazy of a thought to ever say aloud.

The first time those prison guards snapped my bones, I screamed at them. Said they were the monsters, not me. I told them that they were punishing me for trying to fix *our* home. They only laughed.

That was the first seed of regret, the first inkling of *maybe I was wrong to kill.*

I don't like to think much about those seeds and what they did to me. They festered inside my soul, rotting me from the inside out.

Michael was the last seed, his name getting the final slot on the list of things I try not to think about. I hated the fact that Ky's assailant helped me gain back a little piece of my own humanity right before trying to kill my friend, even if it was accidental. I hated the fact that such a man showed me that I was ready to move past the Bloodhound, that I was ready to forget about the past that had haunted me so.

I woke in Ky's hospital room the next morning. The doctors said he was lucky. The stab wound had missed major organs and only took ten stitches to cover up. They said if his vitals stayed normal all night, he could be released when he woke up.

Ky slept on the white hospital bed, hooked up to an IV machine, gauze wrapped around his midsection. He slept soundly, but that also might've been the heavy morphine running through his system.

Ky's phone began to buzz. *Ivelisse Grace calling...*

I pressed the "accept call" button and slipped out the door into the hallway. "Hello?"

"Hi."

The other side went silent for a second. "Ember? Where's Ky?"

"That's a long story. He's okay, though."

She sighed. "I don't have time to ask questions. I need to see you. I've tried calling Roman, but he's not answering, and the phone in my apartment leads me to voicemail every time. Can you meet me by the checkpoint to the Common District?"

"No. I'm kind of in the middle of something."

"Look, Ember, I don't care what you're doing. It's not as important as this. It has to do with Kadjar. And you going back."

A slow fear thrilled through my veins. The second I thought I'd be okay with never seeing my home again, something pulls me back in. If I went home, I'd have to face the Bloodhound again.

I'd have to face the demons I'd spent the month running from.

"Please," she said. "I need you to do this one last thing for me. And then I'll never ask you for anything ever again."

"Fine." I glanced back through the window of Ky's room. He slept soundly. "But make it quick."

Chapter Twenty-One
Roman

"Um, hi. What are you doing here?"

Natasha, my therapist, knocked on my door at exactly eight in the morning. I had been up since five due to meetings, but, like every morning, I stopped back by the penthouse between the beginning of a Senate meeting and a department meeting so I could grab a bagel.

I was hoping to have enough time to stop by the Grace's apartment to see if Ember had returned. She had been missing since the rehearsal dinner two days ago, and tonight was the party. I'd be too swamped for the rest of the day to check any other time. Last night had been hectic: meeting with the priests and rabbis and preachers who were to bless Ember and me at the party, overseeing all the final touches that Ivelisse was supposed to complete. Ember should have been there.

Ky was, though. He had an excuse for her absence before I even had the chance to ask where she was. He said she was blowing off steam and had gotten a hotel room for the night so she didn't have to stay the night in the palace.

"I have something for Ember," Natasha said. She had thick black sunglasses pushed up in her hair and a thick coat wrapped around her small frame. She handed me a manila envelope. "She needs to get this *now*. I don't know where she is, or I'd give it to her myself."

"I haven't seen her in a day or two. We had a fight, and

I think she's blowing off steam."

"She needs to read this letter within the hour."

"Who's it from?"

Natasha glanced around the hallway like someone was listening in. She thought for a minute before responding. "No, I can't say. Ember will know. She needs to read the letter and get correspondence back to me before tonight. I've made a mistake, and I'm trying to make it right."

"What does that mean?"

"Nothing of your concern, Prince. This is between Ember and me."

"I think—"

"Listen, I have a client in half an hour. Hailing a taxi is going to be a mess in this traffic. I need to go. Please, make sure Ember gets the letter. It's important."

Natasha turned to leave, and I didn't call her back. I made my way to the kitchen where a half-eaten bagel sat on a glass plate.

I placed Ember's letter on the counter making a mental note to tell her about it the next time I saw her. If I didn't know where she was, surely I couldn't be faulted for not getting her the letter. But, then again, Natasha made it sound important. I grabbed the envelope.

Technically, opening someone's mail was illegal. At least, it was for the common people. If I slipped the contents into another envelope, Ember would never know.

The date at the top was from two weeks ago. Dirt stains

lined the crumpled corners. The paper that slid out of the envelope was even dirtier, written on with blue, smudged ink.

Ember,

I've gotten word from the king. I know you failed, and I know he freed Mara upon your escape. I've gotten my end of the deal—I don't care how it happened. If this is what's keeping you from returning home, you mustn't worry; I've publicly exonerated you.

I need you back. I need your help with the rebuilding efforts and, more importantly, the retaliation. I want to work with you. I want you to come represent the people. Show me what needs to be fixed. Show me how to be a better empress.

I need someone like you: someone who knows what it's like to live just as they do. I've erased the name of the Bloodhound, but I want you to come back and build the name of Ember Levin, Speaker For The People.

AS *SOON* AS YOU GET THIS LETTER, RETURN IT TO NATASHA ROBELIS. I need to know if you're coming home and when. Do not disappoint me, General.

—Empress Analita Ibrahim

I held the note in my hands, staring at the blurred, barely legible words. This was it—this was her way out.

She'd wanted to leave for so long, and I had pushed her away. It was easy, everything was falling into place. She'd jump at the chance to leave and be someone great back home.

My hands shook as I shoved the letter in the nearest drawer, along with forks and spoons and butter knives. No— she wouldn't want to leave. She couldn't. I'd give the letter to her later, and surely, surely she'd stay. Surely she wouldn't leave.

Surely she wouldn't leave me for a chance to represent her people.

The one thing that she's been aching to do since she got here. I am the only thing standing in the way of her finally going home. I could give it to her. I could let her go, with a wave and a promise to keep in touch. I could bring Ivelisse back. We could get married like we were supposed to. I could forget all about Ember Levin.

I knew that that was a lie.

I stared at the letter sitting on top of the utensils. I almost took it back out. Instead, I shoved the drawer shut.

The watch on my wrist beeped, indicating that it was time for me to leave for the department meeting. I slid the bagel into the trash can and went for the door. It opened on its own, stopping me in my tracks.

My father stood on the other side, dressed impeccably in a suit and tie, just as he was for every Senate meeting. "You're late." He said, flatly. He brushed past me to the kitchen and retrieved a water bottle from the fridge.

"I still have ten minutes. It takes me five to ride the elevator to the Senate hall."

"A king is always early, never late. Haven't I taught you that by now?" He stopped in the middle of the living room. "Where is Ember? She has a meeting to attend at noon—one with the head of the Department of National Security. He wants to run through basic Angelesan procedures with her. Get some opinions on what Kadjar does versus what we do."

I shrugged. "I don't know. Keeping up with her is not in my job title."

A smile grew on my father's face. "Good," he paused. "Taking those rules to heart, aren't you?" My father took a seat on the couch. "Sit with me, son. The Senate will wait for us."

Son. My heart began to beat faster. I was never his son. I was Prince Roman; nothing else. I was never worthy of the title of his son. I was only worthy of the title of prince by birthright. I took a seat next to my father on the couch, albeit hesitantly.

"You and I will begin private lessons this week, after your official eighteenth birthday and after the party tonight. It's exciting, don't you think? To learn all the secrets of Angeles that have been kept from the rest of the world?"

I nodded. "Yes, I suppose."

"But with training and knowledge such as this, there comes a price you must pay. Those rules are just the beginning. Have I ever told you about Loren Gillian?"

"No."

"She was a girl that I was madly in love with before I began my training. She and I had something inexplicable. I was promised to your mother, but Loren didn't care about that. All she cared about was *me*. I'd never had someone care about just me and not my title before. When it came time for my father and I to begin training, I couldn't let go of Loren. I had spent my entire life searching for what she gave me and losing that—losing her—was a loss I didn't think I was ever going to come back from." He stopped, waiting for a reaction.

I was quiet. My father had never given me even the inkling of emotion. He was only plastic smiles when there were cameras around and expressions of blood and steel behind closed doors. I think a part of me forgot that he was even capable of emotion.

He continued when I didn't speak. "Do you know what my father did to Loren and me when he found out that I hadn't cut ties with her?" I shook my head. His gaze fell down to the rug beneath our feet. "He killed her. Took us both down to the prison, tied me to a chair and forced me to watch as he shot her at point-blank range."

Cold fear rushed over my body. "Why are you telling me this?"

My father pulled out his phone. He turned it to face me, the screen lit with a blurry picture of two figures on a balcony holding each other. "Joseph Clark pulled it from the overhead surveillance footage." He zoomed in on one of the figures. "Can you look me in the eyes and tell me that's not you? And that's not Ember?"

I saw her white hair. I saw my hands holding her waist. I saw myself smiling for the first time in God knows how long.

"I thought no one else knew about the rules? Why did Joseph send you this?"

"Because I knew Joseph had access to the drone that would pass by your balcony. I told him what to look for because I knew that's the only place you'd take her. That's the only place you thought wasn't bugged."

I nodded. "I didn't think the drones flew over the back of the palace."

My father put his phone away. "I don't want to see you fail. Angeles can't afford a weak king. This girl, this love that you think you have, is going to drive you insane. Do you know what love does to men like us? Love weakens a king. Love lets in a maelstrom of emotions that make a king irrational and afraid. I know you wouldn't risk the crown for a girl."

"You want to see me fail." I said, not daring to look at him. "I know you do. You want me to fail so you can overthrow me and rule until you die."

"That's a lie, Roman."

"You don't get to act as if you care about me now."

"I do. I've always looked out for you."

"No, you haven't. Mom did. You made me wish I was dead just so I didn't have to wake up and fight you and your words every day. But guess what? I found a reason to keep living. I'm going to live, and I'm going to rule. I'm going to make sure you pay for what you've done to me and what you did to Ian."

To my surprise, he didn't fight back. He rose to his feet and went to the kitchen. I watched from the living room as he began brewing a pot of coffee.

He didn't turn to face me when I entered the kitchen. "Those words came from a different man. An angry one. I'm not him anymore."

"That's it? That's your only excuse?"

My father went silent. There were no perfect words he could say: all of his soul-healing words were written for him, by people who had trained their entire lives to write speeches for people like my father. Without those words, my father was utterly, terrifyingly human.

"I am the king," he finally said, voice trembling with rage. "I need no excuse."

"You might be king, but you are no better than the criminals you execute." I shot back. He slammed his coffee mug down on the counter so hard that it cracked.

"You are the author of her fate, Prince Roman. I've told you that time and time again, and now you've forced my hand to end it."

"What?" I watched as my father stormed out of the kitchen to the living room.

Ember.

No.

I'd watched her kill a man before—I watched her snap

that guard's neck back in the jail, when we were rescuing Mara. Maybe now was the chance to kill my father before he had a chance to touch her. All it would take was a single snap. I just had to get my hands on him.

He burst through the living room.

I ran after him and pounced.

I latched my hands around my father's neck bringing him straight to the ground. He grabbed at anything he could— my shoulders, my shirt, my hair. I didn't react. It was almost as if I were witnessing the fight rather than participating.

The once great and powerful King of Angeles managed to pry my hands from his neck. He grabbed a fistful of my hair and slammed my head into the wooden floor. Sparks of pain and light shot through my vision. I let out a groan, reaching up for my head.

He caught my face in his hands. I stared at my father as the world moved in slow motion. *This* was the man who was supposed to teach me how to rule a nation, how to become a man, how to do all the things that a normal father should have, but instead, he left me with scars that would never heal.

He reeled his fist back and punched my face. I tried to fight him, scratching and clawing at whatever I could, to no avail. I fell onto my back on the floor beside him as my father grabbed a fistful of my shirt, pulling me close to his face.

"You are *never* to defy me *again.*" He hissed.

I was reduced to the shell who only had a mouthful of *yes* and *thank you* for his father. I didn't say anything, though my instinct was to agree with him. I just covered my eyes with my hands before he could reign another blow onto my face.

Some noise barely resonated in the back of my mind. I didn't pay it any mind. All I could hear was the sound of my own blood pounding in my ears. I waited for the blow that would end my life. I counted the seconds that ticked by.

Ten long seconds waltzed by before I opened my eyes. The world around me was a light red. I was bleeding just above my eyebrow, I think. I wiped the blood from my face, tried my best to blink it from my vision. My head pounded with every beat of my heart.

"Oh my God." *Ky.*

I pulled myself into a sitting position, still smearing the blood on my face. Ky stood in the doorway of my apartment, stone-faced and still.

"I just—oh, my head." Ky slid to his knees before me, wiping the blood off my face and trying to pull me to my feet. "We need to get out of here. He's going to…" My words dissolved into a sigh as a wave of nausea hit me.

"He's not going to do anything."

"What? Why?"

"Look," Ky pointed towards my father. I glanced over, and he was lying face down on the floor. Not moving. A gaping bullet hole pierced his back.

My head spun and not just from the pain. From the confusion, the anger, the weight of all the guilt he had rested on my young shoulders crashed down on me. Ky's hands were underneath my armpits pulling me to my feet.

"C'mon, Roman. We gotta get you cleaned up. We

gotta go."

"Ky, my head. I just want to sleep."

He half-dragged me into my en suite bathroom, only stopping at the sink where I saw myself: disheveled hair, blood-soaked face. "Here. Wash your face." He handed me a washcloth and left. Slowly, I began to scrub at my face. There was blood along the collar of my shirt.

The person that I saw in the mirror was someone that startled me. I didn't know this man. This man had wet, smeared blood running down his cheeks and crimson stains on the chest of his shirt. This man was terrifying. This man didn't look like Roman Stone. No. This man looked like Nero Stone.

I broke away from my reflection as quickly as possible, staring down into the pink water rushing into the sink. Out of the corner of my eye, I could see Ky pacing in my bedroom. I remember him doing the same thing when we were little, toy car in hand. I'd try to keep up with him but usually ended up getting distracted. Mom would say that Ky was going to end up pacing a hole in the carpet if he didn't slow down.

I took a dry towel from the rack and scrubbed at my face a final time. As some of the initial fog cleared from my head, I went back into my bedroom. Ky threw a shirt at me.

"Change into this. You've got blood all over yours." I did as I was told. He continued. "How are we going to cover this up, Roman? What are we going to do?"

"Ember," I said, pulling my head through the shirt. "She'll know what to do."

281

"What?" Ky paused in the middle of my room.

"Ember—she'll know. If anyone is going to know how to cover up a murder, it's going to be the assassin."

Ky clapped his hands together. "Alright, I guess we can go from there. Let me call her. Do you have her number?"

"She doesn't have a phone. She refused to take the one that Ivelisse tried to give her."

"So we have no way of contacting her?"

I shook my head. "Not unless you know where she is." I said, only half-joking.

"I do."

I raised an eyebrow. "Where is she, then?"

Ky's voice got quieter. He crossed his arms over his chest. "With Ivelisse. Since last night. I haven't heard from either of them."

"That doesn't sound like a good combination. At all."

"Ivelisse swears Ember is fine. Said she just needed some time to cool off after everything happened."

"Everything?"

Ky blanched. "Yeah. Everything. I'm not dropping another load on you now. It doesn't matter. Let's just go."

"No, what happened?"

"Roman, I really—"

"You promised. Remember? *We* promised honesty."

Ky crossed his arms over his chest. "Fine. I was out the night before last. I was attacked. I spent a few hours in the hospital but I'm fine. Ember was with me. Everything is fine. We don't need to worry about that now. It doesn't matter."

"Who attacked you? What happened? We'll jail the bastard. We'll—"

"Roman! What I need right now, more than anything, is for you to call Ivelisse. Track Ember down, and let's get the hell out of here before I'm crucified for killing the king. I need you to call her. I don't think…I don't think I can speak to anyone else right now."

Ky pulled his phone from his back pocket and brought up Ivelisse's contact. He set the phone on speaker and handed it to me.

She picked up after the third ring. "Hello?"

"Hey, it's Roman."

"Roman, hi. What do you want?"

"Can I speak with Ember?"

A moment of silence dripped by. "Why?"

"It's really important. Just—please. I need to speak with her. Only for a few seconds, I promise, and then I'll be out of your hair. Okay?"

There were a few shuffling noises, some hushed words, and finally, I heard her voice. "Hello?"

"Hey, Em, I need to talk to you."

"Why?"

"Can we meet somewhere? I can't—I can't say anything over the phone. Is there any way you could meet me? I'll come to you, even."

"You don't sound good. What's wrong with you?"

"It's urgent, Em, I really need you."

"What's going on, Roman?"

I swallowed a breath of air. "I need to speak to you—to see you. Can I come to you? Or can we meet halfway? I know what I told you, and I know what I did to you, but please just hear me out. One last time."

"I…I guess we can meet somewhere. I can meet you by the checkpoint in the Common District."

"Yes. Yeah, that works. I'll be there ASAP."

The line went dead. I handed the phone back to Ky. "So?" He asked.

"Let's head to the Common District checkpoint."

He nodded and was out of the door before I could catch up with him. I stopped, though, in the living room where my father's body lay. Thick red blood pooled around him. I kicked him, rolling him over. His eyes were wide and his mouth was half-open like he had been in the middle of a sentence that would never be finished.

I stared down at his lifeless body.

There was no shock, because I had known that this day was coming for a long, long time. I had known that I would be my father's downfall ever since he started to berate me. There was no sadness because I would never be able to find it in myself to grieve for such a monster.

There was only anger.

Pure, unadulterated anger.

I was angry that he took away my brother and my mother. Angry that he tried to take Ember from me. Angry that he ripped every good thing from my hands before I even had a chance to know what it was. And angry that I couldn't be sad over the man I was supposed to love.

Most of all, I was angry that he convinced the little six-year-old boy that I once was that he was never going to be good enough for anything but the throne; he warped that little boy's sense of reality into thinking there was no life for him outside the throne, that happiness was a luxury that he'd never get to see.

I was only sad that I didn't get the chance to pull the trigger.

"Roman! Come on." Ky's voice came from the hall-way.

I followed him into the hallway and into a new light.

Chapter Twenty-Two
Ember

The checkpoint to the Common District sat at the very end of a busy dirt road. Beat up cars that Ivelisse called 'clunkers' and vans were waiting for their turn to pass through to the Business District. The ones that were turned away usually went calmly or else they had to be forced away, which was never a pretty sight.

"How long have we been waiting for Roman?" Ivelisse asked. We sat on one of the few wooden picnic benches by the checkpoint meant for the workers to take lunch breaks on. They weren't in use, so it didn't seem like much of a problem.

"An hour. How long does it take to get from the Royal District to the Common District?"

"Four." She dropped her head into her palms. "We don't have time for this. He can't just keep us waiting."

"He sounded like he was crying on the phone."

"He's a drama queen if I've ever heard one. He probably broke his wrist and thinks it's the end of the world. That's actually happened before."

I didn't say anything back to her, though I did kind of want to know the story. I shouldn't have even agreed to meet Roman. I shouldn't have let him in again. But the crack in his voice had felt like it had the strength to rip my own heart open.

Gods, why did I let myself fall for a prince like this?

She snapped her head back up. "You know, Roman

does know where my grandmother lives. If he really wants to find us, he could. Maybe we should just head back."

I shook my head. "No, I told him I'd meet him here. You can go back."

"No. I'm not leaving you."

"You're kind of clingy. Do you know that?"

"I am not clingy!"

"For the past three days you haven't left me alone. I kind of feel like I'm being held hostage. I was supposed to do something for you, remember?"

"And Miles has that thing for you to do. We just…need to wait."

"I can't go back to the palace while we wait?"

"No!" She snapped. "You need to stay with me. Here. It's safe."

"And the palace isn't safe?"

Ivelisse paused. "No."

"Are you going to tell me why?"

Silence rested between us. Ivelisse's gaze fell down to her lap. She looked up again but didn't meet my eyes. "I will. If you answer one of my questions first."

"Okay, whatever."

"How was he? I mean, before you left?"

"Who, Roman?"

She nodded.

"He was okay. Better."

The thought of his lips against mine and the sweet, whispered words that made the very hair on the back of my neck stand flashed through my mind. Oh, how his words could shatter every barrier I once thought I had. I couldn't tell her that, though.

Maybe I should tell her how every time we were in the same room together, we either ended up fighting or kissing. How our very dynamic confused me to no end. How we both wanted each other with a fire that was almost frightening but were too afraid to fight for it.

Maybe I should ask her if she hated him and loved him at the same time? Did she ever feel something so strong that she wanted to run at the very thought of it? Were we really that different?

Despite the abundance of words on my tongue, I said nothing.

"And now you're going to tell me what's so bad about the palace?" I asked.

"There's bad people anywhere you go in Angeles. Or, in the world. Their headquarters just so happens to be in the palace."

"So that's why I'm here? Because there's bad guys?"

Ivelisse hummed slightly, thinking of an answer, and crossed her arms over her chest. "I think you've had enough turmoil for your lifetime. All I'm trying to do is save you from extra heartache."

"I've spent my entire life facing bad guys. A few more can't hurt."

Ivelisse nodded. "I guess it's also an apology. A getaway for you, from everything going on right now. I was angry. I was angry at Roman, and I was angry at you. I shouldn't have acted like I did."

"You haven't really done anything."

"I know. I just feel like I have."

"Well, you shouldn't. You're fine."

Ivelisse nodded, and that seemed to be the end of the conversation. She stood, smacking her hands on the table. "Let's head back to my grandmother's. Miles should be coming soon. Roman knows where the house is if he needs to find us. You deserve a proper makeover before you head back to the palace before the party tonight. Am I right?"

I glanced back at the long line streaming down from the checkpoint. A massive highway stretched from one checkpoint to the other. I couldn't even see the next checkpoint.

"Yeah. I guess it'd be better than sitting out in this heat, right?"

Ivelisse grabbed my hand, and we began walking toward the Common District. It was a small city made of mud roads and cracked, holed sidewalks. The buildings were laden with faded graffiti and broken glass patched up with wooden boards. The people who walked the streets called out in a million different languages that I didn't understand. Children burst through the throngs of people, chasing each other and giggling with glee.

It looked so much like home.

Ivelisse stopped in front of a fruit vendor. She pointed to a mango, and he responded with, "*Miǎnfèi de.*"

289

"*Zhēn de ma?*" Ivelisse said back, raising an eyebrow.

He nodded and set two mangoes in the bag. "*Duìyú jìnhū nǚwáng hé xīn nǚwáng lái shuō, shì de.*" He said. She paled and turned away without thanking the man.

I ran after her. "What did he say?"

She shook her head. "I don't like that man. Here, take the stupid mangoes. I don't want them anymore."

"What happened?"

"I don't want to talk about it. Besides, it doesn't translate well in English."

"Was it something bad?"

"For me, yes. You don't need to worry about it."

"What did he say."

Ivelisse stopped. She ran a hand down her face. "He said they were free for the 'almost-queen' and the 'new queen.' Talking about *you*. I don't even know why I stopped. I don't even like mangoes." She huffed.

We walked the rest of the way in silence. I think the Royal District was easier to understand than the Common District. The Royal District was made of streets and cross-roads that made the world easy to navigate, but the Common District was one long road that split off into little backstreets and dead-end neighborhoods. Almost everyone who lived here either worked in the little shops on the main road or in the factories of the Agricultural District.

"Hey! Hey, stop! Ember!"

I whirled around. Gods, I'd almost completely forgotten about him: Roman. Part of me was afraid to see him again, but another part of me knew the urgency in his voice during that phone call wasn't for nothing.

He was running toward me at full speed, pushing through the crowd of people and before I knew it, I was running back to him despite Ivelisse's calls. We stopped just short of crashing into each other. Ky, who was at Roman's side, was doubled over.

"Holy shit," he huffed. "I should have run track."

"What took so long?"

Roman glanced over at Ky, who straightened himself. Ky wiped the sweat from his forehead. "We paid for one of those buses that takes you from the Royal District to the Common District in less than two hours. And then when we got there, we saw you two walking away and couldn't catch up." Ky explained.

"Why are you here?" Ivelisse, who had just now managed to get through the crowd of people, stood with her hands on her hips.

Roman caught my gaze—and I swore, in that second, we were the only people in the world. Nothing else mattered but him, as he walked towards me, stopping only a foot away. With some effort, I tore my eyes away, only to find myself staring at the dried blood on his face and neck. I reached up and brought my hands to his face, hoping he wouldn't reject me, again.

"What happened to you?" I asked.

He pulled my hands away from his face, shaking his head ever-so-slightly as if to say *not now*. This was not the time to get distracted by the split-second of his touch.

This boy was driving me insane.

"He's dead," Ky said, lowering his voice as much as he could.

"Who?" Ivelisse stepped up to say.

"Nero."

I froze. Ivelisse sucked in a breath of air. "What happened?" She asked. Roman kept his eyes trained on my face, but I couldn't bring myself to look at him.

"They were fighting, and I thought Nero was going to kill Roman. So, I shot him." Ky let his eyes fall to the sidewalk underneath our feet.

"You *shot him*? Since when do you carry?" Ivelisse's voice raised. Ky and I both shushed her.

"Do you want to get us all killed? We don't know if anyone has found his body yet. And, to answer your question, I always carry during big events. You don't know when some rebel group is going to try something."

Ivelisse snapped, "Do you realize what you've done? What you've unleashed? Two royal deaths only months apart from each other is going to ruin Angeles."

"I did what I had to do. If I had to give up Jude because of—" Ky stopped himself. "You know what, nevermindnever mind. Miles is ready to take us to Calais. I've already called him and gotten everything settled. We just have to be there in twenty minutes. You all in?"

"Calais?" I asked, at the same time Ivelisse said, "we can't go to Miles."

"I thought I was going to?" I asked her.

Ivelisse held a hand up for my silence. "Miles is already coming to the Common District. I called him."

"Called him?" Ky and I both echoed.

"Yes. So he could take Ember back to Kadjar."

"And you didn't tell me that?" I hollered.

Ivelisse whirled around to me. "I didn't know if you were going to run or not! You do happen to have a habit of being flighty."

"I do not!"

"Both of you! Quit it. Let's just go meet Miles and get ourselves the hell out of this mess. The only thing is, he—" Ky pointed a finger at Roman. "Can't go to Kadjar."

"So we'll go to Calais." I said.

"No." Ky insisted. "No one is going to Calais. That's completely off the table. We'll find somewhere else."

Roman huffed. "What, you think we're just going to find some uncharted colony that's going to accept us with open arms? Ky, Calais is our only option. I can't go to Kadjar, Ember can't go there either—"

"Why not?" I asked.

He paused. Glanced at me. Blinked. "Nevermind. Let's just go meet Miles. Where is he supposed to be?" Roman asked Ivelisse, pulling his gaze away from me. Burning questions pressed in my mind, but I didn't let them slip. Not now. Not when the world around us is crumbling.

"Hold on a minute." Ivelisse said. "Think about this. Are the three of you, two of whom are the future leaders of this nation, really going to abandon it now? After everything you've done?"

"Everything we've done?" Roman questioned.

"Everything *you've* done," Ivelisse echoed. "I've picked up your slack for the past how many years now? I put in the work while you were off partying with Ky or sulking up in the Healing Room. You owe it to Angeles to stay and fix what you haven't bothered to even look at these past years."

"Do you realize what's going to happen to me, to Ember, when my father's men find out that he's dead? They're going to know that it was me. He told me that even in death he'd find a way to make my life hell. I refuse to go down without a fight, and this is me fighting."

Ivelisse shook her head. "Fine. If you really think that you have to leave, leave, but I have something for you first."

"You have something for me?"

She nodded, once, curtly. "I need you to take it. It's something that I never gave back from a few years ago. I'd hate for you to leave and not have this."

"What is it?"

"It's your mother's necklace."

Roman paled. "Why do you have my mother's necklace?"

"She let me look at it once and accidentally left it with me. I figured that I'd give it to her when she got back to the palace, but I'd rather give it to you now. My grandmother's house is on the way to the checkpoint, where I am to meet

Miles. Will you come?"

He nodded. Without another word, Ivelisse began leading us through the crowd. It thinned as we turned down one of the narrower backroads. In the very distance, just above the crest of a small hill, I could see another checkpoint and a highway backed up with people, cars, and horse-drawn carts.

The road before us smelled heavily of car oil and hot garbage, poorly masked by the remnants of the fruit vendors on the distant main road. Houses sat squished together, wall-to-wall. Very few people walked the streets. Some carried baskets of laundry on their heads, some carried children on their hips, and some carried nothing but hunched backs and gazes focused on the orange clay beneath their feet.

Ivelisse stopped in front of one of the last houses on the dead-end road. This house was one of the cleaner ones. She stepped up the creaking wooden steps to the porch. Ky, Roman, and I followed. She knocked on the door and waited a few seconds for it to open.

This place looked so much like home. Sure, the people might not have been as friendly, and the Common District was about ten times bigger than the East Sector ever was. Still, they looked so much alike. If there wasn't such a possibility of Angeles falling into hell, maybe I would've stayed here in the Common District.

I could've pretended that Mara and Mama and Papa were all here with me. And that the sun would rise every day in these pretty blue skies, and there wouldn't be a single cloud in existence. I could find a place in this world. A place where

I belonged. Where I was loved. Where I didn't have to fight to get by. It was a beautiful dream.

But I've since learned that dreams don't mirror reality.

Ivelisse's mother, Li, opened the door. She glanced past Ivelisse at the three of us and stepped aside to let us in. The room around us was small, holding only a couch and three chairs. The air was musty, and the only light came from a window on the opposite side of the room. The wooden floor underneath my feet creaked with every step. Li disappeared behind a second door.

"Where's the necklace?" Roman asked.

Ivelisse shut the front door behind her. Locked it. My eyes trailed down to the padlock that she twisted a number combination into. None of us were getting out of this house. A strange feeling settled down deep in my stomach. "What are you doing?" I asked. She kept quiet and refused to look at the three of us.

"Ky," she finally said. "I'm going to give you the chance to run."

"What?"

"You can leave. This isn't your fight to witness." Ivelisse still didn't look up.

"I don't understand what's going on."

"Do you want to leave or not?"

He shook his head. Ivelisse shrugged. She went for the first door, twisting the knob. I should have trusted my gut and bolted out the front door. But my gut has been wrong before, and I was too focused on the two Kadjarian-uniformed guards walking through the door.

The blood in my veins crystallized. She walked in after them, and she looked ethereal. Even in plain civilian clothes, she looked like a goddess. There were no ceremonial robes, no beautiful dresses, just a t-shirt and jeans. She looked utterly normal, and that was terrifying.

She turned to her guards. "Leave. Secure the plane for me. This won't take long." Ivelisse opened the padlocked door for them and locked it once more.

"What's going on?" Roman asked.

"Is that any way to greet an empress?"

"What is going on?" He repeated slower this time.

She glowered. "I refuse to be ignored. For two weeks, my Bloodhound has ignored my letters, ignored my promises of safety for *this*? For *you*? I had to come see it for myself. I had to come end it myself."

"What promises of safety?" I asked.

"My letters to you. I've promise you your freedom, an entire legion under your control, and yet you reject me."

"I don't know what you're talking about."

Empress Analita smiled despite it all. "You can play coy all you want," she removed the black handgun from her belt. "But you aren't fooling me."

I tensed, backing away. "I don't know what you're talking about, Your Majesty. I didn't do anything, and I haven't received any letters."

"Look at what he's done to you. He's brainwashed you!"

The same fear that I should have felt on the day of my execution coursed through my veins. I couldn't die. I had Roman. I had Roman, and I had a whole world to look forward to. I couldn't let her kill me.

Roman, where was he? From the corner of my eyes I saw him and Ky standing at the back wall, watching wide-eyed. *Stay,* I prayed. *Please, don't move. Don't come in the way.*

"Empress, please listen to me. No one has brainwashed me."

"You killed Prince Ian Stone. You killed an innocent child this time—, not some government official that you've decided is corrupt." She flicked the safety off her gun. Aimed. "You can't *stop* killing. Gods only know I should have ended this last month."

I shut my eyes and braced for the impact. A force knocked me to the side with such power that I fell to my knees. When I looked up, I saw him shadowed in the light of the window—Roman.

"What the hell are you doing?" I said, clambering to my feet. "Roman, get out of the way."

I attempted to push him, but he blocked me. "Empress, the letter was my fault. Natasha gave it to me, and I took it. I only took it so I could keep it safe, while I waited to give it to her, but the right time never came. It's at home, in my kitchen cabinet. My father killed Ian. I was there. I witnessed the whole thing. Ember has done nothing other than comply with my father out of fear."

298

The empress flicked the gun to the side, a swift instruction for Roman to move. "You expect me to believe you? After the havoc she wreaked back in Kadjar? I tried to be forgiving, but no more. No longer will I show mercy to this Bloodhound. This ends here and now." She tightened her grip on the gun.

Roman took a step forward as I pulled on his arm. "You have to understand, she—"

"I don't have to understand anything, Prince Roman. I was nice. I offered her a deal that she couldn't refuse. I don't want to hear your *lies*. My spy told me that she hand delivered the letter to Ember and not to you. I am *done* being nice. You won't fall into my trap, then I'll have to drag you."

"Trap?" I echoed.

"You think I'd really offer you exoneration and a safe job? After everything you've done? After the blood of thirty-six of my colleagues and *friends* has flown through your hands? You think that the king hasn't destroyed my nation enough, so I thought it would be best to bring our assassin back? *That* was the trap. I want you dead. You wouldn't come to me, so I came to you."

"Please, Empress Analita," I choked out. "I know what I've done. I know who I've killed, and I think about what I've done every day. But they had to pay for their crimes in some way. You would've let them die slowly in your prison had they not been your friends."

She ignored me. The empress took a step forward and pressed the gun to Roman's temple. "I am going to shoot you

299

if you do not move. Don't test me." Roman didn't falter. Hot, angry tears began to pour down my face as I pounded my fists on Roman's back in some meager attempt to get him to move. I couldn't lose him. I couldn't lose him.

"Roman, please," I cried out. "Move!" A single, solitary whimper fell from my mouth.

The empress looked from me to him. "You're telling me you'd die for this monster?"

"Yes," he replied.

"You are just as much of a fool as your father made you out to be."

Roman, almost instinctively, backed up when the empress lowered her gun. I took his hand in mine. It was clammy. He held my hand so tightly I was sure I'd lose circulation. It didn't matter though. What mattered was that we were here together.

"I have enough rounds inside this gun to kill the both of you. I've been through hell and back these past few weeks. This is *nothing* to me. Step away, Prince Roman, and let me finish what I started. You have three seconds."

"No."

"One—"

Together.

"Two—"

Together.

"Three."

Faintly, I heard someone calling my name. The piercing screams rose above the endless bullets ripping through my skin. Pain shattered every single grip I had on reality. As if in slow motion, Roman's arms wrapped around my waist and pushed me to the ground.

I wanted to push him off of me, but I couldn't. I couldn't move my arms. Out of the corner of my eyes, I could see Ky and Ivelisse at the door, screaming at each other. Ky fell to his knees, clawing at the wooden floor like he could somehow burrow out. His mouth was wide, in a scream, I'm assuming. I couldn't hear his cries. All I could hear, all I could feel, all I could think was of this pain.

Stop it, Roman, I wanted to say. *Don't protect me. Save yourself. It's not you she wants.*

But he didn't, and he wouldn't even if I could have told him.

He looked at me one last time, a million emotions crossing through those green eyes. Pain, fear, anger, and one emotion that made every single fight worth it: love. He smiled. Blood trickled from the corner of his mouth.

I am here.

He is here.

Finally, we are together.